THE DEVIL REVERSED

ALEX MCGILVERY

The Devil Reversed

For information contact:

http://alexmcgilvery.com

ISBN 978-0-9959926-7-2

BEGINNINGS

TEN OF SWORDS

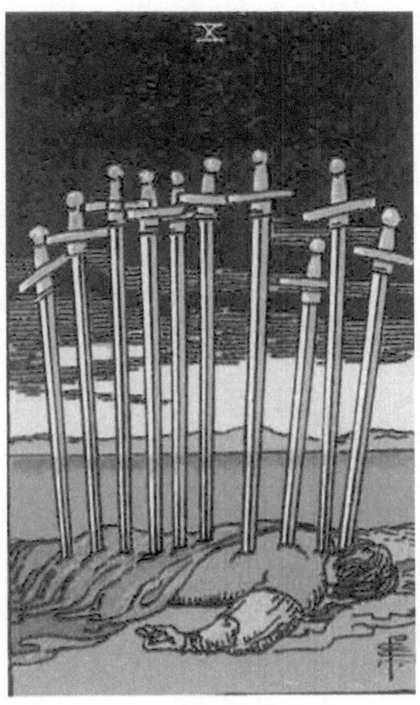

Arthur waited on the bridge huddled under his damp cloak, cursing himself as a fool. *Don't know if even a noble's daughter is worth standing out in this weather.* His boots thumped on the wooden planks as the cold spring rain and the night wind cutting through his cloak started his teeth chattering. Marriette had promised in her letter that she would meet him on the bridge near the Broken Dog Tavern.

She was a nice enough girl, though timid for Arthur's taste. Her noble blood kept him returning to their brief platonic meetings. One last time, he shook the icy water off his head. Damn, I've waited long enough, she's stood me up, again. He turned to go back to the warmth and camaraderie of the Broken Dog.

Two men waited at one end of the bridge. A chill ran through him that had nothing to do with the rain. Arthur turned, two more men at that end. Under his cloak he wiped his hand on his pants and gripped the wooden club at his belt. The four men walked casually toward him. Though muscular enough from helping to load and unload his father's wagons, these men looked bigger and tougher than Arthur. One drew a sword while the others had clubs like Arthur's. *Either he's noble or he doesn't care about hanging.* He tried to slow his breathing. *Neither option is good for me.*

At the last possible second, he whipped around and struck at the man holding the sword. His opponent blocked it easily then forced Arthur back with his own attack. Three clubs came down on Arthur's head and shoulders driving him to the rough wooden planks of the bridge. Curse the pride that made him play at courting a duke's daughter. His club fell from numb hands as Arthur tried to protect his head from the beating.

"Careful, lads," the man with the sword said, "his lordship said no mortal wounds."

The three stepped back from their work. Good, just a hard lesson. He'd lived through bruises before.

"What difference does it make?" one said.

"The difference is: his lordship is paying us to toss a living body into that river. He isn't one to put up with loose interpretations of his orders."

Arthur gasped and tried to crawl away, but a casual kick knocked the wind out of him.

"What?"

"He means we do what we are paid to do," a second one said. "Grab his legs." They picked up Arthur, ignoring his incoherent pleas, and pushed him over the railing.

The frigid water of the flooded river made Arthur scream as it swept him away from the bridge. He couldn't fight the fury of the spring flood and the weight of his clothes dragged him down. Even after stripping off his cloak and kicking out of his boots, Arthur barely reached the surface. His entire attention focused on getting out of the water.

The river was crueler than the men who had beaten him and tossed him to the flood. It brought him close enough to the bank that Arthur hoped escape was possible, then it yanked him back out to the center of the stream. As it played with him, the water sucked the heat from his body until even breathing was too much work. Nothing remained to Arthur but the faintest regret that his father would be hurt by the disappearance of his wayward son. Then even that was gone, and cold darkness overwhelmed him.

His body floated down the river for miles. It bounced off a few rocks, but somehow never hung up on any of the fallen trees or eddies. At midnight, Arthur's body arrived at a sudden widening of the river. The current slowed and an eddy dumped the body on the sandy shore of the bend.

The servant who had been sent there to wait for the body dragged it out of the river. He hoisted the sodden mass to his shoulder and began the long climb up the bank to his master's castle. Once in the castle, he carried it up the steep winding stairs to his master's workroom, carefully placing the flaccid corpse in the center of the diagram carved into the oak floor. He left without word or acknowledgment from the man who meditated on a platform at one end of the room.

THE DEVIL

With a flash of light, the devil named Zeb crashed into a world painful in its concreteness.

"You dare call me to this place?" He reached to tear the fool's head from his body to begin its punishment, but his hands met a searing barrier. His howl shook the stones of the tower.

The foolish mage fell to his knees bleeding from nose and ears, yet kept his incantation going, finishing before he let his shaking hands fall.

"Be silent, Devil. I called you and you will obey me." The puny mage's voice was rasping and thin, yet it contained power that Zeb struggled against.

"You are tired and hurt, human. How long will you be able to keep up your feeble spell? Death will be just the beginning of your suffering."

"You will obey. You are mine."

The devil's laughter rolled over the mage. The mortal screamed with the pain, and almost lost his control of the barrier.

"Almost had you," Zeb chuckled cruelly. "Why don't you just give it up? Eternity isn't that long."

The mage fought back to his feet and began a new incantation. Zeb fell silent, for the first time since he had been yanked into this room. This one had a depth that he hadn't imagined. The mage smiled, as Zeb threw himself against the barrier trying to break through, fighting against the power crushing him like a great hand. Zeb howled, then shrieked and finally whimpered, but to no avail. The mage slowly and torturously brought the devil to its knees.

"You are mine. You will serve me and do my will in all things," the mage said.

"I am what I am because I refused to serve one who is infinitely greater than you. Why should I serve you?" Even in his humiliation the devil's voice made the human cringe.

"You will serve because I will compel it. I will wrap you with chains even you will not break. The mage began a third incantation. The word began to crush the demon again. Zeb fought a long weary battle, but knew himself to be the inevitable loser. He had misjudged this one from the beginning. Yet, one day, he would hold this human's soul in his hands and crush it to dust. The spell pushed him toward a body that lay sodden on the floor. In blind panic, Zeb fought to avoid that fate. He never knew how close he came to breaking loose as the spell forced him into suffocating darkness.

In the black, a voice came to him and spoke with agonizing power.

"You are mine, and you will do my will as by my will you are bound."

Zeb twisted and turned to hide from the excruciating voice, but it surrounded him with unendurable pain. Still he refused, until the devil was but a weak voice whimpering refusal.

"No. I will not serve."

Finally, when the voice reached the point of snuffing out the devil's existence, it stopped.

"Then I will bind you by flesh and power. This is the geas that I lay upon you. You will slay the king of this land at the time of my choosing. Only by his blood will you buy your freedom. Defy me and I will send pain. Obey and you will live. Anything you claim, I will seek out and destroy. Whether you say it or not, you are mine."

The power vanished with a snap and Zeb threw himself at his tormentor. Rough hands caught him and threw him to the floor. A boot kicked him and he struggled for breath. He had never imagined the agony involved in breathing. The rancid odour of the humans in the room assaulted him. Lifted to his feet again, a hard hand slapped him. As often as the devil had dealt and received pain in the spirit realm, nothing prepared him for the white heat of physical pain. To his disgust his body cowered from a man who wasn't any taller than the body Zeb inhabited. Twisted by scars that covered every visible part of his body, his hair grey, yet the man's eyes glittered with a cold blue gaze as if hoping that Zeb would attack again. Zeb hung his head.

"Enough," said the mage, "you know what to do with him."

"Come on, ye reeking sack of bones," the man pushed Zeb toward the door. "We got work to do."

The stairs were yet another torture for Zeb. He wasn't sure of his legs yet. Walking in his 'reeking sack of bones' was like trying to control his feet by pulling strings tied to his toes. Several times, Zeb stumbled, and the men ahead or behind caught him, roughly pushing him to his feet.

They finally arrived on the main level. Zeb was led to a cart and pushed in the back.

"The master wants ye trained, so trained ye will be, though the devil knows what he wants with ye."

The devil does know, and it is nothing good. Zeb quickly fell asleep. Dreams of the mage's cruel voice flaying his spirit and laying him open troubled him. He only woke when the One's light entered his dream, banishing the dark visions of the mage. Zeb sat up with a shout with something banging in his chest like an animal trying to escape. The demon tried to curse in the language of his own kind, but his mortal lips couldn't shape the words.

When the men driving the cart saw that Zeb was awake they made him walk.

"Ye can't fight if ye can't walk," the man the mage gave him to for training said.

Zeb swore at his tormentor. The man just laughed.

"Y'll call me Trainer, I don't care what other words ye add in." He snapped the reins and set the horses to a faster pace.

Over the next week, Zeb learned to walk, then run. Fortunately, his body remembered how to eat and deal with other functions that Zeb had only known of in the abstract. It was one more torment that his 'trainers' stood over him and jeered and commented on every disgusting detail. He was forced to bury the stinking results with a wooden shovel little better than a flat stick.

They arrived at a castle with low walls surrounded by a moat filled with turbid green water. By this time, Zeb walked, and even ran, easily.

"Ye won't want to be drinking from there, or you will die of the chills." Trainer spat into the water. "Tis cursed by the master himself."

They put Zeb in a small, windowless room with a cot and a bucket with a lid. Sounds of men training and working came through the thick wood of the door. The room smelled musty, but it wasn't damp.

"Work hard and I give ye more. Cause trouble and I take away what ye got."

Zeb began a routine of eating whatever food his trainers put in front of him, then working through a series of exercises that tested the limits of his control over the body he inhabited. Gradually, he learned to live in his prison of flesh. He even learned that it could feel more than pain. He began to notice the taste of the food he was given, liking some dishes and not others, though he ate them all. He discovered pleasure in his increasing control of his body.

His training took place in an open yard surrounded by stone walls. The rank smell of the moat floated over one wall. A gate gave a view to another yard with stairs up to the wall and the gate to the outside. The only door was the one they led him through each morning.

A chair and small table appeared in Zeb's cell. The day that they handed him a weighted club the length of his arm he attacked Trainer with all the fury pent up inside him. Trainer just laughed as he danced away from Zeb's attack and covered his pupil with bruises. When Zeb was barely able to stand, Trainer knocked him down.

"Ye might just do, if ye can control that temper. Anger will make ye strong, but it will make ye stupid too."

After that, Trainer took every opportunity to push Zeb to lose his temper, then taunted him as he beat him to a pulp.

The weather grew warmer and the pace of training picked up. Trainer took to making Zeb run through the woods while he rode a horse and whipped him with a thin rod when he slowed too much. Now Zeb was being matched against two or three opponents at once.

One morning, Zeb walked into the training yard, to find Trainer standing by a table covered with swords of different lengths and shapes.

"They're blunted. So if ye got any ideas forget them. Pick up a weapon and get the heft of it." He described each as Zeb handled it. "Short sword, good for formation work, but ye won't be doing any of that. Someone with a long sword will cut ye to pieces. Long sword is better, but tis heavy. Ye need to be strong and fast. If ye go up against some fancy boy with one of these rapiers, he'll stick ye in the eye before ye get a swing at him. This one with the teeth looks scary enough, but it will stick in chainmail and ye'll look the fool trying to free your sword while someone else chops ye up. There are other weapons, too, but we ain't got time to deal with them."

Trainer put Zeb through the basics of each weapon, but then handed him the long sword.

"This is what ye'll be using."

Sword drill was the same as with the clubs. Mistakes were punished with bruises, triumphs rewarded by a grunt of pain from his opponent.

The day came when Zeb held a sharp sword as he faced a nervous opponent.

"What's the matter, Johnny, don't think ye can take this bag of flatulence? If he kills ye, I'll take away his piss pot."

A strange expression crossed Zeb's face—a smile. Stretching it into a feral grin, he saluted Johnny with his sword.

Johnny swallowed and brought his sword to the ready.

Zeb lunged at his opponent, but Johnny stepped aside and was able to block. Zeb kept up a barrage of attacks, but each parried by an increasingly confident Johnny. They chased each other back and forth across the yard.

"Enough," Trainer finally called. "Y're almost ready."

"For what?" Zeb asked.

"Don't know, don't care," Trainer said. "Master said get ye ready. Y're almost ready." He took the sword from Zeb and dismissed Johnny. "Y're wasting energy trying to overwhelm your opponent. Watch and learn; yer enemy will teach you his weaknesses, and then you use them to defeat him."

Zeb wasn't given an edged weapon again, but he was soon matched against multiple opponents once more. His sparring partners took to wearing light armour, as Zeb made no pretense of trying to pull his blows. Now that he was trained and aware, he reveled in the physical sensations of combat. The feel of a blow landing on an opponent, the look of apprehension on their faces, even his own bruises became pleasures.

Zeb gave no thought to the mage, so it was a shock when he turned from training to see the figure in a black robe watching. He bared his teeth and would have lunged to the attack, but his muscles failed and dumped him in the dirt. The mage came over and nudged Zeb with a toe.

"Good enough." Power rumbled in his voice. "It will be convincing. The fool king will die at your hands." He walked away leaving Zeb to struggle to his feet.

The next day, he was brought a clean set of clothes. When he arrived at the training square in the rough homespun, Trainer was waiting for him.

"It is time for you to serve your master's purpose; we will take you into the city and you will be told what to do from there."

The black knot building in Zeb since the previous day exploded. The mage might be able to turn his muscles to water, but not Trainer. Zeb moved faster than he had yet in training and snatched the trainer's sword from his belt and cut the man's throat. Men ran from all corners of the yard to attack Zeb, but he slaughtered them as fast as they arrived. Bruises and pain had been part of training, now blood spattered the sand and put the taste of salt on his lips.

Zeb picked up a second sword and cut and slashed his way to the gate. The stink of spilled guts and blood set him to laughing. Men, eyes white with fear, blocked his way with spears, he couldn't reach them with the swords. He fled up the stairs to the wall and jumped off into the moat. The slam of the water dashed the swords from his hands, but he didn't need them now.

By the time Zeb crawled from the moat and headed for the forest, archers had made it to the wall. Their arrows fell around him as he ran. One struck him in the back, but Zeb ignored it as he ran through the forest.

No sounds of pursuit followed him. Killing Trainer should confuse them enough to let him escape. The arrow was a nuisance but he'd deal with it later.

For some reason, he lost speed, bumping and crashing into trees. Zeb kept running until he reached a road. Instead of bursting onto it to overpower whoever was there, he staggered out and collapsed in front of a cart being pulled by a donkey.

As darkness swelled to drown him, he bared his teeth.

"I will not serve.

EIGHT OF SWORDS

Marriette wandered through the market. The sun shone warm after the cold spring rain, but she still kept the hood of her cloak up. Marriette's hair was an unremarkable brown, and no poets were going to sing the praises of her beauty. Her father paraded her around enough that even here a servant from another great House might recognize her. If word got back to him, he'd be furious.

After all, Art had. He was so kind to her. His strong hugs and gentle smile brought a different warmth to her face. The market's bustle was so different from the austere elegance of her father's home. She breathed in the scents and sounds of the city as it enjoyed the return of warmth. Even the fecund smell from the pens of the animals couldn't crush her mood.

Marriette didn't manage to escape her father often, and the punishment was dire, but she couldn't sit ladylike in her cold, shadowed room. The stolen servant's dress was much freer and more comfortable than any of her fine gowns. She walked through the market with an easy stride that would have turned her father's face dark with anger. The thought of him made Marriette shorten her walk to something more refined, then she gritted her teeth and lengthened it again. He might be the most important person in Bellandria next to the king, but she wasn't going to let him push her around anymore.

A cloud covered the sun as she strode out again, and the sudden dimness and coolness made her father seem near. Marriette's heart pounded. Foolishness, but her mood was spoiled. Even when he wasn't there to control every part of her life, her father made her life miserable. Her face crumpled and tears leaked out of her eyes.

"Stupid girl," she said to herself, "pull yourself together. You are not going to disgrace the deLanguiers by crying in a common market." The cold, uncaring voice of her father in her head dried up the tears and lifted her head. All he ever worried about was his importance, and the possibility of another House taking his position.

As much as she loved the experience of being free and unchaperoned in the market, Marriette couldn't ignore the effect she had on the people around her. They watched her from the corner of their eyes. In spite of her rough dress and cloak, they made it obvious that she didn't belong. Though she had no basket to carry purchases, she stopped and looked at the stalls and displays. She didn't talk to the people behind them, not knowing what to say. The crowd flowed around her. Even in the midst of the so many, she was alone.

Marriette was more used to being invisible. She no longer wondered at it. At home, her father's cronies let their eyes slide past her without ever stopping. Even the servants came and went through her rooms as if she wasn't there, on her father's orders. Her mother died when she was just a child of eight. In the decade since then the Duke of deLanguiers worked to crush her and form her into a tool for his use. Running out into the city was one of the few ways Marriette had left to assert her own existence. He would beat her for it, but she was used to that. Her father had been punishing her for one thing or another since her mother had died. She wasn't going to let a potential beating stop her from her purpose today.

Marriette walked toward the end of the market where the wagons came in and were unloaded. Horses and oxen steamed as men hitched and unhitched them. The wagons were unloaded with rough efficiency. She recognized some of the men from her previous trips to the market, but they ignored her. She knew she wasn't pretty enough for their whistles. The way the barmaids talked to the men when Arthur took her to the Broken Dog astounded her. What must it be like to banter so freely?

Art had been the first person to see her in as long as she could remember. She still didn't know what it was that had made him look up from his work and come over to talk to her. Ignoring the complaints and jeers of the other men, Art took her to a little tent where they drank weak tea and talked. Not only did he notice her, he listened. Over the next few months, Marriette crept out of her father's house, again and again, to meet the strong, blond man who made her heart beat with something other than fear.

The long, cold winter had offered little chance for Marriette to escape her father's house. In desperation, she chanced sending Art a letter asking him to meet her, but her father suddenly announced that they must attend a ball at another duke's city house. Trussed up in clothes meant to make her beautiful, she spent the evening dancing awkwardly in the arms of young nobles whose hungry gazes were for her father's wealth, or listening to her father explain how much she was disappointing him.

Today, Marriette came to surprise Art, and to apologize for not showing up at their assignation. She watched the men at work for a while looking for Art. A young girl stood off to one side with a board making marks as bales and boxes were moved about.

"Excuse me," Marriette said, "could you tell me where to find Art?"

"You mean Arthur?" The girl didn't look up from her work. "Haven't seen him for a couple of days, Father is furious. This is our busiest season and Arthur is supposed to be learning the business."

"Would you give him a message for me?"

"Sure, assuming he can still hear after Father is done with him. You know what fathers are like."

"Oh, yes," Marriette said. "Just tell him Marriette was asking after him and said sorry."

The young girl looked at Marriette for a long moment, then nodded.

"I will, promise. You had best be getting on. It is almost time for break and this is a rough bunch. My name is Joan, if you come around again. I'm Arthur's sister."

"Thank you."

Marriette walked back toward the market. The day grew warmer, and she was uncomfortably hot. She envied Joan both her lighter clothing and her quiet confidence. Marriette pushed the hood back away from her face and reveled in the cool breeze. Even though she wasn't going to see Art, Marriette was reluctant to go home. The day was so beautiful, she couldn't bear to be locked up in her room any sooner than need be. The breeze caressed her face, and the young woman walked in whatever direction the playful wind led her.

The wind failed and left her in the midst of a strange section of the market. The people in the stalls were dressed in bright colours and embroidery. Unlike the people in the market, they made no secret of their suspicious looks. Marriette swallowed and tried to remember the path that had brought her to this unfriendly place. Tears pushed at the back of her eyes, and she rubbed angrily at them. She was not going to cry just because she had got herself lost.

Marriette couldn't help staring at two young men whose braids might have been as long as her own. They said something to her in a strange language, then laughed and walked away. A familiar heat burned her face. She didn't know the language, but she did know mockery all too well. They sounded like the young men her father forced her to associate with.

"You must be thirsty, m'dear."

Marriette started and spun around. The speaker was an old woman. Her hair was grey, though her eyes still looked sharply at Marriette.

"I am, a little, now that you mention it." A sudden raging thirst clutched at her throat, dust coating her tongue.

"Come, I make you some cool tea. Maybe I tell your cards." The woman led her into a tent. She pushed Marriette onto a cushion on the floor. "Wait. I come with drink. Ease thirst."

Marriette was too thirsty to be scared. How had she become so dry so quickly? She might fall into dust any moment. The woman came back with a tray with glasses filled with a clear red liquid.

"Rose tea, make you beautiful, make the boys want you."

Marriette took a glass and barely remembered to nod in thanks before she sipped at the glass. Indescribable liquid flowed through her mouth. Lemon, but also something tasting a bit like the smell of a rose. She finished the glass, and a second without concerning herself that it wasn't ladylike. An oversize deck of cards lay on the tray.

"What are these?"

"Those are the cards of fate. They will tell you your past, and your future." The woman handed them to her. "Hold them and think your question. Do you have silver? No, your father is a hard man who doesn't give his only child any money of her own." She took the cards back and began dealing them out.

The first was a man lying with swords stuck in his back.

"Ten of Swords."

Another card showing a woman surrounded by more swords.

I look like her.

"Eight of Swords."

The third showed cups floating in the air filled with fantastical images.

"Seven of Cups. The cards of your question. You are trapped in a life that is killing you. To break free will cause great pain, to stay will bring greater pain yet. Wishful thinking that you will escape without pain. Put it off now, make it worse later."

More swords. "Three of swords: you lived through heartbreak and loneliness, hope betrayed to pain. Ace of Cups: love in your future, not what you expect."

Another card laid under the line, a skeleton in black armour. Marriette's heart fluttered as she gasped for air.

"Death: your life will change, and change and change again before you hold the cup in your hands."

The next card was worse. A malignant creature held a man and woman in chains.

"The Devil traps you. He keeps you hopeless and ignorant." She began laying out yet more cards and talking of future struggle and pain, always pain. Marriette stared appalled at the cards and wondered why she bothered living. There was a tower struck by lightning and falling. She knew how it felt. More swords, more cups, a man blithely stepping off a cliff, another hanging from a tree. Her head swam. The drone of the old woman became a voice thundering doom. Marriette held her head and tried to shut out the cards, but they burned their way into her mind. The woman laid the last card in the pattern, a person in a chariot perfectly balanced between light and dark.

"This is the crux, to choose," the old woman said. "It doesn't make sense now, but it will in time."

It was too much for Marriette; she let out a thin scream and fainted.

"Take her back to her father," the woman said to a man who came in from the back, "when you get back, we leave."

FIVE OF WANDS

Marriette awoke in her bed still wearing the servant's dress. The cloak hung by itself in a closet that once held her gowns. Her father was standing watching her, his face hard and cold.

"So, now you must humiliate me by walking the streets like any common strumpet. If you prefer to be clothed in rags that will be all you may wear." He leaned over her. "It isn't enough that you go out consorting with some merchant's son, ruining my reputation, you are brought home in a drunken stupor by Wagoners! Foreigners!" He slid his belt from around his waist. "You have shamed me for the last time."

"Then kill me and have done with it." Marriette turned to face the wall.

"Oh, no, I need you, but you will be properly punished." The first blow came as a shock, as it did each time. Some part of

Marriette protested. This was her father. He wasn't supposed to treat her like this. It quickly gave up the protest, as it did each time. The blows struck an increasingly numb body. She tried to withdraw into herself completely but the pain of the bruises and cuts refused to let her go. Marriette tried facing her father since she didn't think he'd mark her face. Soon the dress hung in tatters from her body, and her father was breathing heavily and licking his lips. This was when he would run out the door and leave her for a servant to come and clean.

Today, he fumbled with his pants as his eyes looked glazed and distant, like he was seeing someone else in her place. The last fragment of Marriette fled screaming in horror as he pushed her to the bed and began a whole new kind of torture.

"You witch," he muttered as he lay on top of her. "Would you seduce me too? You witch...."

When he was finished, her father pushed himself away and snorted in disgust. He slapped her face harder and harder until she moaned in response.

"Look what you've done," he said. "Clean yourself up, then you can clean this room." He picked up his belt and stalked out. Marriette looked at the blood spattered on the walls and felt the pain in her body and soul. She stumbled to the washstand and began washing blood and worse from her body. Then her stomach revolted and she vomited until she had no strength left. She fell to the floor whimpering and wishing that she were dead.

The servants found her and roughly cleaned her. They put her in bed and left her. Marriette lay listlessly in the bed and tried to die. She held her breath as long as she could, but her body always rebelled and started breathing again. She thought about breaking the mirror and using the edges to cut herself, but she'd have to get out of bed to break it. Despair weighed her down and trapped her into living.

A man in a doctor's smock came and examined her impersonally while her father watched.

"Yes, it is as you suspect, my Lord Duke. She is no longer a virgin. I will leave some herbs that will prevent any complications," the doctor said to her father. "Take care not to use too much if you want her to bear children later." He stood to leave. Marriette tried to summon the strength to say what had truly happened. It was too much for her and she fell into a troubled sleep.

She stayed in the room, while the welts on her body healed. A maid rubbed them with an ointment to prevent scars. Marriette learned that her father decided it was time for her to get up when the servants dragged her out of bed and dressed her. They marched her through the halls of the great house until she began walking with them. After that, she was allowed to walk by herself, shadowed by a servant charged with keeping her obedient. Marriette didn't care; although her heart beat, she was dead inside - a ghost in her own body.

A week after she had been dragged from her bed, servants dressed her in one of her fine gowns. It hung on her like rags, but they led her down the stairs to have dinner with her father. They ate in the formal dining room. Her father never ate anywhere else. The huge room never warmed up, no matter what fire burned in the grate or candles on the table. Marriette shivered as they directed her to the hard wood chair at her father's left.

"You are too thin," he said, "eat something before you starve yourself."

Hope bloomed and she turned away from the table refusing to sit down.

"You will eat, or I will have a servant force you."

She spat in the soup and glared defiance at her father.

His face darkened and he moved to slap her. Marriette lifted her face.

"Go ahead, Father," she said, "you enjoyed yourself so much the last time."

"You try to seduce me again?" he hissed, but sat back in his carved armchair. "You ought to be burned at the stake as a witch."

"Better burning in hell than another day in this house!" Marriette screamed. The words burned her throat like acid. She drew breath to continue, but her father nodded at the servants and two men pushed her down into the chair. She fought against them with her weakness, but they ignored her.

"My loyal servants know how troubled in mind you have been, Marriette. They will know to treat whatever you say as the ravings of a lunatic. Now, will we eat as civilized people, or will you be fed like a sick animal?" Her father's cold voice shattered the hope and the rage. Marriette became a ghost again. She let her arms fall to the table.

Her defiance shattered, Marriette slumped in her chair and ate the soup. The next day, she was again brought down to dine with her father, and every night following. He talked at her as if she hung on every word. He was already important, but schemed constantly to improve his position as if the whole world conspired to cast him down from his pinnacle. Marriette only cared that he didn't demand she respond. Her body filled out her dresses again. She tried to find her anger with her new health, but it was buried deep. The only emotion she felt was self-loathing.

One evening, he looked especially pleased with himself.

"You want to escape my house?" he asked. "I have arranged a marriage for you. He is willing to overlook your...unfortunate virtue because he is growing older and needs an heir."

"How fortunate for you, Father. How much was he willing to pay to marry the daughter of the Duke deLanguiers? Have you recovered the cost of raising a woman of dubious virtue?"

"Careful," her father said, face darkening, "I will not be mocked."

She looked in his face and saw an awful hunger in his eyes.

"Very well, Father," she said, "I will be the dutiful bride."

The wedding day came far too slowly for Marriette who counted the days to freedom from her father. She couldn't imagine that this groom would be any better than her father, but he couldn't be any worse. She woke in the night with nightmares of a man lying on top of her as her father had, causing awful tearing pain. Some nights, her father grunted and muttered in her dreams, other nights it was a man identical to the duke, but lacking a face.

Cold-faced women fitted her for a grand gown in the softest white. A veil would hide her face and gloves would cover her hands. I will look like a ghost. Marriette almost smiled. Her father lectured her each evening at dinner on the importance of this union. She would bind this man closer to him.

The night before the wedding, her father came to her room.

"Remember, daughter, you are mine. I brought you into this world. You will do as I say whether you abide here or in your husband's home." He looked hungrily at her, breathing hard.

Marriette just nodded.

"I must rest, Father," she said, "if I am to look beautiful and do you honour tomorrow."

Her father spun and left the room. She heard the lock click into place. She didn't care. Tomorrow she would be free. By some blessing, she didn't dream at all.

Early in the morning, the servants came and dressed Marriette in her wedding dress. They pulled her hair into an intricate arrangement of braids and flowers. They put makeup on to add colour to her face, then placed the veil on her head to cover it. The carriage came and took her and her father to the cathedral for the grand wedding.

The church was full, as befitted the marriage of the daughter of the Duke of deLanguiers, the most important noble in the realm apart from the king. The king himself was there looking much younger than Marriette thought a king ought to be. He had to be there on the off chance that he would forbid the marriage and claim her for himself. It was a tradition that Marriette's father had explained carefully. She wasn't sure whether her father wanted the king to notice her or not. The queen certainly wouldn't approve of the king claiming her. The king just nodded absently at her when she walked in on the arm of her father.

Huge windows surrounded her with a riot of colour contrasting with the flat grey stone making up the columns and walls of the cathedral. People filled the vast space and added their own colours and scents to the mix. If she looked up, she would see the carved ceiling. Right now, she was determined to make it to the front of the cathedral without tripping or otherwise humiliating her father. She could see the archbishop in his gold robes at the front, waiting patiently for her to arrive, so he might begin.

The only people she knew were her father and the archbishop, who had visited and lectured her at length about the ceremony and what was expected of her. Her oppression from the stares increased as she walked up the long aisle. She wondered what they thought about her, what her father had told them. They arrived at the front and her father joined her hands with the stranger who was going to be her husband. The groom was older than her, not as old as her father, but much older than Art. She could see dimly through the veil that there were lines around his eyes and he leaned on a cane. She thought it an affectation until she saw the twisted leg that no amount of tailoring could hide.

He looked almost as nervous as Marriette, but then, if he knew what kind of family he was marrying into, he should be terrified.

"Friends, we have come to celebrate the joining of Count Torrance leBraun and Marriette deLanguiers..." the archbishop began the liturgy. Marriette stood, knelt and spoke as required. It seemed like the ceremony lasted forever. Finally, the archbishop concluded. "...I pronounce you husband and wife. You may kiss the bride."

As her husband lifted her veil back, Marriette got her first good look at him. The lines around his eyes crinkled as he smiled wryly. His brown eyes were warm.

I could learn to like this man.

"So, will I do?" he asked quietly.

"I think so," she said just as softly.

He kissed her gently on the cheek then led her after the archbishop to put their signatures in the immense register. After centuries of use, it was little more than half full; not many people were important enough to get married in the cathedral.

A grand celebration followed the wedding service but Marriette didn't remember anything but the brief awkward dance with Torrance. Mercifully, she was able to politely avoid dancing with the eager young men who flocked around her trying to use her to gain her father's ear. At midnight, Marriette and Torrance were allowed to escape, leaving the party to wind down without them. Torrance handed her up into a coach that wasn't nearly as grand as her father's but more comfortable without his presence.

"I understand that you don't know me at all," her husband said taking her hand, "but I expect we will learn more about each other as time goes by." He stared off into the nighttime streets for a long moment. "I will endeavour not to let the ghosts of the past come between us, but someone of my age has as many scars inside as out. There may be days that they claim my attention and it will seem that I am cold and distant. I apologize in advance for those times."

"We each have our scars," Marriette said.

"Your father told me of your experience at the hand of the Wagoners."

Marriette opened her mouth to explain the truth, but she remembered the look her father had in her room the night before. Just how long was his reach?

"I am not ready to talk of it," she said.

They rode the rest of the way in silence. Marriette found that she liked the warm strength of Torrance's hand on hers. The carriage pulled up to a house that was not nearly as large as her old home, but there were flowers set out and a staff of servants awaited their arrival. Torrance introduced her to them, then led her across the threshold of her new home.

"I cannot carry you across as custom demands," he said, "but this is now your home as much as it is mine. If you need anything, you just need to ask, and, if it is in my power, I will get it for you. I will protect you to the limit of my strength." He led her to a suite of rooms decorated in subtle blues and greens. "My staff begged permission to redo the master suite in your honour."

Marriette wandered through the rooms marveling at the love and care that went into decorating them.

"They wouldn't let me see them either. I have been living in the guest rooms for a month." He came up behind her and put his arms around her waist. Marriette stiffened and Torrance began to pull away. She put her hands over his.

"You just startled me," she whispered. "I am not used to a gentle touch." She turned and took Torrance's face in her hands. "I will try to be as good a wife as you plan to be a husband, but all this is new to me."

Torrance ran his fingers through the tangle of hair and flowers that graced her head. He kissed her forehead gently. She lifted her face and he kissed her lips. Her hands clutched at his back as the kiss grew stronger. Torrance's hands wandered to the fastenings at the back of Marriette's dress. The heavy gown slid to the floor leaving only her underdress. She shivered uncontrollably and buried her face in his shoulder. The ties for the underdress were under his fingers. Marriette made herself nod, and soon it, too, slipped to the floor. She gasped for breath, but allowed Torrance to step back and look at her. His eyes were sad as he pulled a sheet from the bed and wrapped her in it. As soon as the soft material covered her, she was able to catch her breath.

"I know I am not beautiful," she said softly.

"No!" he said. "You are more beautiful than I deserve. I need to cover you so I can control myself. I will not force myself on you. Our marriage bed is for pleasure, not fear." He led her to the huge bed. She could see a deep, deep sorrow in his eyes. "I will sleep on the couch."

"Please," she said holding his hand, "please, just hold me tonight. I don't want to be alone."

So he lay down beside her and she laid her head on his chest and wept quietly. He stroked her hair and whispered gentle words in her ears.

ACE OF CUPS

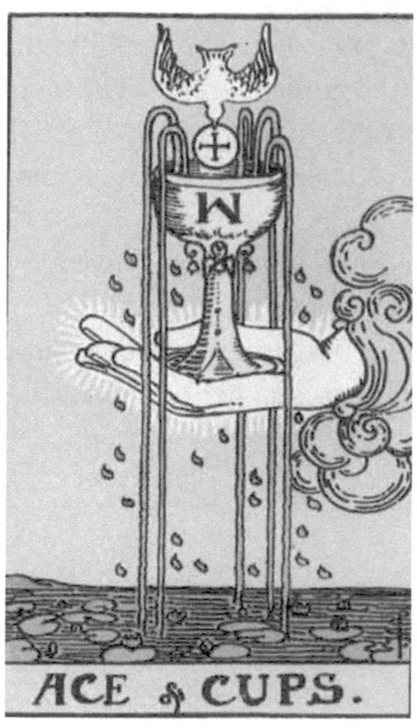

Marriette woke with strange warmth at her back; an arm came around and held her gently. A vision of her father dropping his belt hit her, and she sat up with a gasp. A man slept beside her. She tried to get away, only managing to tangle herself in the sheets. Her struggles woke Torrance who rolled away from her flailing hands. That freed her to fall out of the bed with a thump. He came over to help her to her feet. She stared at him for a moment before recalling the wedding, and started to giggle.

"Not quite the awakening people expect after their wedding night," she said, and again caught a brief glimpse of sadness before Torrance smiled in his turn. He turned her around to face the mirror.

"See how beautiful you are?" he said. "Doubt that the sky is blue, doubt that winter is cold, but never doubt that you are beautiful." He stepped away from her and removed the remains of his wedding finery, considerably more wrinkled than the day before. He stood behind her naked. "I have seen you. If you will look upon your husband, you will see what a poor bargain you got."

Marriette turned and looked at Torrance. His face held painful vulnerability, but she forced her eyes down across his strong chest and stomach. A brief flash of her father standing over her made her eyes jump to his legs. His right leg was straight and muscular; his left was twisted and thin. She marveled that he could use it at all. Marriette looked him in the face again, here might be a friend, if not truly a lover.

She touched his face.

"I think you are gentle, and strong," she said, "I would dearly wish to be with you as wife and husband, but there is too much ugliness in me yet. I am sorry. I will understand if you send me back to my father."

"Heavens no!" Torrance said. "You are my wife, the archbishop himself said it. We will find our way, together. Yet, may I ask that we get dressed? As much I enjoy watching you, it is...distracting."

The servants came in a while later and found them wrapped in soft robes laughing and talking. They set the breakfast tray down and slipped out again.

So started the new pattern for Marriette's life. She slept beside Torrance in the huge bed then woke to stare at his masculine body. As hard as she tried, she couldn't get past the memories of her father. Yet other feelings started flowing through her veins. Torrance told her so often that she was beautiful that she almost believed him. Even if passion didn't awake in her, she found that she looked forward to spending her day with this man.

She filled the rest of her days with learning to run the old house that the leBraun family had called home for generations.

"Anna," she called to her head housekeeper.

"Yes, Mistress."

"I feel like having greens with dinner today. Perhaps Cook could send a couple of girls down to the market to find some."

"Certainly, I will ask her." Anna bustled away while Marriette walked through her home.

Only a few weeks, and I am more at home here than I ever was at Father's house. She pinched dead blossoms off houseplants as she passed, and occasionally rearranged the placement of ornaments. The only thing she never touched was the small painting in the front hall of a woman holding a baby. It had a black scarf draped across the top of the frame. Anna had told her once that they were Torrance's first wife and his son. He never talked of them, just as he never mentioned the awful wound that had crippled him.

All his staff adored him, and that fondness transferred to Marriette.

"My Lady," Anna said, "the cloth merchant is here with samples for the East Room. He'd like you to approve his selection. She led Marriette to the small room being done over as a guest room for Torrance's people visiting from the estate in the country. The cloth merchant had fabric laid out on the bed.

"Here, my Lady," he said, "this isn't the finest fabric available, but it's sturdy and will be welcoming."

Marriette ran her fingers across the fabrics; one had a smooth texture which kept calling her fingers back to it.

"My lady has fine taste," the merchant said. "I included a bolt of fine fabric so you might know the difference. The other is good enough."

Anna stood in the door with a slight frown on her face. Was the frown for the fine fabric or the cheap? Marriette closed her eyes and went over the bolts one more time. If she had traveled into the city to do business with Torrance, she'd want to sleep next to the smooth texture of the fine fabric. Why not treat all visitors as important?

"This is the count's home," Marriette said. The frown on Anna's face eased slightly. "All the rooms should be suitable for the count or any guest he invites. We will use the finer fabric."

Anna smiled now and nodded.

"Of course, my Lady," the cloth merchant's face turned pink as he pushed the other bolts aside.

"You had my lord's interests in mind," Marriette said. "I am not upset, let us discuss colour…."

As the days passed, the best thing Marriette discovered—in this house she wasn't invisible. The servants didn't bow and cringe as the servants in her father's house did when he passed them. Instead, they smiled and nodded.

She found her way to Torrance's office. Marriette had never known her father to do any work other than scheming for more power. Torrance spent a great deal of time looking over the accounts of his city house and, more importantly, his estates to the south.

"They work hard so we can live easy," he said. "They deserve my attention. I will take you there in the fall and show you off. Look at the estimates for the harvest." Marriette went over the reports with him until they were called away for lunch. They laughed and joked through the meal, a strange but welcome experience.

One morning, while she was supervising the arrival of supplies, Marriette discovered Joan with her board checking off the order as it was delivered.

"Joan!" she said. "How are you?"

"So, you are married now," Joan didn't seem as confident as last time they met.

"My father arranged it."

"But you are happy."

"Yes," Marriette said, "I am happy."

"I'm glad for you," Joan said, "I truly am. It's just…Arthur hasn't shown up. He's never been gone this long before and Father is beside himself with worry."

"I'm so sorry. Torrance will ask his people to keep a watch for him."

"He will look for your old boyfriend?" Joan asked.

"No," Marriette said, "for the brother of a new friend."

Torrance was glad to help out his young wife's new friend and descriptions of Arthur went out with the people who travelled back and forth between the city and the leBraun estates. Joan became a regular visitor at Marriette's home, bringing not just needed supplies but someone for Marriette to talk to. Joan rearranged her schedule of deliveries so they could share tea.

One day, Joan showed up red eyed and silent.

"What is it, Joan?" asked Marriette. "I can see something is bothering you. You've hardly said two words all afternoon."

"You'll think it's foolish."

"Hardly."

"Wait here," Joan said, and went out to the wagon. She came back holding a boot. It was moldy and torn, but hardly the subject for tears. "I just found this on a rag picker's cart. He told me that he found it on the riverbank just downstream from the bridge to the Broken Dog. I think it is Arthur's. He had a pair of custom boots that he was ridiculously proud of. See, here is the marking on the side. It is supposed to be a wagon wheel. I always teased him that it looked more like a pie." Joan dropped the boot and burst into tears.

"Where did they find it?"

"It was in the river. When Arthur disappeared, it was in spring flood. If he had drunk too much and fallen into the river he would never survive. More than a few people have drowned in that river."

"I am so sorry, Joan."

"What is the upset?" Torrance asked, coming into the room. "Anything I can do to help?"

Marriette showed him the boot and explained Joan's fears.

"That's a bad stretch," Torrance sighed and handed the boot back to Joan. "I can ask if the river walkers found anything after the river dropped. I know it isn't what you want to hear, but at least you will know." He left to return to his office and send a secretary out on the grim task.

"How are you doing?" whispered Joan when the door had closed. "He was your lover."

"No," Marriette said, "he was never a lover. It might have been easier if he were. Then I would have enjoyed the sin my father accused me of."

"I've heard whispers that you were assaulted by Wagoners." Joan shook her head. "They say that is why you were married off to a lesser house."

"Don't let Torrance hear you call his house 'lesser'. The Wagoners brought me home with my virtue intact, if not my reputation." Marriette sighed bitterly. "It wasn't them."

"One of your father's servants? Why would he protect...." Joan saw Marriette's shaking head and the tears. "My God, Marriette, he didn't!" Marriette nodded her head and burst into tears. Joan clung to her and added her own sobs. Torrance came to the door, but left again without speaking.

"Have you told him?" Joan asked a long time later.

"I couldn't. I can't. He would hate me."

"I don't think he has it in him to hate you, but he deserves the truth."

"You're right." Marriette dabbed at her eyes with a lace handkerchief. "He's been more than understanding. I'll try."

Joan left soon after carrying the boot and its sad news to her father.

Marriette planned to talk to Torrance that night about her father and what he had done to her. Maybe Joan was right, maybe if I tell him then the awful visions won't come between us anymore. She hurried off to find her husband.

She found him in his office holding a letter with a look of wonder on his face. When he saw her, he came around his desk and hugged her. Marriette stiffened as she always did, then deliberately relaxed into his strong embrace. She held him for a long time and breathed in his slightly musty scent.

"You need to get out of this office more," she said into his shirt. "You are beginning to smell like it."

"Speaking of getting out more," Torrance let her go to show her the letter, "we have been invited to the Summer Ball at the palace. I think the king is taken with you. He specifically asked for you to be there." He was so pleased that Marriette let him sweep her off to the dress shop immediately, leaving no time to talk.

Somehow, there was never a good time to talk. Evening was too close to bedtime, and even knowing Torrance would never hurt her, going to bed with him was a battle with black waves in her head which threatened to drown her. He let her get changed by herself and only came in when she was ready, but as many nights as not she shivered in the bed fighting visions of her father.

Mornings were better, but Marriette loved the warm casual chat over breakfast and couldn't face despoiling it with the horror of her reality. The rest of the day was caught up in managing house and estate. There was little space, or privacy, for the opening of hearts. Now preparing for the Summer Ball took even more time.

All excuses Marriette admitted when she woke in the night beside the warmth of her husband. The truth was she feared his reaction. She couldn't bear being shut out of his life. But how could he still welcome the evil person she was into his home?

The longer Marriette didn't speak the harder it became to imagine what she would say. She convinced herself it was better this way. So she kept her silence.

Torrance reported that no body matching Arthur's description had turned up along the river. Joan's father refused to believe that Arthur was dead without a body. He had told Joan that he was sure he would feel if his son were dead. Poor Joan was torn between her father's hope and her own certainty that her brother was gone. As the Summer Ball approached, there was less and less time for the young women to talk.

The dress Marriette was wearing to the ball was a lush gold fabric with more lace and pearls and fancy work than Marriette imagined possible. She loved it, even though it made her feel guilty. Since she helped with the accounts, she knew what it cost.

"You could feed a village with this!" she said one day to Torrance.

"Well, let's sell it and find out." He laughed at the face she made. "Look, you help me with the accounts, so you know what these figures are." He pointed to the ledger.

"That's the cost for maintaining your estates and the land around them."

"Right, but it isn't just maintenance on fences and such." He flipped through the book. "Here, last winter a storm dropped a huge amount of snow all at once. Being farther south they aren't used to those loads and a roof collapsed. This is what it cost to fix it. Over here is our payment to the list that the parish has to make sure that everyone gets enough to eat. Here is the bonus we paid for an especially good harvest...." He closed the book and took Marriette's hand.

"It is part of our job to represent these people and make sure that they are fairly treated. Yet, to represent them, we must be dressed so that our voices are heard. You will meet some of those people when you go with me in a month or so. There will be people who come to me to resolve disputes. That is their right. It is not all privilege, we have some responsibilities too."

"Though, there are those who would take the privilege without the responsibility. They say that they are born to rule while the people are born to serve. I say that rule makes us accountable for how we treat *all* our people."

"This sounds like an old argument," Marriette said, thinking again of the difference between her father and her husband.

"Older than I am, and unlikely to be resolved soon." He stood up, "I think I heard the bell for supper."

SEVEN OF CUPS

The day of the king's summer ball arrived. The entire household was in an uproar as the servants tried to get Marriette and Torrance looking good enough not to embarrass themselves. Marriette's hair was teased and arranged, then rearranged, as the heat made it go flat. She was made up, perfumed, and fit into the golden ball gown. Finally, just as the sun touched the horizon, she was helped into the carriage while Torrance climbed after her. The driver's muffled voice ordered the horses to walk and Marriette and Torrance were driven off to the palace.

The attendees of the ball arrived in reverse order of importance, so Torrance and Marriette, while not the first ones there, had plenty of time to check out the decorations and the food. Flowers and greenery dotted the walls. Birds in cages sang sweet melodies over top of the hum of the people talking. The banquet table groaned under berries and ices and cold meats. Yet, as colourful as the room was, the people outshone it. Women in fine gowns of every colour blended or clashed with their men whose own outfits rivaled a peacock's.

Torrance and Marriette chatted with the people who were already there. Marriette remembered some from occasions when her father had dragged her along. She was amazed how much she enjoyed their conversation now that they didn't see her as a path to her father.

The moon had started to rise when Duke deLanguiers arrived. Smoke from the candles made the air hazy, but the looks of desire and fear sent toward the duke were clear enough. He strutted past the crowd, which parted before his red and gold splendour. His demeanour announced there was no one present worthy of speaking to him. He stopped in front of Marriette and stared coldly at his daughter.

Torrance had gone to fetch drinks for Marriette and himself and the people she had just been speaking with turned away as if she and her father were in a bubble, alone in the room.

"I would have thought my daughter would have come to visit her father before now," he said.

"You must know that a wife's first duty is to her husband." Marriette astonished herself with the courage to defy her father.

"You *will* visit," he said, leaning over to speak quietly, "I have questions you must answer."

Torrance maneuvered across the floor, glasses with ice and punch in each hand. His presence gave her courage. She could never betray him. He nodded at her and disappeared back into the crowd.

"I will never again set foot in your house while you are alive," Marriette's stomach ached and she tasted bile at the back of her throat. "And I will not answer any of your questions now, or ever."

"Foolish girl, you don't know what I can do to you," her father said as he gripped her forearm. She would have bruises in the morning.

"I doubt that it would be much worse than you have already done." Marriette took a deep breath and tried to pull her arm away.

"It is pleasant to see father and daughter reunited," the archbishop said. "Henri, you are wrinkling her lovely dress. Whatever plot you are hatching will just have to wait."

The duke dropped Marriette's arm like it was suddenly red hot and stalked off.

"One advantage of my age is that I no longer fear political repercussions," the archbishop said. "My dear, you look even more radiant than you did on your wedding day. If you ever need to talk—about anything—just stop by the cathedral."

Marriette looked into the kindly face of the archbishop and smiled.

"Thank you, Your Eminence."

He wandered off again. Marriette went and found her husband. He was arguing politics with a man dressed in a simple black suit that made him look like a crow among the exotic colours of the rest of the crowd.

"Marriette," Torrance said, "this is the king's Justicar. Tamas, my wife Marriette."

Tamas bowed over Marriette's hand.

"If all our nobles were as wise as Torrance and as beautiful as you, our land would truly be blessed."

"Oh, please," Marriette said, "I can see a dozen ladies from here who outshine me tonight."

"Perhaps, perhaps, but I must look deeper than appearances." The Justicar winked and slipped away into the press of nobles.

"He is a good man, if a little odd," Torrance said. "His views on responsibility and the law are even more radical than mine." He led Marriette over to the buffet and filled a plate for her.

White moonlight shone through the windows when the majordomo thumped his staff on the floor.

"Lords and Ladies, his Majesty King Harald and the Queen Sarandia." Everyone bowed in their direction then slowly returned to their conversations. The king and queen walked opposite directions around the ballroom talking to a few lucky people.

They were followed by guards whose eyes flitted across everyone in the room. In addition, the king was shadowed by a large man who looked lighter on his feet than most of the dancers, and a much shorter man who peered about as if he couldn't quite see anyone clearly.

"The big man is the king's marshal," Torrance whispered. "He is part bodyguard, and part champion, and all dangerous. The other man is the king's cousin, vonFromme, he's a bit fussy, but harmless."

Marriette nodded. Torrance saw people as having a place and value in society, a contrast to her father who only saw tools to be used. Servants walked through the crowd carrying trays with bite sized food and tiny glasses of wines and liqueurs. She breathed in the warring perfumes of dozens of fine ladies and smiled. It was like being in the garden with her mother, before both the garden and her mother died.

The king walked past and nodded at Marriette, but didn't stop to talk. She wasn't sure if she was relieved or disappointed. As important as her father was, he'd never brought her anywhere this near royalty. The music began soon after the royal couple arrived and Marriette watched the dancers wistfully. She enjoyed dancing; just not the political maneuvering that usually went with it.

After the first couple of sets, a younger man, who Torrance introduced as a business associate, asked her to dance. With Torrance's permission, she joined him on the dance floor. She kept checking on Torrance, but he encouraged her to enjoy herself. She relaxed and let her husband's friends escort her. She saw her father frowning at her and turned away.

The moon had set when the king's cousin asked her to dance. Marriette was tired by now, but one more dance wouldn't hurt.

"I am so glad you are enjoying yourself," Lord vonFromme said as he twirled her expertly about the floor. "Torrance is a good fellow, but a little intense. It is really too bad about his leg." Nothing he said was insulting, but his voice set her teeth on edge. It was as if there was some constant underlying message that she couldn't quite hear. She would just enjoy the dance. They finished their set and he returned her to Torrance. She caught a look of disappointment on vonFromme's face. She couldn't imagine why.

She headed back to where Torrance awaited her. The duke talked to the king and looked tremendously pleased with himself. Marriette turned away to find her husband.

Torrance's face was grey with pain. Marriette was shocked that he looked so bad so quickly. She put her arm around him to try and support him. He patted her arm absently but watched her father.

"I wonder what he is up to?" he said.

"I don't want to know," Marriette said.

"That is the problem with politics," Torrance said with a sigh, "most often what you must learn is what you wish to know the least. Ah, the king is leaving; if you don't mind, my dear, I think I must get home and off my feet."

Marriette took his arm and began heading toward the door. She was afraid that Torrance would collapse before they had made all their goodbyes. Their carriage waited at the front. Torrance pulled himself in with a grunt and settled into the seat.

"This cursed leg has turned me into half a man," he complained.

"You are a whole man to me," Marriette said.

"Am I?" Torrance asked then shook his head. "I apologize, Marriette. I am tired and out of sorts."

Marriette nodded and rode the rest of the way in silence.

The staff met them at the door and helped Torrance into the house.

"You would have enjoyed it tonight, LisAnne," he said to the picture.

"You still miss her?" asked Marriette.

"We never got along. We fought like cat and dog all the time, but we both loved our son, Niklas." He took Marriette's hand, "I am very glad you are here. I just wish you could have met Niklas." Torrance limped away to the bedroom while Marriette stood looking at the picture.

"Anna, please clean that black cloth and put it back, and put some flowers under the picture. Daisies, I think."

"Yes, my Lady," the housekeeper looked pleased.

In their quarters, a maid helped her out of the ball gown.

"I will take this to have it cleaned," the maid said.

Torrance sat on a chair trying to rub the cramps of his leg.

"Let me," Marriette made him move to the bed, then sat beside him and rubbed his calf. The muscles relaxed under her touch. After some time, she moved her ministrations to his thigh. She loosened his belt and pulled the pants off. Working her fingers into the knots of his muscles she concentrated on easing the pain her husband was feeling. He rolled onto his back and she continued working on his leg. His skin was warm and soft. She enjoyed the knowledge that she was helping him. Marriette allowed her eyes to close.

It was a shock when he sat up and embraced her; a worse shock when he kissed her with desperate urgency and reached under her dress. She gasped and tried to pull away, but Torrance didn't stop. His caresses became more intimate. Marriette's heart pounded painfully. She could hardly breathe. The vision of her father dropping the belt and fumbling at his pants came to her and she pushed away violently. The thin material of her underdress tore and Torrance fell heavily to the floor, but Marriette didn't notice.

"Father, don't, please, stop, stop, STOP!" She huddled on the bed crying and rocking. Torrance came around and tried to put an arm around her but she pushed him away again. "Don't touch me!" she screamed. "You are just like him."

"Your father?" Torrance said, choking. "Your father?" He stumbled from the room and shut the door behind him. Marriette threw herself onto the bed and wept until she fell asleep.

In the morning, she was still alone in the bed. She missed the warmth of Torrance at her back. She pulled the sheets around her and huddled in the bed rocking. Torrance hated her. Why else would he run away and not come back? The truth disgusted him. Marriette began crying again. The maids came in, took one look at her, and ran out.

Anna came in with a tray.

"Poor dear." She put a cup in Marriette's hands and made her drink the hot sweet tea, then tucked her back into bed. "Rest. The day will go on without you."

Marriette hid in the room for the next few days being cosseted by Anna and the rest of the staff. She didn't see Torrance the entire time. Part of her was relieved, and part was disappointed. Finally, she made herself get out of bed and dress.

Wandering through the house, Marriette tried to recover the contentment she had felt just a short week before. It had vanished, and in its place lay the certainty Torrance was avoiding her. Her misery deepened. In desperation, she decided to go to the cathedral. Maybe the archbishop would have some advice.

Marriette had only been in the cathedral a few times, and not since her wedding. Empty of people, the sanctuary was filled with light and the dance of dust motes in the air. Marriette watched entranced until the archbishop interrupted her.

"My staff said you were here. I decided to come and see for myself." He sat himself in a pew next to her. "I'm thinking it isn't just the beauty of the architecture that brought you here?"

"My husband hates me," Marriette said bluntly.

"I would have said that he dotes on you."

"I…I can't be with him as a wife with her husband."

The old man sat in silence. Marriette tried to recapture her enchantment with the light, but a knot in her stomach twisted ever tighter.

"I want to, but I can't." She hung her head and whispered in the softest of voices. "Not after what my father did to me. He said I seduced him, that I am a witch." She lifted her head heedless of the torrent of tears pouring from her eyes. "Why? Why did it happen to me?"

The archbishop sighed deeply.

"I don't think the Duke deLanguiers sees anything but his own need." He pulled out a handkerchief and dried Marriette's tears. "There is no law on heaven or earth that we have not broken. Listen to me, child, this is not your fault. This is your father's sin and he will pay the price for it when he stands before God."

"But he told me—"

"I am sure he did, but his words can't lay responsibility for his crime on your shoulders."

"So, what do I do?"

There was a long silence before the old man sighed again.

"You go home and make up with your husband, because what your father did is not his fault either."

Marriette left feeling both better and worse than she did before. When she got home, she went looking for Torrance. She found him in his office surrounded by mounds of paper. He looked up.

"Hello."

She tried to tell him about the tangle of feelings in her heart, but couldn't find them.

"I was young when I married LisAnne," Torrance said, as he stared out the window. "Young and impatient. She wasn't ready for our wedding night. I don't know what she had been told about what happens between a man and a woman, but she just lay there without moving or talking. I took her anyway, even though she began crying before I was done. We never slept together again. Niklas was conceived that night, in lust and pain, yet we both loved him. I loved him so much I wanted to have another child. She wanted to leave, instead of submitting to me again. Niklas cried as we shouted at each other through the window of the carriage."

"The horses spooked. I tried to catch them but was too slow. The carriage ran over my leg and shattered it. Without a driver, the horses ran out of control through the city. It finally crashed and both LisAnne and Niklas were killed." He looked at Marriette. "I almost didn't survive myself, but my mother still lived then and was determined I would live. I swore when I agreed to marry you that I wouldn't make the same mistakes with you. How can you trust me, if I can't trust myself?" He crumpled paper under his hands, but made no move to look at Marriette.

"I don't know," Marriette fought to stay on her feet when her legs wanted to let her drop to the floor. Every breath was forced past a lump like a knife in her breast. She wanted to hear him say he wanted to be with her, even now, but when Torrance didn't say anymore, she left him with his accounts. She went to their room and heaved the contents of her stomach into the washbasin.

A servant girl must have heard, because she took away the basin and brought a clean one.

Torrance didn't come to their room that night, or any night after. Marriette missed his warmth in her bed, and the conversation in the mornings. Speaking with Torrance was awkward, as if a barrier had gone up between them. She didn't know how to reach him and he didn't touch her or say more than he needed to her.

They were invited to more balls, and made their appearances, pretending everything was fine. Torrance went to talk to the Justicar and others while Marriette danced with some of the young men who continued to cluster around her. Her father never talked to her, but the king's cousin made a point of escorting her on the dance floor at least once each evening. His conversation continued to be innocuous, but at the same time laden with meaning. Marriette was sure he was playing some game that was beyond her, but she didn't care - just one more chore to get through.

She whiled away the time between balls, wondering what her life would have been like if she'd run off with Arthur. She would have had to work, like Joan. There would be no balls, no gowns, no servants. She wondered how long Arthur would have lasted before he too demanded his due from her.

After arriving home from the latest ball, Marriette undressed, then dismissed the maids and threw herself on the bed. She was as unhappy now as she had been happy before that horrible night. She had to talk to Torrance. He was staying in the guest room, so she put on a loose robe and went to find him. As she approached his room, a woman she had never seen before left his room. Marriette leaned against the wall and tried not to cry out loud.

She had lost him. Somehow, she found her way back to her room and fell into bed and screamed into her pillow until she was hoarse. She was no true wife and he'd turned to someone else for comfort. She hadn't imagined how much it hurt to be betrayed.

She had a dream that night of the old Wagoner woman and the cards. Marriette had forgotten them, with everything that had followed. She tried to hear the woman's words, but she heard shouting instead. Suddenly, the man and woman in chains on the Devil card were Art and Marriette. Arthur shouted at someone who was attacking him. He fought desperately, but the Devil's chain kept holding him back.

Marriette woke with a start. She tried to forget the dream, but she couldn't shake it. It haunted her through the day. She didn't dare talk to Joan about it for fear Torrance would hear. She had the dream again the next night and the night after. Art's wounds grew worse. No one could survive them, yet he still fought against the chains.

Art was alive and needed her. The dreams showed they were connected. She would find out what had happened to him and what that connection meant.

Marriette found some clothes to travel in, then left a note for Torrance.

I am not the wife you need. I hope you are happy with your new woman. I have gone to find Arthur.

She folded it in half and wrote Torrance's name on it and left it for the servants to find in the morning.

FIVE OF SWORDS

Zeb came back to consciousness slowly. The ache where the arrow had been removed from his back and the rub and hurt of other scrapes and bruises from his run were present, but not as bad as he expected. Hands ran firmly up and down his body exuding warmth and confidence. He began to take in the murmur of voices in the room.

"He should be dead. The wound itself should have killed him, even without the blood loss."

"Yet, here he is, alive, and it is our duty to heal him."

"The only good thing about the bleeding was it may have kept the infection out of the wound."

"We can only pray."

"Pray—but clean and dress his swounds."

"Of course, Brother Stephen."

Zeb opened his eyes to see two men in plain brown robes over him.

"Your patient is awake, I will leave him to your healing." The speaker glowed within with a hard, clear light. Zeb blinked at the light. The door shut firmly, leaving him with the other man.

Brother Stephen sat beside him. A chubby, old man with wispy white hair, shaved in the center of his head, he shone with a warm light that hurt Zeb's eyes. Zeb tried to sit up to escape, but the flesh that he inhabited betrayed him and he fell back to the bed.

"Easy, friend, you are safe here." Brother Stephen's voice was as soft as the rest of him. "The abbot has given you sanctuary, so nothing may disturb you, but by the will of God."

Zeb gnashed his teeth at the mention of the One, but his weakness wouldn't allow him more. The darkness swallowed him.

He woke again quickly and completely. Brother Stephen slept slumped in a chair beside the bed. Zeb would have crushed him, but the cursed flesh of his body refused to obey. His struggle did wake Brother Stephen. Zeb opened his mouth to rail at the monk, but no words would form. Every time he tried to speak his throat closed and he'd cough. Brother Stephen spoon fed Zeb and helped him to use the bucket in the corner.

"You took a terrible wound from that arrow, then you lost much of your blood running through the forest. Twas God's grace that you fell in front of that farmer and he brought you here."

Zeb opened and closed his mouth several times trying to speak, but could make no sound at all.

"I fear that the shock of your wound has rendered you silent. Try not to trouble yourself over it. There are many in this place who find silence preferable to speech. Because I am a healer, I am permitted to speak to you or others as I need," the brother smiled, "or perhaps it is my joy in speaking that made me a healer."

Zeb tried to growl at the fool and railed at the weakness of the flesh he was imprisoned in. He had no strength to silence this chattering mortal.

"You need rest, so I will not disturb you further with my prattle. If you need me, clap." Brother Stephen demonstrated. "God willing, you will heal without infection." He pulsed with light at the mention of the One, so Zeb cringed away. The brother left the room and Zeb was alone.

He could have howled at the irony of these foolish monks bringing him in to heal him. Couldn't they see that he was not just another mortal? But then, how they could see anything past the light pouring from them was a mystery.

The next days were slow torture for Zeb. His voice did not return, and he developed a fever. He wandered in and out of consciousness, sometimes shaking with cold, sometimes sweating with heat. Brother Stephen stayed with him constantly, not talking, but praying. Even through his closed eyes the light from the monk burned. Other brothers wandered in on errands. They all glowed, but none with the intensity of the healer. The abbot came in and frowned at Zeb a few times, but said nothing.

The fever broke after a week, to the joy of Brother Stephen, but it left Zeb helpless. He consumed vast amounts of thin broth. After a few more days he graduated to having a chunk of rough bread with the soup. Though not as hearty as at the castle, the food slowly gave Zeb his strength back. His voice still refused to work. He ground his teeth at the humiliation of needing to summon Brother Stephen then pantomime his need.

A week after the fever broke Brother Stephen had Zeb up out of bed. At first just walking across the room exhausted his strength, but soon he was walking the hallways. He wandered out into the yard and was slowly put to work shoveling out the barn and weeding the small garden that grew within the walls. He enjoyed his freedom from Brother Stephen's prattling, but mostly from the blessed light that shone from the old monk night and day.

The other monks grew used to seeing Zeb around, and since most of them were under vows of silence, his involuntary silence wasn't much of a burden. The abbot continued to stay aloof. He didn't mingle with the others except when they went into the tiny chapel. Zeb had refused to enter the chapel under any circumstance, though Brother Stephen asked him at every opportunity.

"I fear that your silence is the result of your body and spirit at war," he said. "To speak again, you will need to resolve that conflict. What better way than to come into the presence of the Almighty?"

One day, almost a month after Zeb's arrival, Brother Stephen was being especially persistent. Zeb pushed him away and snatched a shovel to strike him down. Strength flowed through him and he grinned. Now he would be free of this monk and his light. Brother Stephen scrambled away and ran from him. Zeb pursued him. He didn't pay attention to where the monk led him.

When Zeb stepped through the door into the chapel, he met a figure so bright he couldn't see its face, standing between him and his intended victim. Zeb shouted and swung the shovel at it. A searing white sword shattered the shovel. Zeb was thrown back through the door of the chapel to land in the dirt of the yard. He woke to find the abbot standing over him.

"Bind him in chains," the abbot said, "and lock him in his room."

They confined Zeb to a small cell with chains fastening him to the wall. A bucket was left within reach in the corner, and bowls of the thin soup pushed within his reach. He tested the strength of his chains, but they were too strong for him to break. Trapped, Zeb sat on his bed and nursed his fury.

He lost count of the bowls of soup he drank before sounds from outside roused him from his lethargy. It sounded like fighting. Zeb was certain that he heard the clash of arms and the moan of wounded men. He gathered his strength and waited.

The door to his room was kicked open, and a man Zeb recognized from the castle stared at him then laughed.

"So, these monks aren't as foolish as I thought. They have you tamed. They converted you to their God yet?" He stepped into the room with sword lowered.

Zeb screamed and threw himself at the foolish mortal. Zeb took the man's bloody sword and used it to cut him open. The perfume of blood and guts called him to battle. His unwitting saviour sat trying to push himself back together as Zeb hammered the chains until they broke.

With the chains, the hold on his voice shattered. Screaming blasphemies, Zeb ran through the monastery killing anyone who stood in his way, both monk and soldier. He painted the walls with blood and smashed in doors looking for either the abbot or Brother Stephen. They weren't to be found, the monks had fled along with the soldiers. *Time for me to leave too.* They will search the roads, I will return to the woods.

He left the road and walked into the shadow under the trees. The forest was dim and cool. The leaves on the large trees blocked the sun so there was little undergrowth. Walking was easy, but Zeb was soon lost. He washed in a river. Zeb didn't particularly care about the blood, it might make him easier to trace.

Zeb carried the sword with him as he wandered through the forest. He didn't want to be without a weapon, but it was no use in catching food. It was too early in summer for berries, and the animals and birds stayed well clear of him. Hunger cut through his stomach. He drank more water, but his body demanded food. Zeb didn't know how mortals lived with the constant demands of their bodies. He took pleasure in the physicality of flesh and blood, but it was so weak.

He'd been traveling under the trees for several days when he heard voices. Zeb headed toward them. Voices meant food. He crept up on a group of rough looking men sitting around a fire. They had a couple of rabbits roasting on sticks. The smell made his mouth water. He hefted the sword and stepped into the clearing.

"I want some meat," he said.

"So what?" said the largest man, who towered over Zeb when he stood. "They're our rabbits, go get your own."

In the brief time it took to look around at the half dozen men who were sitting there, Zeb decided that it would be easier to let them find food for him to eat, so he didn't kill the big man. He kicked the man in the knee then in the head. He had the sword at his throat before he hit the ground. The other men hadn't had a chance to move.

"Give him a leg, boys," the downed man said, "I think Chancy will like him." He rolled to his feet and sat across from Zeb surreptitiously rubbing his knee.

Zeb ate the rabbit with the sword in his hand and grease running down his face.

"Ye don't need to be holding on to that sword," said one of the other men as he gnawed on his own chunk of meat. It ain't like we are going to steal it. If ye can't eat it, we ain't interested."

Zeb learned the big man was called Oaf.

"We're all here 'cause it keeps us from the gallows," Oaf said. The others nodded or shrugged. "Now, Chancy, he's got real houses, with roofs and everything. We winter with him and help out with things."

They wandered without any clear direction throughout the summer. Zeb learned how to knock a squirrel or rabbit down with a stone. One of the men insisted on picking and eating various bits of green plants that they found along the way. Not as good as the meat, but welcome on the days when the stones missed their targets.

The summer passed in the green light of the forest. They saw no other people than themselves. Oaf showed Zeb the marks that told him that another group had crossed their path.

"Why don't you take what you need from the peasants?" Zeb asked one day when they were all hungry.

"If we start hurting the farmers, they complain to the lords. Then we get hunting parties coming through with bows and dogs. If we leave them alone, they leave us alone." Oaf gnawed on an old bone.

"Chancy don't like us messing with the farmers," another said past a mouthful of leaves.

They told him it was a lean year. He couldn't argue with them. As summer progressed, there were more days that the little group chewed on leaves or went hungry. Even the berries when they began to appear didn't appease their hunger.

Their first raid on a farm came almost by accident. They were walking along the edge of a field when they heard the sound of chickens. Upon investigation they found the birds pecking the dirt at the edge of the forest. A house was just visible across the field. Zeb's stones knocked three birds down and they grabbed their kill and ran back into the forest. There was no sound of pursuit.

The birds vanished into the men's bellies quickly. The day after, they were hungry again. Zeb led them back to where they had found the first birds, but nothing was there. As they walked in the shadow of the trees, they heard the sound of chickens again. This time, it came from across the field. When the men refused to cross the field, Zeb adjusted the sword in his belt and headed off alone. He found a fenced area and a dozen of the delicious birds. It was a matter of a second for Zeb to snatch the closest and walk back to the forest.

He wouldn't let the others eat until they promised that they would go the next time. The men did convince Zeb that they should spread their theft out so they rarely returned to the same homestead. Zeb didn't care, as long as he had sufficient food to feed his body.

What began with chickens soon progressed to larger animals. They took whatever they could carry easily. The men had never eaten so well.

Fall came, and the men began talking about the hardships of surviving the winter. It didn't sound like something Zeb wanted to experience. He started going into the farmhouses and taking supplies they could keep through the winter. The men didn't like it, but they had grown so used to following Zeb that they didn't do anything more than grumble.

The first time they were interrupted in their raid, the farmer's wife just swore at them and ran off. They were gone before she returned with help. The next time, a farmer with a pitchfork tried to stop them. He was no match for Zeb. Even Oaf was white-faced as Zeb stepped over the body to ransack the house.

A farmer with a bow managed to kill one of the group before Zeb got to him. Zeb took the bow, but he couldn't get the hang of it and broke the three arrows they had been able to find. The men quit asking Zeb to stop. They had caches of food through the forest.

"We are going to eat better than Chancy this winter," Zeb said as he gnawed on a ham bone. The other men didn't argue. They were too busy eating.

PAGE OF WANDS

The early fall days stayed warm, but grew shorter. The leaves falling off the trees were more a concern to Zeb and his group. They made it impossible to walk quietly, and the shade, which had hidden them from unwelcome attention, disappeared with the leaves. They moved deeper into the woods to escape the roving groups of farmers that walked the edge of the woods to collect nuts and watch for bandits.

The food caches were all dried or preserved food, and meant for the deep winter. The men didn't want to eat the food that was going to keep them from starving when the snow fell. Instead, they went back to hunting rabbits and squirrel and collecting nuts and berries. After the rich eating of summer, their stomachs growled and complained, but they told themselves that it would be worse in the winter, and much worse if they ate their stores too early.

A more serious problem was the cold. Zeb didn't pay much attention to the temperature, though it annoyed him when his hands didn't work. The others buried themselves in leaves and woke shivering in the morning. They all had sniffles and sneezes, and Oaf developed a wracking cough. If Zeb didn't want to lose his band of men they would have to make another raid on a farm - this time for bedding and clothes.

The next morning, they set out to the edge of the woods. It rained for the first time since the leaves fell. In the summer the rain barely made it through the canopy of the forest. Now there was no escaping the cold rain. Soaked and miserable, they reached the fields. No one was out and about.

"They are all inside staying warm," Oaf said between coughs.

"Of course," Rat, the smallest of the group, said, "so we go and take blankets and stuff. How are we going to keep them dry?"

"How does Chancy do it?" asked another one: Zeb didn't care about their names.

"He has houses, Chancy does," Oaf said.

"We don't need Chancy," Zeb said. "We need something to keep you dry and warm." He pointed toward the farm that was barely visible through the rain. "They have what we need. Let's go get it."

He started walking across the plowed field, his men straggling along behind him. It took them a while to make it to the farmhouse. The mud from the field coated their boots and weighed them down. It also made the ground slick; two of the group fell and were covered with the cold muck. When they made it to the farmyard, Zeb scraped the muck from his boots with his sword, while his men did the same with whatever they could find.

When he looked up, there were three men holding farm tools standing in his way.

"Move or die," Zeb said, "we need clothes and such to survive the winter."

"We don't want to hurt you," Rat said, "but we will if you force us to."

The farmers looked at each other, then at the motley group in front of them. The bandits looked more miserable than dangerous, but Zeb ignored the rain and the chill as he waited for the farmers to decide if they wanted to live or die.

"We have some old coats and blankets, some oilskin to keep it dry," one of the men said. "You can warm up in the barn while we fetch it."

"Rat, Oaf, go with them," Zeb ordered. "Take us to your barn."

They were shown to the clapboard barn. Heat from the animals warmed the air. Steam rose from their clothes. One man stayed with them in the barn while the other two took Rat and Oaf to fetch the clothes. He pulled out an oilcloth and gave it to Zeb.

The other two men returned with wool coats that were worn and ragged, but still warm. Zeb's men put them on gratefully. Zeb set his down by the oilcloth.

"We will be watching. You tell anyone that we have been here, I will kill you."

"Take what you need then leave us alone. That is all we ask."

A chicken wandered out into the open.

"Supper," Zeb said.

"No!" came a high pitched shriek and a tiny girl ran out of a stall and poked Zeb with a pitchfork, but she was too light to wield it effectively.

Zeb swept his sword against the wooden shaft and it snapped. He raised the sword to kill the child, but his arm refused to strike. Zeb shook with the effort of trying to make his arm do his bidding. The man stepped in front of her and shielded her.

"Please," he begged, "she is just a child. A chicken won't feed all of you. There is a young pig in the last stall. Take it instead."

Zeb nodded and waved his hand at Rat and Oaf. They went to the stall and led out a small pig on a rope.

"Give me your shirt," Zeb said, secretly relieved that his voice worked. He lowered the sword. The farmer stripped off his shirt and handed it to Zeb, who dropped it into the bundle. His men rolled up the oilcloth and they left the barn. Zeb went last, looking hard at the three farmers. This time they walked along the edge of a pasture to avoid the mud. Oaf led the pig, which squealed and complained at the cold. The forest was as cold and damp as the fields but their wool coats were still warm in spite of the wet.

Zeb drove his men deep into the forest. They found a rare pine tree to shelter under and looked over their spoils.

"Look at this," Rat said, "oilcloth, ropes, rags, even coats."

"Don't forget supper." Another poked at the pig rooting in the forest floor.

"That was quite something with the kid," Oaf said. "I thought you were going to kill her for sure." He shook his head. "I wouldn't have thought about threatening her to get more from her old man. He must love her something awful."

"Love?" Zeb said. "He was just weak."

After some experimenting, they got the oilcloth hung up so that they could sleep almost completely dry. Rat got a fire going. The meat from the pig lasted them almost a week.

The day after they finished it, the first snow fell.

The snow curtailed their movement. Not only did it soak into their boots, making their feet cold and numb, but also give away their position to any who sought for them. People were looking too. They found out from a man who stepped out of the snow one day and looked at their camp with a mixture of approval and concern.

"Nice set up you have here," he said, holding up his hands to show them empty of weapons.

"We're doing alright," Oaf said. His cough had vanished with the coming of the snow.

"Be careful. Some folks were raiding farms this summer. That always gets them riled up. There will be squads through doing 'winter training'. If they find you, it'll mean trouble."

"We are fine," Zeb said.

"The usual invitation is out," the man said, "if you want to join Chancy you are welcome. We could always use some extra hands through the winter."

"And how can Chancy be so generous?" Rat asked.

"He has...connections. We sell lumber and do some other little jobs."

"These are mine," Zeb said, "I will take care of them."

"Alright, then, good hunting." The man vanished into the snow as quickly as he had come.

The snow started coming thick and heavy. Zeb sent Rat and Oaf to fetch supplies from the caches they'd made. Though he didn't say anything, his side bothered him where the girl had scratched him. The constant cold made healing slow. The men huddled under the oilcloth and tried to stay warm with their tiny fire.

Zeb trained constantly with his sword, as much to test that he again had full control of his body as to stay warm.

Day by day, a cold ache worked its way through his body. It wasn't a result of the winter weather, but the mage's curse at work. Zeb wasn't moving toward the mage's goal and pain was the price for disobedience. He counted each small ache and went to sleep telling himself that he would not serve any master in this world or any other.

Winter grew colder, and even with the food caches throughout the forest, their diet grew bland and thin. Even Zeb's drill with the sword couldn't keep the mage's curse at bay. He fought the pain, but started losing his grip on the sword. Rat had him chewing willow bark, which was as disgusting as anything Zeb had yet eaten, but it helped for a time.

They spent more time sitting around a tiny fire in the shelter of the oilcloth and talking about what had driven them to the life they were living.

"Big man like me," Oaf said, "everyone wants to test themselves against me. If I pound them in self-defense, I am a bully. If I let them pound on me, I am a coward. All I want is to be left alone."

"Heh," Rat said, "at least you could fight back. I had no chance at all. Even the boys were beating on me. Only thing they wanted from me was the cures I learned from my ma. Then a new priest come to town who didn't like the folks going to Ma. They burned her while they made me watch. If I so much as whispered a complaint, they would have burned me too. Left as soon as they turned their backs."

The other men had similar stories. Tales of how life had treated them poorly. All Zeb would say was that he would serve no master. The men nodded and went back to their own complaints.

THREE OF SWORDS

Oaf's cough started up again, and his constant hacking echoed through the woods. The only good thing was that they had fetched food from another cache the day before, and had plenty to eat. Rat was mixing up yet another vile batch of moss and dried herbs to try to help Oaf.

They were running short on supplies. Zeb had misjudged how much food they needed to get through the winter. Even making their meals smaller, they weren't going to make it.

"We should go to Chancy," one of the men said, whose name Zeb didn't care to remember.

"And this wonderful Chancy is going to just let you walk in and take his food and shelter?" Rat sneered.

"Every year, Chancy invites the forest bands to join him."

"So, why don't you go?" asked Rat. "It would give us more to eat."

"I don't know the way," the man said. "You just walk west, and they find you."

"I need you here," said Zeb.

"There is more to life than what you need," said the man.

"Is there?" asked Zeb. "I showed you how to get food easily. I can kill you too. You are mine now."

The man's face grew set.

"I don't belong to anybody, least of all you. I'm going to find Chancy, and I'd like to see you stop me."

Zeb was up in an instant with his sword at the rebel's throat. The man rolled to the side and drew a knife.

"Come on, then," he sneered, "I know those hands of yours can barely hold that sword." He circled around whipping the knife through the air making it whistle.

Zeb just watched in silence.

The man shouted threats and called the others to help him, but Oaf blocked the others from interfering. The man made a quick lunge toward Zeb and impaled himself on the sword suddenly extended toward him. With a moan the man dropped the knife. He tried to say something, but Zeb twisted the sword then pulled it out. The man's eyes rolled up as blood gurgled in his throat. A last twitch of the hand and he died.

"Get rid of him," Zeb ordered as he wiped his sword clean.

There was no more talk of finding Chancy. There was little talk of any kind. The men gave Zeb a wide berth, as if they had just realized he would kill them as easily and with as little regret. Rat and Oaf went to get the last of the food from the furthest cache. On their return, they were dragging a small deer.

"You should have seen Oaf," crowed Rat. "He jumped on the deer and wrestled it to the ground until I could cut its throat. He's a crazy man."

The arrival of the food and the good fortune of killing the deer put the band in a better mood.

They sat around the fire gorging on the meat.

"Hey, boss," Rat said, "you killed that idiot with the knife."

"He wasn't useful."

"Yeah, well that's my question," said Rat, "you killed him, and I've seen you kill others with no more concern than I would kill a bug. So, why didn't you kill that kid that stuck you with the pitchfork?"

"We got more with her alive."

"We could have killed them all and taken everything. We did before."

"Hey, back off," Oaf said. "I don't like this talk of killing kids. It's bad enough we've killed adults, but killing kids will send us to the worst part of hell."

"There is no worst part," Zeb said.

"What do you mean?" Oaf said. "There has to be a worst part."

"Why?" Zeb said. "It is all bad. Imagine the most horrible place you can, and hell is worse than that."

"What, are you some kind of priest?" Rat asked.

"I came from hell," Zeb said, "I will go back there."

"So, you're some kind of devil?" Rat said laughing.

"Whatever you say." The conversation moved on, but Zeb wondered at the men's determination to keep their fate after death separate from their lives, as if they believed in Heaven and Hell, but not their power in this world. Even when he as much as told them what he was they just laughed and changed the subject. Perhaps that was the mage's strength, he knew there was power beyond this world. He believed he could summon it and control it.

"I will not serve," Zeb said, but no one was listening.

Their first warning of the attack was the bolt that appeared like magic in Oaf's chest. He gave one last cough then fell across the fire. The other men shouted in panic and tried to run away, but bolts found them as well.

Zeb rolled away under the tent when Oaf had been hit. His small group were slaughtered as he watched. He didn't care about them, but they were his. Whoever fired those bolts would pay the price. His sword settled comfortably in his hand as he crouched behind the tree. The distinctive click of a crossbow arming meant he needed to get into the middle of them, where the bolts were as likely to hit friend as foe.

Six attackers came out of the woods holding their crossbows casually.

"I think we got them all," one said.

"Where's the sword?" another said. "At least one of them had a sword and knew how to use it."

"No swords here," the first one said, nudging Oaf's corpse.

Zeb stepped up behind him and ran him through. He grabbed the dying man's crossbow and shot another man from point blank range. The bolt went through him to strike the man behind. The remaining men shouted in surprise, and their shout was answered from a distance.

Zeb jumped on them in an instant, and dropped two more while they fumbled with their crossbows. A bolt danced off his ribs and blood dripped down from the wound. The last man dropped his crossbow and drew his sword. The shouting got closer. The other man glanced away to see how close his friends were. Zeb stabbed him and ran away into the forest.

He heard a large group shouting and cursing, then the crash of people following after him. With the snow on the ground, he wasn't going to lose them, so Zeb put his energy into running.

Zeb held his own easily at first. He snatched up moss Rat had used to stem bleeding in the others. Zeb had no desire to collapse again from blood loss. He and his men had explored the entire region around their camp, so he knew the fastest paths to take. He sprinted along, and the shouts faded behind him. Too soon his body began to let him down. His obsessive training with the sword hadn't included running, so he gasped for air. His lungs froze in his chest, and he started coughing. Still, he pushed himself. Yet it wasn't long before the pursuit behind him was audible again.

Zeb crossed into country he'd never seen before. The flat terrain became hilly and uncertain. Deep ravines cut across his path. The snow got deeper too. The few inches that had marked his trail without slowing him became a foot or more that made his legs burn with effort. He was finally forced to stop and rest.

He picked a ravine, filled with a tangle of broken branches and stumps, to take his break. Making his trail look like he ran straight into the mess was simple. Then he pulled himself up into a tree.

The aches and pains of his abused muscles and joints were worse when he stopped, but Zeb ignored them. He concentrated on breathing through his nose to ease the constant irritation in his chest. While he waited, Zeb tried to figure out a way to escape without leaving a trail. Jumping from tree to tree might be possible, but he didn't think they were close enough to each other to make it work.

Three men arrived at the ravine. They were gasping for air, but not with the same urgency as Zeb. He watched them drink from leather wrapped flasks.

"Oh, great," one said, "if he's gone into that mess we may never dig him out."

"My brother's blood is on his sword. I will follow him to hell if I need to," a second said. The third just nodded.

Zeb's throat chose that moment to rebel, and he coughed violently. The three gave a start and looked around. Zeb swung out of the tree and kicked the first man out into the ravine. Drawing his sword he slashed at the other two. They retreated and drew breath to yell for help. The one who hadn't spoken began coughing, so Zeb ignored him and attacked the other man. There was a brief clash of swords before Zeb's opponent slipped and Zeb stabbed the man's leg and kicked his sword away. Just as he turned, the third soldier's sword caught in Zeb's coat. Zeb punched him in the throat with the edge of his sword and the man went down.

Looking for the first man, Zeb saw that he was impaled on branches at the bottom of the ravine. Blood dripped from his mouth and a branch poked through his neck.

Zeb quickly killed the injured men, and took their water bottles and hard rations then set off running again. This time, he kept his pace slower, just enough to stay ahead of the people following behind him.

The ambush at the ravine, though not planned, had gained him more time. The mortals had a need to cry over each death. Zeb didn't understand it, but he was willing to use it. He found another good place for an ambush that evening—a high cliff overlooking a valley floor littered with sharp rocks.

Zeb circled around so he would come up behind whatever group was behind him. There were four of them this time. They traveled with their swords drawn, one with a loaded crossbow in his hand instead of a sword. They walked cautiously, constantly scanning the forest around them while the fourth read Zeb's footprints. None were looking behind them.

Zeb waited until they'd bunched together not too far from the edge of the cliff. Then he charged them, holding a log crosswise to add weight, and pushed them over the edge. The man with the crossbow twisted and fired at Zeb as he fell. The bolt cut through the sleeve of Zeb's coat, but he didn't stay to marvel at the man's skill.

He was running again before the four hit the rocks far below.

All night, Zeb half walked, half ran through the forest. His legs screamed in agony even with the slower pace, but he refused to stop. In the morning, it started to snow. Within minutes, the footprints behind him filled in. Minutes later, Zeb couldn't see further than his outstretched arm. He stumbled and pushed his way through the storm using the sword to check the footing in front of him. Yet now that he no longer needed to push himself to the extreme, the flesh he inhabited failed him.

He fell, and when he stood up couldn't make his hands pick up the sword. Shouting in fury, Zeb left it behind. He refused to give in. As he walked, Zeb muttered curses against the mage who had trapped him in this weak flesh. Still, this cold torture was preferable to serving another being willingly. Slowly, the cold seeped up his arms and legs and into his body. Finally, he could go no further. Zeb fell into a bank of snow and let darkness take him.

THE MAGICIAN

The mage tapped his fingers on the rough table in a cheap room upstairs in an anonymous tavern. His co-conspirator came in late and sat across from him. There was no need for them to meet here; they saw each other on a daily basis. The other man poured a glass of wine, then made a face and pushed the glass to the side.

"Well?"

"I trust you weren't followed." The Mage picked up the other man's wine and waved his hand over it before pushing it back to him.

"It should be more suited to your palate now."

The other frowned and pushed it away again. The mage shrugged and took the glass for himself and drank. The wine was trash under the glamour of his magic, but drinking it showed it wasn't poisoned.

Their first meeting had only come about after they had tested and counter tested each other. The mage soon determined that they shared the same moral standard: namely, none at all. They would do anything and everything to feed their addiction. People would be sacrificed, love would be shattered, hope would be betrayed; all on the altar of their desire for power.

So they met to keep an eye on each other. Each knew that they would betray the other in an instant if it would work to their advantage. They watched each other with suspicion and hatred, which is why the mage played his games, tasting the wine after he'd glamoured it. The other never yet drank so much as a sip.

"What is going on?" the other man said. "I had the body sent down the river as you requested. Here it is, fall, and nothing has happened."

"He is out there with my geas laid upon him," the mage put down his glass. "Be patient. He fights my chains, but they tighten around him."

"Bah, speak clearly. You have no idea where he is or if he will ever show up. He could be lying dead in a ditch, for all you know."

"He is not dead, or I would have felt my power returning to me. I am not sure he can die. He has been grievously injured twice and recovered both times. Twice, he has left havoc and death in his wake. My spell will pull him to me, and when it does, he will serve our purpose."

"And then what? If he can't be killed, how will we be rid of him?"

"What can't be killed can be dismissed, leaving only empty flesh to take the blame. What about your part?"

"She will help to destroy him, whether she wishes or not. With him gone, that whole group will fail. He is the glue that holds them together."

"And how are you so sure?"

"Your magic isn't the only way to bind someone to your will. She is twisted around my finger."

"I am sure you enjoyed the...twisting."

"As much as you enjoyed forging your chains."

"Then you enjoyed it a great deal. Just be certain that she doesn't slip your will. She hasn't spoken to you all summer."

"When I am ready, she will come to me. Even if she doesn't, I have another arrow to let fly. There will be no escape."

"So we wait."

"We wait."

The mage watched the other man leave, then pulled a flask from his pocket and washed the last taste of the wine from his mouth. His magic reached out to tug on the one he'd so carefully prepared—a reminder the mage was not a patient person.

The mage considered what he would do when this buffoon he conspired with was no longer useful.

***

Months later, they met again.

"It is winter. Where is he?" The mage's co-conspirator leaned across the table in another anonymous upper room. Its legs creaked in protest.

"He slaughtered a squad of the local baron's bandit hunters and escaped into a blizzard. He is out there fighting me with every breath, and with every breath he is closer to losing his battle. It will be worth the wait."

"I grow impatient with your excuses."

"Perhaps it would be more to the point to grow impatient with your daughter. I hear she has left her husband and vanished from the city."

"Can you not find her?"

"To answer your question, no, I cannot find her for you. I have no connection with her. I thought that you had her completely under your control? Twisted around your finger were your words. Perhaps you needed to use more than your finger."

"She is stubborn like her mother."

"Her mother died rather than submit to your will."

"She burns in hell for it. Suicide is forbidden."

"Incest is not?"

"She isn't mine, her mother betrayed me."

"No, there was no betrayal. The girl is your flesh and blood. You are as damned as her mother."

"Damned or not, I will have my way. She will serve me, or her absence will."

"What about your 'other arrow'?"

"When the time is right."

"So, still we wait."

"We wait."

This time the mage left first. Undoubtedly, the other spun webs to ensure the mage's downfall. The mage grinned into the falling snow. He looked forward to when the masks came off.

73

WANDERINGS

EIGHT OF CUPS

Marriette left the house with no idea where she was going. She couldn't stay with Torrance. His needs and desires as her husband had become entangled with the memory of her father's eager face as he raped her. Escaping the house helped her calm down, but what to do next?

She wrapped her cloak closer about her and shivered in the cool fall night. Lanterns gave pools of illumination, but no heat. First, she must get out of the cold. Marriette walked through the dark streets hiding whenever she heard footsteps. None of the doors she passed made her feel safe. Raucous laughter spilled out into the street along with the stink of beer and smoke.

Walking kept her warm until she arrived at the market, more tired than she'd ever been before.

My feet are smarter than I am, I will talk to Joan.

The first wagon arrived just as Marriette reached the far end of the market. Joan was there wiping sleep from her eyes as she checked the load.

"Marriette!" she said. "What are you doing here?"

"I can't stay with Torrance," Marriette said. "He is just like my father. Are all men so hateful?"

"I don't know," Joan said, "I don't think so. I thought Torrance to be a good man."

"I told him about...my father, and he ran from the room. Then he wouldn't even look at me anymore. Like I lived with a stranger."

"Maybe if you talked to him some more?"

"How can I talk to him? I went to find him and saw another woman coming from his rooms."

"Oh, Marriette—"

"I am going to look for Arthur."

"Arthur is dead."

"No, I had a dream. He was in a place and fighting for his life. There was a horrible shadow hanging over him. You told me that your father didn't believe he was dead. There was no body."

Joan sighed and was silent for a long time.

"Torrance heard nothing from his people in the south, so if Arthur is alive, he must be north of the city. If you are going to travel, you will need money. Do you have any?"

"I couldn't take anything from Torrance."

"You're his wife."

"Not in the way that matters."

"I can't understand you, Marriette." Joan made a few more marks on her board. "I think that you have more than a few things backward."

"I don't understand it myself," Marriette swatted at the tears on her face. "But I can't live with Torrance and the dream tells me Art's alive and needs me. I have to go, please help me?"

"Don't be silly, of course I'll help you. I just wish it wasn't to run away." Joan sighed again. "Come with me, when I'm done here, and see my father. Don't tell him who you are. He has a thing about nobility. He wants so desperately to be noble that he can't see that he is better than most of them. He'll keep you all day, if he thinks you're noble, and, more to the point, tell all his friends. We need someone in Northdale who can do numbers. You said you did accounts with Torrance. Once you are there, you can look for my brother."

Marriette watched Joan as she worked. Her young friend was quick and thorough. Nothing escaped her, but she bantered with the men so they didn't resent a girl the age of their daughters supervising them. Marriette was sure if anyone threatened Joan that these rough men would run to her rescue. Marriette only hoped they would be as sympathetic with her.

Joan's father looked like an older version of Arthur. He had the same blue eyes and Marriette detected a vestige of Art's roguish grin, but the last year hadn't been kind to Master Candler. His hair was thin and grey where Art's had been wavy and blond. He walked with a stoop, as if he carried a burden that was too heavy for him but was unable to put down.

He absently listened to Joan's lies about Marriette and why they needed to send her to Northdale.

"Certainly, you may travel with one of my wagons. If Joan thinks you can do the books, that's fine then. I'd send Arthur with you, but he hasn't come home yet from drinking…."

Joan drew some money from a box in the corner and dragged Marriette out of the room.

"I'm going to go and buy you some clothing," Joan said. "You stay here under that cloak, and keep out of sight."

Marriette sat in the parlour, pleasantly decorated, but without the richness of Torrance's house. Her father would have sneered at it as being only slightly better than a hovel.

I will have to get used to it, for most people this is luxury.

An odd sensation, thinking of herself as privileged. Marriette considered that life had treated her with great unfairness when she thought of it at all. Yet, here were people whose hearts were at least as torn as hers, but did not have the instant access to comfort she did. Perhaps part of her problem was her relationship with Torrance was the only thing in her life that she had to worry about. Everything else was handed to her on a silver platter; very few people were as fortunate as she was. She had almost talked herself into returning to Torrance when Joan ran in.

"Here, get changed into these. Quickly. There is a wagon leaving for Northdale. I am holding them up for you."

Marriette changed into the strange clothes. They were rough and itchy and didn't fit very well, and grey with no decoration. Joan redid her hair in a simple braid.

"Now, you look the part of a widow who needs work," she said. "Try not to talk too much, your accent won't match your clothes. Once you get to Northdale, it won't matter, they won't notice." She handed Marriette a bundle. "Here's some more clothing, warmer things for the winter. You'll be working for Giuseppe who is from a country well to the south of our kingdom. He won't care who you are or where you are from, as long as you can do the accounts. Don't let him scare you. He is loud but kind." They were outside and almost running. The men at the wagon groaned when they saw Marriette.

"Ye aren't going to saddle us with that old girl, are ye?" asked one. "Why can't ye just come along yourself? We would have a fine time, we would."

"You aren't my type, George," Joan replied.

"What is your type?"

"Younger, much younger," Joan said with a grin. "This is Marie. Treat her kindly, or else."

"Anything for you," George said. He hoisted 'Marie' onto the wagon then jumped up himself. "We're off!" he shouted and cracked the whip at the horses.

After all the rush, Marriette half expected them to take off at a gallop, but the horses started at an easy walk. They plodded along through the streets of Bellpolis, reaching the gate only slightly faster than Marriette could have walked it herself.

"Ah, good," George said, "we made it before shift change. Ye see, lass, they make everyone wait while they go through the rigmarole of handing over command of the gates. Besides, if we time it right, they're more interested in getting us through than in checking our load. Master Candler runs an honest business, but it is good to know." He winked at Marriette. She had made herself a comfortable nest in some soft bundles behind the bench where George and his partner sat. George kept up a running commentary through the day. He pointed out landmarks and told scandalous stories with equal abandon. His partner never said a word.

The countryside around Bellpolis stretched flat as far as Marriette could see. The only thing breaking the monotony was the river that meandered near and far across the plain. George and his partner took turns driving the team. Occasional lines of trees broke the flow of the wind. The hostelry was visible long before they reached it.

When they arrived, George handed her a board like Joan's.

"Make yourself useful, lass, and we'll stand you for supper."

Marriette looked at the board. It was almost identical to the ones that Joan used, with short notes describing the cargo and where it was supposed to go. She took the board and the wax pencil and began checking boxes as they were unloaded. Marriette had a new appreciation for Joan when they were done. Several times, the men had to stop and wait impatiently, while Marriette sorted out her list. Finally, they were done to the satisfaction of both drovers and hostel keepers.

Supper was a little bit of stew and a large loaf of bread. It could have been anything and she'd have eaten it, she was so tired. She spent the night in a room with the innkeeper's daughters. The innkeeper wouldn't hear of her spending the night by the fire, even if she didn't have money for a private room.

Banging on the door woke her and soon they set off at the same plodding pace. George handed her a chunk of bread.

"I always save some bread from supper for the morning."

"Thank you," Marriette said.

It took them a week, at a crawl, to arrive in Northdale. Marriette got faster with the check board, and George seemed reluctant to leave her at Master Candler's office in the village.

"If ye get tired of the dusty books, ye could work with me on the road," George said.

"You aren't my type, George," Marriette said, thinking of Joan.

"So what is your type?"

"I wish I knew."

George patted her on the shoulder before climbing on the wagon. He and his still nameless partner waved farewell as they started on the next leg of their journey.

Giuseppe worked in a tiny office. Marriette wondered how on earth they were both going to fit. He looked her over then sat her at his desk and put a column of figures in front of her.

"Let's see you add them up." When Marriette had completed that, he had another test for her. By the time he was done, her brain was as tired as her body.

"You'll do," he said, "tomorrow I will teach you what I need you to do. If you can do that, I will keep you. Now, come meet my family." He led her through the streets to a cheerful yellow house on the edge of town. The yard was filled with flowers blooming even into the fall.

"Hey, Nanna," he called, "we have a guest to share our supper." A graceful woman with long black hair stuck her head out of the kitchen.

"Oh, Pappa," she said, "it is a good thing I always cook too much." She smiled at Marriette, "Welcome to our home. Gracia will show you where to wash up."

A little girl ran up and hugged her pappa, then shyly showed Marriette to a washstand where she was able to rinse the worst of the dust from the road away.

"I am Gracia, my sister is Karitia, and my other sister is Therese."

"My name is Marie," Marriette said, "thank you."

Gracia was the youngest and Karitia the oldest. Marriette thought they were among the most beautiful girls she had ever seen, with their dark hair, brown eyes and bright smiles. They were all younger than Joan and they chattered happily about their day. After supper was done, Karitia showed Marriette through their home while Therese and Gracia cleaned up.

"Here is where you will sleep," she said, "Therese is moving in with me."

"I can't put you out of your bed!" Marriette said.

"It's alright," Karitia said, "why would I have a bed if not to share it with a stranger?"

"But it is your bed."

"It is only mine if I can give it away. If I can't let go of something then it owns me."

"You are a wise girl."

"Pappa taught us. He came here before we were born because the people where he lived wanted to own the world."

Marriette slept well in Karitia's bed. She had every intention of finding her own place to live, but Giuseppe wouldn't hear of it. She was family, and since Agathia, his wife, and the girls didn't mind she gave in.

Marriette had never experienced anything like this family. Life with her father had been lonely and painful. Life with Torrance had been better, yet still it had been the two of them surrounded by people whose work was to make them comfortable. In Giuseppe's family, they all worked, and they all shared. Marriette was surrounded by eager chatter. Her advice was asked, and they just as freely gave their opinion to her. They appeared to relish loud discussions on every topic.

Giuseppe's method of keeping accounts was completely new to Marriette. He kept separate columns for expenses and income.

Torrance's accounts had them jumbled together. Marriette wondered, now, how he ever kept them straight. She caught herself imagining how much he would like this new system. Then she shook her head. Torrance would hate her even more now for running away. He probably had that other woman installed in their bedroom.

Marriette discovered she couldn't have chosen a better place to gather news and rumours about what was going on in the northern part of Bellandria. The drovers were as fond of gossip as any old woman. They competed with each other to find the most outrageous stories to tell Marriette. There were plenty of stories. One man told bitterly how his wagon had been commandeered to haul bodies away from a castle. He described, with ghoulish delight, the wounds on each of the men.

Another man countered with the tale of a bandit raid on a monastery. They had been serving a man who was demon possessed. He'd desecrated their chapel then called in his minions to wreak havoc on the defenseless brothers. Only the abbot and an old blind monk had survived because they'd been traveling at the time.

Later, a drover told her about a bandit who raided and pillaged the farms along the great forest that formed a buffer between the farms and mountains. He was supposed to be huge and cruel, leaving countless bodies in his wake. It was so bad that the local baron talked about putting together a raiding party to clean out the forest.

George, on one of his visits, had the most interesting story. He had swung farther north than he usually did to make a delivery to a town at the very fringe of the forest. He met a man there who swore he'd met the demon bandit. The man told how a blond man with cold blue eyes had walked out of the rain into his farmyard followed by a group of ragged men. They demanded clothing and supplies. The farmer was sure they were going to kill everyone. He'd heard stories of the murderous bandit. When a chicken ran out, his granddaughter tried to protect it, but instead of killing her, the bandit held the sword over the girl as though something was holding his arm back.

This story troubled Marriette's dreams.

As she tossed and turned, Art became the demon bandit. She saw him running from a stone building with blood running from a sword in his hand. She saw him standing with the same sword, looming over a tiny redheaded girl. The worst part of the dream was that when she looked into Art's eyes she saw only hate and pain. What could have happened to turn Art into such a monster? She became certain that her dreams were true and that Art was lost to himself.

She woke tangled in her blankets. The dream came back other nights, each time the blood redder, and the pain in Art's eyes deeper. She'd followed one dream to this place. Time to follow another even further north.

"I need to go north, Giuseppe," she said one day.

"What do you seek in the north?"

"There's someone I must see."

"And how do you know this person is to the north?"

"I've been having these dreams," Marriette said.

"Ah, dreams," Giuseppe said, "they are rarely what we think them to be, yet, right or wrong, we can't ignore them." He looked up at her. "We will miss you."

"You will let me go?"

"Of course, you are my friend, my associate. There is no asking or begging, just blessings."

Marriette packed up what little she had. Tomorrow, she would find a ride with a wagon heading north.

The girls cried they would miss her, she must come back to see them. They hugged her tight and wet her dress with their tears. Agathia looked worried, and said the winter was a dangerous time to travel. Marriette hugged them all then went to find her ride.

THE TOWER

Marriette found a ride with a wagon carrying supplies to a monastery up north by the mountains. John, the drover, knew the town George had talked about and said he would be passing through there on his way. She bundled herself up in heavy wool blankets and sat on the seat beside John. He talked as much as George on the road, but where George had pointed out landmarks along the road, John pointed out the sites of tragic events. Given the amount of snow on the road, and in the fields beside them, she was nervous. His stories made her fears worse.

Here, a family was accosted by bandits and killed. There, a drover lost a wheel in a blizzard and froze to death. The longer and more torturous the death involved the more John relished the telling of the tale. Marriette had never realized that life in the country was so dangerous. If it wasn't bandits, it was the weather, if it wasn't the weather, it was animals. There was a spot where a man had starved to death while pinned under a tree that had fallen on him. He had time enough to scribe a last letter to his family in the wood of the tree before he died. She wrung her hands and held tight to the seat. John finally noticed her agitation.

"Don't you worry, as long as the wind doesn't blow up too hard we will be fine. I have a fine strong wife who would kill me if I died out here."

In spite of the never-ending tales of death and destruction, their journey north was uneventful. They arrived in the village and parked by the local inn.

"You've been good company, Marie," John said. "If you finish your business quick enough, come back and wait here for me. I will take you back down to Northdale."

"Thanks, John," Marriette said, "I would appreciate it."

Since John's whole load was destined for the monastery, there was no unloading. They went in and ordered supper. The inn looked and sounded a lot like the Broken Dog Art had taken her to once or twice. Plenty of talk; but most of it harmless. The trick, Art had said, was to know when someone got serious about making trouble. No one here looked serious.

John was well known in the inn, since he often brought supplies to the village. He was going all the way to the monastery because the farmer who used to take the monks their food refused to go back. By the time they were done with supper, John had wrangled the tale out of the bar man.

"You won't believe this, Marie," John said, "but the man who did the supply run to the monastery was him who picked up a man who fainted right in front of his donkey. He took him up to the monks, and that was the one they're saying was possessed and killed all those people. The farmer's here tonight." Marie smiled and told him to go and find the man. John grinned like a kid given a candy and vanished into the crowd.

Shortly after John went searching for the farmer, an older man sat himself at the table across from Mariette.

"We don't see many women visiting our inn," he said. "Welcome. If anyone bothers you, just let me know, and I will have a word with them."

"Thank you," Marriette said, "but everyone has been very kind."

"Your friend seems to have deserted you."

"He's off trying to find the farmer who picked up the man on the road." Marriette shook her head and pretended to shudder. "He collects horrible stories."

"Well, Ganther will give him plenty of those. I swear the story grows every time he tells it. First time I heard it, it was just some ordinary man who fell on the road. Now blond hair has become writhing snakes, and blue eyes flaming eyes from the pit."

"I am sure John will be delighted," Marriette said trying to calm her pounding heart. "Are there any other storytellers he should be looking for?"

"Young William has quite the story. He met the demon bandit, as they are calling him now, and lived to tell of it."

"Is he here tonight?" asked Marriette.

"No, he has sworn off drinking and spends all his time with that red haired granddaughter of his."

"Where would we find him, then, this Young William with a granddaughter?"

The man laughed. "Old William has been dead some thirty years, but we still call him Young William."

"What do they call his son?"

"Bill," the man said, laughing even harder. "Though, truly, I'm his son-in-law." He reached across the table. "Pleased to make your acquaintance. The girl is my sister's daughter. Your John will be driving close enough to their farm tomorrow. You will know it by the carved rooster on the gatepost. Just tell them Bill sent you. I'll give you some soft cider to bring my dad since he no longer drinks the good stuff."

John returned a few minutes after Bill had left. He told her Ganther's story in all its bloody detail. He was delighted to carry Mariette up to Young William's farm the next day and hear the old man's tale.

The morning dawned crisp and cold—Marriette was very glad for the blankets that she had wrapped around her. John was content in his heavy wool coat and gloves. He turned them out so she could see.

"Sheepskin," he said proudly, "leather on the outside and wool on the inside. They let me drive and keep my hands warm."

They drove through the morning in silence, and Marriette realized that John had never been up this far before and didn't know the stories of the road. His nose twitched when they passed a marker on the side of the road, but he just sighed and drove on. They reached Young William's farm just before noon of the short winter's day. True to Bill's word, they were welcomed with open arms.

Young William insisted they stay for their noon meal, so they sat off to one side and listened to the old man tell his story as a variety of children set the table with cracked plates and chipped mugs. Cheese and meat on a platter were set in the center.

"It was just as the rains had come on heavy. We had the crop off and the field was plowed. They walked across the plowed field, then scraped off their boots, as bold as brass. I told the family to hide then went out with my Janie's husband and his brother to run them off. Only the young fellow with the sword stared right through me, like I was no more to him than a bug. Had the coldest eyes I ever saw. He'd have killed me as soon as look at me, only I think he was tired from walking across the mucky field in the rain. Told me to move or die. So, I asked him what he wanted. If I could get him satisfied and off my land, I was going to give up drink and start going to church again. They wanted some cold weather gear. We always have extra around here. I put him in the barn while the brothers went with a couple of his men to fetch the stuff."

"The barn was warm and I could see they were getting more relaxed, so I just oiled up the cloth I was giving them and watched them. The boys came back with the other two and coats for all of them. I had rope and rags with the cloth by then. I was hoping they were all set to move on. That's when Fran's prize hen wandered out of the stall and those fellows saw supper looking up at them."

"Fran, my granddaughter, wasn't too pleased with that. I told them to hide, so, of course, she had come out and hid in the barn. She grabbed a pitchfork and tried to stick the young one with the eyes with it. Didn't do much damage, but he had his sword out ready to take her fool red head right off. Only he didn't. I can't explain it. A man like that should have killed her like I would kill a dog that bit me, but his arm stuck. Him wanting to kill, but his arm saying no; I'm mighty glad his arm won. Sent them off with a fine young pig. When they vanished into the rain, I grabbed my family and headed into town. We come back a couple of days later, but they hadn't been back. I poured out my drink and I been scaring the young priest at our church every Sunday since."

"His eyes were sad." Marriette jumped as a little girl spoke up behind her. "Papa says he was a mean one, like the dog we had that killed the chickens, but his eyes were sad."

Young William ruffled the girl's hair.

"She might be right at that. All I know is that I looked in his eyes and saw death. I know for sure he killed other folk up and down the forest boundary. The baron's sent a group of his soldiers into the forest, just today, to search him out and kill him, and I can't say I am sorry to hear it."

"You said he was young?" asked Marriette.

"Yep, he wasn't much older than you, except for those eyes."

"Did they call him anything?"

"Not that I could hear. I think he called one Rat and one Oaf, but they didn't talk to him at all, though they watched him almost as hard as I did."

Fran's mother called them to the table and decreed that there would be no talk of bandits at her table. Marie told them about Northdale and even a little about Bellpolis. Then it came time to get on the road again. She and John decided she might as well ride up to the monastery and back with him, so off they went. The day continued cold and clear, and stayed cold through the night.

They arrived at the monastery in the early morning. The young monk at the gate had to run for the abbot since, by custom, women weren't allowed in the monastery. The abbot, however, was very understanding. He watched with approval while Marriette checked the load out of the wagon.

"Come inside for a bit and warm up. It doesn't hurt to remind the monks of their vows now and again." The abbot led them into his office. He poured out some tea for them and cut some rough bread. "It isn't much, but we try to live simple lives of contemplation here. Too much comfort makes it hard to focus."

"So you keep yourselves hungry?" asked Marriette, curious. The abbot wasn't at all like the archbishop in the cathedral.

"Not hungry, but our diet is simple and predictable. We put the effort we would have used to wonder about what's for supper to use asking what God has in mind for us."

"That must be hard, after this summer," John said.

"Yes," the abbot said, "the monks who died were like sons to me, and the strangers were also God's children."

"What about the demon?" John asked.

Marriette tried to kick him under the table but feared she'd kick the abbot instead.

"There was a man who may or may not have been possessed by a demon. He had some of the signs, but not others. Since he escaped during the attack, we may never know. I fear the bandit we have heard about in the forest may be him." He stood up. "It is time for you to go, before the weather changes."

As they stepped outside, the wind sucked the heat from Marriette. It howled like a living thing as it drove snow into their faces. The abbot pulled them back inside.

"You may stay in the guest rooms until the storm has passed. Feel free to use the chapel, if you wish. If a brother speaks to you, you may talk to him, but otherwise please respect the silence of our community." A young monk showed them to rooms. They were tiny, but warm and clean. Marriette stretched out on the bed and was soon asleep.

A bell woke her, and for a moment she didn't know where she was. Once she remembered, she realized the bell must be a call to prayer. Marriette no longer felt tired, so she followed the sound of the bell until she saw a line of monks entering what she guessed was the chapel. She walked in after them and sat herself at the back. She didn't understand the prayers. They were in some ancient and sonorous language, but they warmed her. She stayed through the prayers then remained in the chapel after the monks had filed out.

In the silence, Mariette let her mind wander where it wanted. The day in the market, her father, Torrance, her fears, the old woman's voice speaking about a terrifying future and everything fell into place as the answer to a question she didn't know how to ask.

"May I help you?" Marriette turned. An old man stood holding a stick and as his eyes stared off into nothing.

"I am waiting for a question," she said.

"Most people wait for answers," he replied.

"I think I know the answer, but it is the question that is important."

"The abbot told us that we had a fair visitor. He didn't say you were wise." The old monk sat himself on a bench near her.

"Not very wise, I'm afraid," Marriette said.

"So, you have achieved the first part of wisdom," the monk said, "to know that you are not wise."

"What is the second part?" she asked.

"To know that God is." He pushed himself to his feet. "I will leave you to your contemplations."

"Brother..." Marriette began.

"Brother Stephen," he said.

"Do you think the abbot would let me stay?" She didn't know where the question came from, but it felt right.

"The only way to learn is to ask," Brother Stephen said, and he walked out of the chapel.

Marriette found her way back to the abbot's office and knocked timidly on the door.

"Come in," he called.

As Marriette entered he looked at her and his eyes widened.

"I would like to stay a while, here," she said, stumbling over her words. "I think what I need is here."

"And what do you need?" asked the abbot.

"I don't know," Marriette said, "I am too tangled up in what I want."

"Ah," he said and waited.

Marriette didn't know what else to say, so she waited with him. It seemed like hours before the abbot spoke again.

"I think you have come here for a reason," he said. "You may stay, but our rules for novitiates are strict, and I will expect you to live by them."

"Simplicity, contemplation, silence," Marriette said.

"I think you will do well here."

Marriette sent a message with John back to Giuseppe that she would be spending the winter at the monastery, then, going back inside, she left the world behind for a season.

TEMPERANCE

Torrance sat at his desk with his glass in his hand. All manner of papers littered the desk, but the only one he looked at was the brief note from Marriette the servants brought him along with the news that she had left in the middle of the night.

I am not the wife you need. I hope you are happy with your new woman. I have gone to find Arthur.

Arthur was Marriette's friend's brother. He read the note again, and maybe something more. Everyone has secrets. Unfortunately, she misunderstood one of his. He turned the note over and over in his hands trying to pull some new meaning from it, but no new words appeared, no new hope. She was gone, and she had taken his heart with her.

He'd never expected to fall in love with her.

The offer of Marriette as his bride had come as a shock to Torrance. He and deLanguiers were at opposite ends of the political spectrum. Torrance believed that his position called him to great responsibility. He worked hard to improve the life of all his people. The Duke deLanguiers saw himself as the pinnacle of creation with everything existing for his own convenience.

There were not many eligible men of a class to suit deLanguiers who would have taken Marriette as a wife after she had been among the Wagoners. The decision may very well have been Torrance or no one, and, politics aside, the leBrauns were as old and rich in history as the deLanguiers.

From Torrance's side, he'd run into brick walls looking for a wife to give him an heir. The rumours of what happened to LisAnne and Niklas had only grown in the telling. So, for him, too, it was Marriette or no one. He'd known the duke would have shaped the girl to his own ends.

The depth of her wounds took his breath away, yet she'd begun to trust him, and perhaps even to choose him over her father.

Torrance put his head in his hands. He'd learned more than he wanted about her wounds. He wanted to talk to her, to hold her, but he didn't know what to say and was afraid that he would fail her again. How could he hold her without becoming her father?

Marriette had refused to get out of bed. She stayed there for days before she finally got up and dressed. Even then she looked like her own ghost.

Torrance told her everything - all about how he had been a terrible husband to his first wife. Marriette's distance from him grew as he spoke.

Then Sylvie had returned. He'd sent her away when he agreed to wed Marriette. He wasn't going to go to his wedding smelling of another woman. Sylvie wanted back into his life. He regretted ever sleeping with her in the first place. From the beginning, she wanted more than he was willing to give. It wasn't Torrance that she wanted, but the prestige of being his mistress. Torrance had refused her. He'd treated Marriette badly enough, he wasn't going to betray her with Sylvie.

Anna had brought him the note.

Now Torrance sat in his office and stared at it.

When the agony of his feelings got too strong, he opened a bottle of brandy. He sat there every day for a week. The only thing he said to the staff was they were to tell people that Marriette had gone south to his estates, and he would be joining her there in a few weeks.

Torrance was interrupted by a brisk knock on the door. Marriette's father walked in. Torrance slid her note under the other papers.

"Henri," he said, "what an unexpected pleasure."

"Where is my daughter?" the duke asked.

"She is south at my estates," Torrance said. "I will be going to join her shortly. I will bring her your greetings."

"Don't lie to me." The duke glared at Torrance. "She hasn't gone to your estates or anywhere else my agents have knowledge of."

"Then perhaps you need better agents," Torrance said. His face grew hot. How dare this man walk in and talk of spies and agents in my own home?

"I will find her," Marriette's father said, "and I will see that she is properly punished for her foolishness."

Torrance pushed himself to his feet. Something cold and eager curled in the duke's eyes, as if he looked forward to causing his daughter pain.

"She is my wife, Sir," Torrance said. "I will deal with her as I see fit."

"You are a weakling and a cripple," the duke said, "but even you should have been able to control a slip of a girl."

"Thank you for your visit, Sir," Torrance forced down the bile that tainted the back of his throat, wishing he had two good legs so he could get satisfaction for the insult. "Harold will see you out." He sat down to read the reports and accounts piled up on his desk, ignoring the duke in front of him.

"I gave my daughter to you, I will take her back," the duke said. "She is mine!" When Torrance didn't look up, the duke turned and stomped out of the house.

Torrance forced himself to continue his work until the beat of his heart returned to normal. Then the work pulled him further in. By the time the bell rang for supper, his desk had almost returned to its normal tidy condition. He looked at the bottle and shook his head in disgust. Picking it up, Torrance carried the bottle with him to dinner, where he handed it to Harold with the request that the staff each be given a drink as they desired.

After supper, he asked his staff to assemble in the front hall.

"Friends, Marriette is off looking for a friend. It is my prayer she will return home to us here. So it is our task to keep this a home she would be pleased to come back to." Torrance dismissed them to their work and went to the bedroom they hadn't shared for weeks. He moved his clothes back into the room and looked around. She'd find him waiting when she came back.

The day came when Torrance was to travel to his estates in the south. As much as he wanted to stay in his Bellpolis home and wait for Marriette, he had a duty to his people. As he watched the staff pack the wagon with his papers, clothes and other things that he needed, he recognized the young girl who was checking the boxes and bales as they were loaded.

"Excuse me? Joan, isn't it?" Torrance said. "May we talk for a moment?"

Joan looked around and sighed. "Let me finish this load."

When the wagon was loaded, Joan gave the drovers their orders then came back to Torrance.

"Is there somewhere quiet we can talk?" she asked. Torrance led her into the parlour.

"You are Arthur's sister," he said. "The same Art that Marriette has gone to look for. Have you heard anything?"

"It was a dream that Marriette had, my Lord," Joan said. "It convinced her that he was alive. She was terribly confused when I talked to her. She thought you hated her."

"Why would I hate her?" Torrance asked.

"Because of what her father did to her." Joan dropped her head. "And you stopped speaking to her or touching her."

Torrance sat down suddenly.

"Oh, my God," he whispered, "I am a bigger fool than I thought. I gave her space, but she saw it as me pushing her away, and she thought...." He looked at Joan, not caring about the tears running down his face.

"I promised her I wouldn't tell where she went." Joan sighed and ran fingers through her hair.

"If you can get a message to her, please let her know I am sorry, I still love her. Better yet, wait here a moment." He hobbled as quickly as he could to his office and scribbled a message. He sealed it and brought it back to Joan. "Here, please, send this on to her."

Joan took the note and placed it in her pouch.

"I will do what I can."

He stood and showed her out. "Thank you, and if there is ever anything that I can do for you, just let me know."

They travelled south for several days while Torrance's heart and mind were travelling north. Business on his estates was usually one of his favourite activities. He walked through his vineyards and put his hands on the trees that had been selected for cutting. It was a time when he was available to all his people. He gave permission for marriages, and gifts to newborns. This year, he wanted to introduce his wonderful young bride to all his people, and show her how special they were. He started going to chapel since that gave him a solid hour to think about Marriette and pray for her safety. He even got his nerve up to talk to the priest who had served in his family chapel since his father's time about Marriette.

"What do I do, Father?" Torrance asked. "I want to love her, but I am afraid of hurting her."

"You did well enough," the priest said, "such a terrible thing hurts everyone it touches. Now, you need to be patient, but you also need to let her know that you desire her. She thinks she is repulsive. Let her see herself in your eyes."

"But what if I cause her more pain?"

"We all cause pain to those we love, no less than we cause God pain. Take heart, God has forgiven you, and your wife will too, in time."

"I want to heal her of her sorrow."

"You can't, you may increase it, but you cannot lessen it. Each of us must heal by God's grace."

The winter deepened and they even had a dusting of snow in the midst of the rain that poured endlessly from the skies. One day, Torrance found a letter on his desk. He tore it open eagerly and tried not to be too disappointed that it was from Joan, not Marriette.

Dear Sir, Forgive me for being so bold, but I have learned from our people in Northdale that Marriette is spending the winter in a monastery at the foot of the mountains. I don't think she would have got your letter before she went there. It will be waiting for her at the inn in the last village to the north before the mountains. Joan Candler.

Torrance sat with the letter in hand until night fell.

"I am going north," Torrance announced when his secretary came in to check on him.

"Back to the city, my Lord?"

"Farther north, past Northdale."

"We don't have any interests up that far."

"I do."

"Ah, I see. If you would permit, I will send young Hans to you. He grew up in that region and will be able to tell you what you will need."

Hans was a fountain of information. He kept remembering things he'd forgotten and running back to Torrance to let him know the newest addition. Torrance finally decided to take Hans with him. They set off in the carriage and travelled easily to the city. Torrance bought the long list of warm clothes that Hans insisted he would need. Two days later, they took the road north.

Travel became more difficult the farther they went. A winter storm kept them trapped in one hostel for a week. Finally, they arrived in Northdale, where Torrance stopped for a couple of days to meet Hans' family.

They travelled to a tiny village after which the roads were blocked. He took rooms at the inn run by a well-organized man named Bill. Sure enough, the letter waited for Marriette on Bill's desk. Torrance settled himself into the small but very comfortable room at the back of the inn and waited for spring.

EIGHT OF WANDS

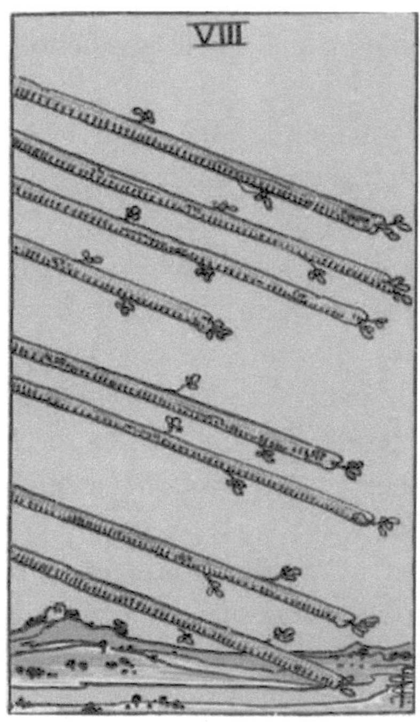

Marriette was allowed to keep her long hair, but the clothes she had with her were set aside for the season. In their place, she was given a novitiate's robe, which draped to the floor and covered her feet. Since it was winter, she was allowed to wear a pair of light sandals to protect her feet from the cold stone.

The first forty days were dedicated to silence. She rose in the morning with the monks and went to the chapel for prayer, then to the common room to break her fast. The rest of the day was an alternation of prayer, contemplation and chores.

The abbot assigned Brother Stephen as her spiritual director. He chose the scriptures she was to contemplate. They ranged from stories of the Christ to odd tales from the Old Testament. Each time, the instruction was the same. She was to put herself in the story as an actor or observer. 'To be open' became her constant prayer during these days. The only time she was permitted to talk was during their brief talks in morning and evening.

Brother Stephen was as comfortable with his blindness as he was with silence. He walked through the halls of the monastery at all times of day or night without hesitation or misstep. Gently pulling Marriette's learning from her with a word here or there, he recited to her the next lesson for her contemplation, but the rest of the time he didn't speak.

"My silence is the silence of good friends who no longer need to fill the space between them with chatter," he said to her one time. "It is chosen, not forced, like wearing a comfortable robe," he said another time.

Marriette's silence grew comfortable after a while. At first, the words tried to force themselves out of her. She wondered that they didn't burst through her ribs and deafen everyone. After a week, their urgency lessened. Many of them were saying the same things. She listened to them and set them aside. Her hatred of her father. Her torment about failing Torrance as his wife. Her fear of the intimacy and vulnerability of sex. All of these wound their way out of her soul, and she sent them spinning on their way to whatever void unspoken words inhabited.

"Marriette," Brother Stephen said, one day in the New Year. "I think it is time to hear your questions."

"Where do I start?" she said.

"Start with what is on the surface."

"I'm a terrible person," she said. "I hate my father, and I have run away from my husband."

"Hate is a strong word."

"Not strong enough," Marriette said bitterly, "my father raped me to punish me for disobeying him. He would say that he had the right because I am his daughter and he owns me." She lapsed into silence. "I talked to the archbishop about it, and he said it was my father's sin, not mine. Yet, I still feel the stain of it on my soul."

"The archbishop is wise."

"Wise, but afraid. He would not condemn my father except privately to my ears alone."

"You are not afraid?"

"I am terrified. I wake in the morning fearing to see him standing over me. I go to sleep trembling lest he come into my chamber. Even in my husband's home, even here."

"The fear is ruling you."

"I can't just stop being afraid. He is too powerful."

"Then you need a connection with someone more powerful, but someone whose power you can trust."

"The king? Even if he believed me, what could he do to protect me?"

"A king, yes, but not just of this land."

Marriette was silent for a long time. Brother Stephen waited.

"How do you do it?" she asked. "You are blind. The walls of this place have been breached before. What if it happens again?"

"What if it does?" Brother Stephen said. "What is the worst that will happen? I will die. I will someday regardless. We all will. I know when I die, I will be with my Lord. Knowing that, I can live fearlessly in the world. It is a great thing to be able to look at kings and powers and know that they have no true hold over you."

"What about while I am alive? Must I suffer beatings and abuse while I wait for death? Why doesn't God do something?"

"Hasn't God done something? Are you not here? It is a rare thing for God to interfere directly with the work of his creation. Yet we are gently guided and prodded to learn what we must learn."

"But it is too late!"

"Too late for what?"

"Too late for me to know love. Too late for me to be anything but wounded and afraid."

"You have already known love. Love is a much bigger thing than just the sharing of bodies. As for being wounded and afraid, who is not? It is by our trials that we learn to turn to God."

"You're a monk. You're supposed to believe that. What do you know of real life?"

The silence grew so long that Marriette feared that she had said the unforgivable. Each breath without talking made her more certain that Brother Stephen was going to cast her out. Just when she was ready to scream to break the silence that wrapped her in its coils, she felt it loosen. He hadn't denounced her. He hadn't stalked off in a rage. He was waiting for her. Marriette didn't have to fear Brother Stephen. She didn't have anything to fear in this place other than what she brought with her. It wasn't her father that made her miserable, but her fear. It was fear keeping her from Torrance, fear preventing her from opening herself to everything he had to offer. Great tears began rolling down her cheeks.

"Forgive me," she said, but Brother Stephen didn't answer. "Forgive me for letting my fear rule me. I don't want to be afraid anymore. I don't know what you want me to do, but I will try." The coils of fear fell away. The silence was no longer something hard or terrible, but comfortable and safe. Brother Stephen wasn't angry. A great space opened up inside her. Light shone into it and showed her herself. The fear, the pride, the rebelliousness were all revealed. She wondered how anyone, even God, could love such a terrible person. Then the light brightened, and for an instant she caught a glimpse of the woman that she could be. Compassionate, strong and at peace.

"I want that," she said to the Light. "Whatever the price, whatever You want from me." The light brightened even more, until it was the only thing in all the world. For an instant she almost understood. Then it was gone. No. Not gone, just no longer so overwhelming.

The bell rang for supper, and Brother Stephen stood.

"It is time for supper, my child."

Marriette opened her mouth to protest then laughed. The light would be at supper too.

"Is it always like this?" she asked.

"No, not always. The world is a hard place to live and may not be as full of the light as you just were, but it is always there, even if we forget. God never does."

Marriette soon learned, even in the monastery, trying to hold on to her experience was hard. Brother Stephen set her the story of Jesus on the mountain. Even he needed to go back down to work.

"It is what we are for," the old monk said, "or at least partly. When we shine, people are drawn to us, and through us, to God."

"Why allow suffering? If everyone felt this, the world would be perfect."

"It has to do with choice," Brother Stephen said. "Love as a choice is beautiful, love without choice is rape. Now that you know that, you can teach it."

"What happens when I go back?"

"Life happens. Real life," Brother Stephen said with a gentle smile. "You will make choices, and so will the people around you. The more times you choose to be loving, the more you make it possible for others to find their light."

"That doesn't explain suffering. Why doesn't God protect us?"

"We aren't here to be protected, we're here to be in the midst of the worst of life and shine anyway."

Another day they walked outside as the air warmed toward spring.

"What about Torrance?" Marriette said. "What do I do about him?"

"Why do you think you need to do anything about Torrance?"

"He's my husband."

"Yes, but he is his own person. You can't fix him any more than he could fix you."

"I have to do something."

"Of course you do, but it isn't about him. It is about you. Love yourself as you are. Love him as he is."

"He's going to be angry."

"He may."

"How could he not be?"

"You would be angry at him?"

"I would be furious."

"Then let go of your anger."

Marriette shook her head and laughed.

"This isn't as easy as I thought. Every time I think I have it right, I get it turned around. Does it ever get easier?"

Brother Stephen waved her to a seat in the garden.

"A farmer brought in a young man with terrible wounds. I was sure he would die, but I argued that we needed to try to heal him. I did heal him. He recovered completely except that he couldn't talk. Some conflict in his soul had closed his lips. I was so sure that I could reach him. The abbot wasn't as sure. He feared that the conflict could as easily resolve to darkness as to light, especially since the young man refused to enter the chapel. One day, I said something to him, and he attacked me. I ran for shelter and the closest safety was the chapel. He followed me in, and there was a being of light so intense it blinded me, yet I count myself fortunate that it was the last thing I saw. The man shouted, and it was a cry of the deepest rejection and fear I had ever heard."

"What happened to him?"

"The abbot had him bound in chains to be sent to the city. He took me to Northdale to see a healer about my eyes. When we returned, the monastery had been attacked and many of my brothers were dead. The young man had fled into the forest. Was I right in my compassion, or wrong in my pride?" The monk laughed. "A long answer to your question. No, it doesn't get easier."

Soon after that day, the abbot called her into his office.

"It is spring. I think it is time for you to rejoin the world."

"Yes."

"Where will you go?"

"I must see Torrance and talk to him."

"And your father?"

"If God gives me the strength."

"It is good, my child. God go with you."

John had come up with the wagon, and was more than happy to carry Marriette back down to Northdale. They left at the morning light. Marriette was again dressed in her own clothes. She fingered the simple wooden cross that Brother Stephen had given her.

"It was rough wood when I put it on before your father was born. Years of wearing it has made it smooth. Keep it and think of me."

The cross and the glimmer of light inside her were the only things she took from the monastery.

The road down to Young William's farm went faster than Marriette remembered. She let John's gruesome commentaries slide past her as she wondered what Torrance was doing. He would be in the south getting ready to return to the city, she guessed. They reached the inn run by Bill in the early evening. Stretching she thanked John and headed inside. She was barely in the door when Bill came up to her.

"I've got a letter for you," he said. "It has been waiting here all winter." He handed it to her and went back to his work. Marriette's hands shook as she opened it. She carried it into the common room and stood by the window to read it.

Dearest Marriette,

Please forgive me for letting my desire overwhelm my sensibilities. I love you so much that I must constantly remind myself that you are real and my wife. There is no other woman. Only you from the moment I saw you at the altar. Whatever you may think, you have made me happier than I have ever been.

Torrance

She stared at the note until the words blurred through her tears.

"I don't deserve someone like you," she said to the letter.

"No, you deserve better," Torrance said from behind her.

Marriette whirled and dropped the letter. She threw herself at Torrance, who stood beside a table covered with papers. He tried to speak, but she clutched him so tightly that he couldn't get the words out. So he just held her.

After a while, she realized that there was a crowd of people in the room clapping and cheering.

"I told you it would work out," Bill said to no one in particular. "Okay, now, give them some privacy." He shooed the people out, leaving Marriette and Torrance still holding each other. They sat at the table and held hands. Marriette couldn't think of anything to say, so she just looked at Torrance and soaked in the sight of him. He looked stronger, more sure of himself somehow. He didn't have his cane.

"There is a healer here who does massages and makes me exercise. He is sadistic and cruel, and very, very gifted. I still need the cane for long walks, but for shorter distances I can do without it." He rubbed his thumb across her hand. "It looks like the monastic life agreed with you."

Marriette started to explain all about what she had done and learned, but her heart pounded and she struggled to breathe. She didn't want to be afraid. Not of Torrance, not any longer, so she kissed him, long and passionately.

"I am sure the monks didn't teach you that," said Torrance when he caught his breath.

"Take me to your room, my love, and I will show you some other things the monks didn't teach me." She caught his hand and its shaking told her he was as afraid as she. "Don't worry. You won't hurt me."

They walked to Torrance's room and closed the door behind them. Marriette led him to the bed.

"Love is greater than fear," she said and kissed him again. His hands found the ties of her dress and it fell from her. She pulled his shirt off and loosened his belt as he fumbled with her underclothes. Then they were embracing, feeling only the warmth of each other in the chill air of the room. Torrance lowered his wife to the bed and looked in her eyes. Marriette saw herself in his eyes. She didn't see any fear or uncertainty, only love.

TWO OF CUPS

Marriette woke in the morning and smiled. The warm security of Torrance sleeping at her back was something she'd missed horribly in the past months. She rolled over and reached down under the blankets. Torrance woke with a start, then a smile to match his wife's spread across his face. By the time they made it downstairs they were far too late for breakfast. They went for a walk while they waited for the noon meal to be served.

The day was warm and bright. People aired out rugs and blankets while the sun shone. Torrance greeted many of them by name. Marriette was surprised at how pleasant it was to just hold hands. She craved physical contact as much as she had feared it before. Several times they stopped for long, passionate kisses. They had missed lunch by the time they returned to the inn. Fortunately, Bill had set a couple of plates aside for them.

"I remember the first week or so after I married my Beth; we would have starved if my ma hadn't put food in our hands."

Even the cold meal was delicious; Marriette and Torrance didn't notice when Bill cleared the dishes away. If they talked, Marriette couldn't remember what they had said. The only sense of passing time was Bill putting a hot meal in front of them. He snorted at their astonished expressions.

The couple stayed at the inn for two weeks rising late and retiring early. After the first few days they tentatively started exploring each other's lives as well as bodies. Marriette could talk about her father more easily while Torrance's strong arms surrounded her. She learned that his guilt over LisAnne had kept him from hearing her before. He had been so afraid of hurting her that he was afraid to love her. They found forgiveness and atonement in each other's embrace.

"Did you find Art?" asked Torrance one day, while they sat on the window bench watching a spring snowstorm swirl through the village.

"No, but I heard many terrible stories about a person that might have been Art. He wasn't a saint, but he wasn't a monster who killed at the slightest excuse. Something truly evil must have happened to change him so."

"The demon bandit might not be Art."

"I dreamed it, love," she said. "In the same dream that I saw Bill's niece was a redhead. We were never lovers, but there is something that connects us. I don't know why."

"We will just have to wait and find out," said Torrance squeezing Marriette to remind her that there was definitely something that connected them.

"There is no chance I will go anywhere without you," she said putting her hand on his. "We are truly joined, body and soul now."

"Just wait, you will get tired of this old man someday."

"Never," Marriette said, facing Torrance to kiss him.

"Hey," Bill yelled, "go to your room if you are going to be doing that!"

They spent their days getting used to being in each other's lives again. They talked of everything and nothing, or didn't talk at all. Marriette discovered all the ways her body yearned for her lover's touch, and all the ways his touch could fulfill her.

On a rainy day, Torrance told Marriette about Sylvie.

"It was a year or so after LisAnne and Niklas were killed. I was dreadfully lonely and slowly killing myself with brandy. She was one of the maids and always flirted with me. One day, I flirted back, and the next thing I knew, we were sleeping together. Not that unusual, though the church frowns on it. It was just fun, but she started wanting more. Dresses, jewels, that kind of thing. I caught her moving her things into my bedroom and knew I needed to do something."

"I thought she took it well when I broke it off. Your father's agents had just floated the idea of marriage with you, and I didn't think marrying you with Sylvie's scent still on me would be a good way to start a relationship. I got her a place with a friend who would treat her properly and not assume that because she shared my bed she should share his. To be honest, I don't think Sylvie is his type at all.

"She started sending me notes telling me how much she missed me. She wanted to come back. I refused. She came and saw me that night to try and seduce me back to her. I told her I wasn't interested. She threatened blackmail, and I lied and said that you already knew about her. That quieted her, but I don't think that you were the person she had planned to talk to."

"She certainly had a smirk on her face when I saw her, poor girl," Marriette said.

"Poor girl?"

"Can you imagine what it would be like to think that was the only thing that you had to offer to someone?"

"I did the best I could by her. There isn't anything she wants I can give her."

Their idle days ended soon after. Torrance got a letter from his secretary saying that they needed him to make some essential decisions. Torrance replied that they would return to the house in the city. It was still a bit early in the season, but Torrance felt it would be more familiar to Marriette than the estates to the south.

They started off the next day, much to Bill's disappointment.

"We don't often get such long standing customers, the place won't be the same without you here." He shook Torrance's hand and hugged Marriette. "Come back and visit."

After both Marriette and Torrance promised to return, he gave them a basket of food to eat in the carriage. Torrance's guide to the north, Hans, had found a girl in town and was still sorting out his feelings toward her, so Torrance left him with a purse of money and a letter of reference. He also told the young man that he was welcome to rejoin Torrance's staff if he ever wished.

As the carriage rolled south, Marriette entertained Torrance with the gruesome tales that John had told her. Soon they were in Northdale.

"I have friends here I would like to see," Marriette said, so Torrance directed the driver to Giuseppe's office.

"Hello, Giuseppe!" she called as they walked into the tiny office. "I'm back, for a visit, at least."

Therese squealed, and ran to hug Marriette.

"Pappa is teaching me to keep the books," she said as she dragged Marriette to the yard where Giuseppe was checking out a wagonload. By the time Marriette had introduced Torrance and explained what she had been doing all winter, it was suppertime. Giuseppe insisted that Marriette and Torrance join them for supper. Agathia was delighted to have Marriette as a guest again. Gracia and

Karitia almost knocked Marriette over with their excitement then went shy around Torrance. He told stories about his winter in the north that soon had them screaming with laughter.

Giuseppe and Agathia said that the couple must take their beds while they roomed with the girls.

"Are you sure?" asked Torrance. "We can easily go to the inn and not put you out."

"The inn is a fine place for strangers," Giuseppe said, "but not for friends. You will honour us by staying here."

"We would be delighted, Giuseppe," Marriette said, "but you must promise that you will bring the girls to visit us in Bellpolis."

"It's a deal!" Giuseppe said.

The girls were sent off to bed while the adults opened a bottle of wine and talked far into the night.

"Yes, yes," Giuseppe said, "our nobles only thought about their own comfort. They fought and quarreled like dogs fighting over bones. It got so bad that they were selling their own people to pay for their pleasures. Agathia and I were lucky to escape."

"I fear that we are headed down that same road," Torrance said. "There are too many of the noble Houses filled with young people concerned only with fulfilling their next whim. Estates are poorly run, and wealth is being squandered."

Marriette and Agathia smiled at each other over their glasses and listened to the talk.

In the morning, the girls hugged both Marriette and Torrance.

"Promise that you will come and visit again," Therese said.

Agathia gave them food for the journey, and Giuseppe slipped in a bottle of wine. It was mid-morning by the time the carriage pulled out of Northdale.

"I like your friends," Torrance said, "and not just because he agrees with my politics. They are a special family. I haven't often met people as generous."

The rest of the journey went far too quickly for Marriette. She found herself getting nervous as they approached the city. *What is Anna going to think? Will they worry that I'll run off again?* She took hold of Torrance's hand for comfort. He gave it a gentle squeeze.

"Almost home."

The sun touched the horizon as they arrived at the leBraun home. It reminded Marriette a great deal of when Torrance brought her home after their wedding. All the staff were gathered and waiting. Torrance helped her down from the carriage. Marriette could hear the murmurs of surprise that Torrance wasn't using his cane. He led Marriette to the door, then swept her off her feet and carried her across the threshold. There were cheers from all the people there—as much Torrance's family as his servants. When he carefully put her back on her feet, Marriette gave him a long kiss that brought more cheers from the staff.

"I am glad to be home," she whispered.

They had supper and soon went to off to bed. Marriette walked into the room and saw it for an instant as the place of all her suffering. Then she closed her eyes and took a deep breath. She replaced the memories of the sorrowful days alone in this room with the thought of the early days when she and Torrance had become friends, if not lovers. When she opened her eyes, the shadows had fled.

"I moved back in the day after you left," Torrance said, "I wanted to be here for you when you came home."

"There is only one problem," she said.

"What's that?" asked Torrance, looking worried.

"You still have your clothes on," she reached behind her to the ties on her dress. "I'll race you."

In the morning, she lay beside her husband, and smiled to herself. Here she was with her husband, in their own bed, in their own house. There was only one thing missing, and she planned to wake Torrance soon and start working on that.

THE HERMIT

Excruciating pain dragged Zeb out of the darkness. He wanted to return to the blissful state of unconsciousness that preceded the pain, but there was no escape. So he opened his eyes. He lay on something soft and warm in a tiny hut. The walls looked like they were made out of earth. A fire burned in the center of the hut and smoke rose up and through the hole in the roof.

Zeb tried to sit up, but couldn't get any of his muscles to cooperate. He tried speaking and managed a rough rasping sound. An old man sat up from a mat on the other side of the fire and came around to Zeb.

"Heh, so y're alive." He picked up a bowl and a spoon. "Try 'n eat some." He fed Zeb carefully, but only managed three spoonfuls before Zeb's eyes closed and he went back to sleep.

Some time later, Zeb woke again, and the old man fed him some more. This time the old man stripped the mat down and washed Zeb before putting some clean clothes on him.

"Y'll be weak like a baby for a while, I figure."

Zeb wandered in and out of sleep each time the hut was lit only by the tiny fire. The old man was always there to feed and clean him. Zeb had no idea how long this lasted. It might have been days; it could have been months. Very slowly, he regained control over his flesh and bones. He was able to use a crude pan instead of messing the cover of his mat. He was even able to feed himself.

The pain gradually receded, as he gained strength.

"How did I get here?" Zeb asked.

"Found ye in a snowdrift. Ye were still breathin' so I brung ye here. T'see if y'd live."

"Why?"

"Why not? I don't mind a bit of company through the winter."

"How do you know I am not going to kill you?"

The old man just snorted.

One day, Zeb was able to sit up on the mat of sheepskins that was his bed. It exhausted him completely, but made it easier to eat. The passage of time became marked by the periods Zeb could sit up. The old man never seemed to sleep. Whenever Zeb awoke, the man would be there watching him. It wasn't a predatory look, the old man showed no interest in having any power over Zeb, but it wasn't the watch of someone who is afraid either. It was as if he watched Zeb simply to watch. Zeb didn't like it. The lack of fear or desire confused him.

One day, the old man wasn't there, when Zeb woke. At first, he couldn't pinpoint what was wrong. When he did see the old man was missing, it was as if a wall had vanished. Zeb closed his eyes and opened them again. The old man still wasn't there. Zeb's heart pounded. He didn't have the strength to do anything for himself yet. He was completely dependent on the old man for his survival. Just before his panic was complete, a leather curtain that Zeb had taken as part of the wall moved and the old man stepped into the hut.

"Heh, y'r awake. Good." He busied himself at the fire.

"Where were you?" asked Zeb even as he despised the fear in his voice.

"Almost lambing season. Had to check the ewes."

"Why now?"

"Check 'em every day," the old man said. "Tis the first day you woke up. Y'r getting' stronger." He went back to stirring the pot.

"Could you show me how to tend the fire and cook?" The old man looked at Zeb, then shrugged his shoulders.

"The fire's coal," he said. "Don't mess with it much. Just put a chunk on in the morning. Soup's the same, mostly barley. Top up the water when you put on the coal."

"I'm sure I tasted meat in the broth."

"Mutton," said the old man. "Old ewe wasn't going to make the winter. Twas kinder to kill her early before she suffers. Just bones left." He lifted a bone out of the soup pot to show Zeb then let it drop back in.

"You kill an old sheep, but you nurse me through the winter?"

"Ye ain't sheep."

After that, Zeb never knew whether the old shepherd would be in the hut or not, but he always returned after a short time. He kept no schedule, but did whatever he thought of at the moment. Sometimes it was bright sun on the other side of the curtain, other times it was swirling snow or black night.

One time, the shepherd came into the hut carrying a tiny bundle. He gave it to Zeb.

"Lamb, the ewe wouldn't take to 'er. Happens sometimes."

"What do you want me to do?"

"Nurse 'er," the old shepherd said, "I'll show you how."

The old man brought a bowl of warm milk over to Zeb along with a cloth. He dipped the cloth in the milk and gave it to the tiny creature to suck on. After a while, the lamb got the idea and finished the milk.

"I'll bring you milk. You nurse 'er."

Zeb felt a curious thing in him as he held the tiny lamb. He wanted to protect her. Over the next few days, he fed the lamb her milk as the shepherd had shown him. In the process, he sat up for longer and longer periods. There was a strange delight in caring for this creature for no other reason than because it needed him. It got stronger and was soon jumping around the hut. Yet it would always come over when Zeb spoke to it.

Perhaps this weakness in him came from his near death in the blizzard. Yet, he had come close to dying in the monastery and remained himself. Zeb worried at the problem as his strength grew. He could hurt the lamb, but he didn't want to. In all his aeons of existence he'd caused pain, or had pain inflicted on him. The idea of not wanting to hurt something was absurd. Still, whenever the lamb pranced over to him, he held it gently, even protectively.

He could hear more activity outside, so one day he crawled out the door. The hut looked like a small hill in the middle of a pasture that was more green than white. The sun made Zeb squint, but the fresh air was so delicious that he stayed leaning against the outside of the hut the rest of the day laughing as Lamb explored the larger surroundings. From that day on, Zeb made his way outside, rain or shine. He gradually was able to walk the few feet and didn't have to crawl.

As he grew stronger, he lifted his eyes to see the mountains surrounding them. Snow still lay white on their slopes.

The days slowly got warmer. Zeb pushed himself now. He took hold of the staff of wood that leaned on the hut next to the door and walked around the sheepfold. The animals had been skittish at first, but now they accepted him the same way they did the shepherd.

Spring greens found their way into the soup as Zeb recognized some of the plants that Rat had picked for them to eat.

"Tis time to move to the upper pasture," the old shepherd said one day. "Are ye strong enough?"

"Yes." Zeb was surprised to find it was true.

The next day, the old shepherd began collecting bits and pieces from the hut and wrapping them in a blanket. He rolled up most of the sheepskins and tied them into a bundle. The next day he came with a fresh staff for Zeb.

"Y'r taller than me. This'un will fit ye better." He was right. Zeb liked the slightly thicker heft of the new staff. The shepherd gave a bundle of sheepskin to Zeb then hefted a bundle that was so large he was barely visible under it. He clicked his tongue at the sheep and started walking. The sheep followed him without hesitation; the lamb ran after the sheep, so Zeb followed the lamb.

They walked through valleys that were still filled with snow, and along hills where flowers were beginning to show their colours.

Zeb had never done anything as hard as keeping up to the old man and the sheep. As each day progressed, he leaned more on his staff, but he stubbornly persisted. Mostly, they slept on the grass under the stars. Only if the shepherd called for rain did he pull out an oilcloth to spread it over them.

Lamb spent most of the time gamboling around Zeb's feet. They walked for days through air that was so clean and fresh it was like Zeb had never breathed before. The old man noticed everything. Occasionally, he would point out the hawks floating high above, or a tiny fern uncurling at their feet.

They travelled this way for a week before they arrived in a huge valley surrounded by steep hills covered with pine trees. A hut that looked identical to the one they left waited for them. The shepherd pushed his way into the hut and swept it out before setting it up the way he wanted it.

The sheep spread across the valley and began cropping the new grass. Zeb slept through the next day. The next he pushed his way out of the hut and walked around the field. He watched the old shepherd and learned what was needed. Mostly it was a matter of keeping the flock together so the sheep were less likely to stray. After a week, the shepherd began leaving Zeb to watch the sheep, while he slept.

Watching the sheep gave Zeb time to contemplate his situation. He'd heard of other devils being forced to possess humans. They were sent to cause as much confusion as they could before being sent back to Hell. Zeb could recall no story in which the devil spent a long time in a mortal body acting mostly like a mortal. He'd experienced both pain and pleasure and learned he preferred the pleasure. Perhaps, by some alchemy the mage hadn't expected, he was no longer just a devil wearing a mortal body.

They had been in the valley only a few days before the first sheep wandered off. The shepherd left Zeb with the sheep and went to find the stray.

"They are silly creatures," he said when he returned with the sheep. "They need each other, but they are always wanderin' off alone. Tis like they don't know what they want."

Several times after, the sheep wandered away. Mostly the shepherd would come back carrying the lost animal on his shoulders, once or twice he returned empty handed.

"Happens," was all he would say about it.

One evening, a few of the stupid animals had wandered up to the far end of the valley. Zeb picked up his staff and walked to fetch them down for the night. Lamb followed along beside him. It was dusk when he got to the small flock. As he arrived, he saw a shadow slip from the forest, then another—wolves. He tried to get the sheep to move faster, but the grass was fresher up here and the sheep hadn't scented the pack yet. Zeb pushed them harder, but they just slid around him and went back to the grass. Then he heard a scream. The wolves had one of the sheep.

Zeb ran over swinging his staff. He clubbed one wolf and knocked it to the ground, but another one came from behind him.

Zeb yelled and the sheep finally realized something was wrong and scattered across the valley.

Zeb stayed in the middle of the pack of wolves as they tried to drag off the sheep they had killed. Wolves nipped at his heels or leaped toward his throat. Zeb's rage gave him strength. One by one, Zeb killed the wolves or drove them back to the forest. Finally, he stood alone with the bodies of the wolves he had killed and the one sheep they had torn apart. Blood dripped from scratches and bites on his arms and legs.

He went to see which sheep had died. It was Lamb. Zeb went to his knees and howled. Tears flowed from his eyes and sobs wracked his body. He didn't know what was happening to him. This pain, this weakness, was entirely new to him.

"Happens, lad," the old shepherd said as he came up to Zeb. "Tis sad, but it happens."

"Why?" sobbed Zeb.

"Tis what wolves do. They pick on the weakest. S'what they are." The old man helped Zeb to his feet. "Come. Grieve, but grieve while ye work."

They spent the rest of the night gathering the spooked animals and guarding them closely. In the morning, the shepherd went up and skinned the wolves. Lamb was gone, dragged into the woods by the rest of the wolf pack. Zeb took to walking the fringes of the forest looking for more of the wolves. The shepherd shrugged and let him. Zeb never found anything more than prints. Several times, the flock was attacked by the pack. Each time, Zeb rushed in with his staff and he managed to kill more wolves, but the wolves also claimed the lives of more sheep.

"Ye can't kill all the wolves," the shepherd said one day when Zeb returned with two more skins. "They have a place too." Zeb spent less time actively seeking the predators, but he was more vigilant with the sheep.

With the return of Zeb's strength came the return of the mage's pain. As if each time he killed a wolf, he made the connection between them stronger. His hands ached so he could barely hold the staff.

"I have to go," he said to the shepherd one day.

The old man just nodded.

"I don't want to," Zeb explained, "but the pain is going to just get worse until I do. This man wants me to call him master and do his bidding. I have fought him as long as I can."

"T'isn't good to call any man master," the shepherd said, "but ye do need to know what ye serve."

"I serve no one."

"Ye served the sheep, kept them safe as ye could. Y'll end up serving somethin' or someone. Might as well be somethin' ye choose. Like them wolves. They were attackin' the sheep, but it was to feed themselves and their pack."

"So, I should be like the wolves?"

"No, ye should be a man and choose what and who ye will serve. Not just what y'r against, what are y're for. Ye go and do what ye have to do. If y're still livin' next winter y'r welcome to come back."

Zeb put together a small pack and took his staff. The old shepherd made him take the wolf pelts with him.

"They're just rough tanned. Won't last the summer. Can't give you money, but y'll get a little for them at market in Westfale."

He hoisted the bundle onto Zeb's back.

"Go safe, lad. Stay west of the forest. There's a slaver calls himself Chancy just waitin' to pick off the weak and foolish."

"Like the wolves."

"Heh, maybe, but he ain't a wolf for you to chase, go around him and land up in Westfale. It will take ye longer, but y're more likely to arrive."

So Zeb walked south out of the valley, and, for the first time, he didn't leave death and despair behind him.

EIGHT OF PENTACLES

Zeb travelled south through the mountains for a week. He steered well to the west staying in the foothills of the range stretching south from the mountains encircling the pasture. The weather stayed clear for the most part. The only day it rained, Zeb spent sitting under a pine tree surrounded by the sounds of the forest.

He gave a great deal of thought to the old shepherd's words. Truly, he had served the flock. It never occurred to him service could be anything but what was imposed on him from the outside. Ever since the Great Rejection, he had given himself to the dual tasks of fighting off the need to serve the more powerful, and enforce the serfdom of those weaker than him.

Having a choice was novel. He re-examined everything that happened to him—he never really made a free choice. He'd been pushed from one place to another, always reacting against whoever was doing the pushing. Time for him to start making his own decisions.

The problem was he didn't know what he wanted. Going back to what he was before didn't seem like an option. He had been close to death without crossing over enough times for him to suspect that nothing on this world could kill him. On the other hand, giving in to the mage and his demands wasn't an option either. Zeb wasn't going to let his first true choice in millennia be giving up his freedom.

The forest made a gradual shift from the conifers of the foothills to the hardwoods he and the bandits had inhabited. Zeb kept a close watch for Chancy or his people, but saw no one. Two weeks after he left the pasture, Zeb found the first hint of a path. It became a track, then a dirt road as he walked. He didn't have any experience of people aside from robbing or killing them, so he avoided the farms and small villages that appeared. The people were content to let him pass, as long as he left them alone.

He had been almost a week walking on the road when the farmer offered him a lift into Westfale. Zeb shrugged and tossed his bundle into the wagon and climbed up beside the farmer.

"Long winter?" the farmer asked.

"Long enough," Zeb said.

"Where'd you spend it?"

"Up in the mountains, with an old shepherd."

"Do you remember his name?"

"He never told me, and I never asked."

The farmer laughed and shook his head.

"That sounds like those old shepherds. Them wolf pelts you have there?"

"A few," Zeb said cautiously.

"I wouldn't want them," said the farmer, laughing again, "but you'll want to see Joseph at the market. He gives the best prices for furs, though he is fussy about quality. What did you use to kill them?"

Zeb hoisted his staff. The farmer whistled.

"Better you than me, friend, but at least there won't be sword cuts or arrow holes for Joseph to fuss about."

They arrived at Westfale before noon. The guards at the bridge waved the farmer through as he asked about their families. They did give Zeb a sharp look, but didn't say anything. The farmer circled around to the market and dropped Zeb off in front of Joseph's tent. Zeb hoisted his bundle and walked into the tent. He was surrounded by the pelts of more animals than he could name. Some furs were smaller than his hand while there was a bear skin on the floor longer than he was tall.

"Hello, may I help you?"

"I have some wolf pelts," Zeb said.

"Winter or summer?"

"I killed them in early spring."

"They might be all right then," Joseph said, "let me see them."

Zeb unrolled them; Joseph wrinkled his nose at the smell, but checked them over carefully.

"Whoever rough tanned them did a good job, he saved them for you, but another week and they'd have been gone." Joseph pointed at a couple of pelts. "These ones are very good, and an unusual colour. I can use them. These ones aren't bad. This last couple are from too late in the season and the fur is uneven." He pushed himself to his feet. "I can give you a gold each for the first two, and another gold for the rest."

"Is that good?" asked Zeb.

"Well, I think it is fair," Joseph said, "but you are welcome to check out some other buyers. Stefan across the way sometimes buys wolf."

"I will take it, then," Zeb said. They shook on the deal, then the merchant paid him not in gold coin, but rather a motley collection of silver and copper.

"Less likely to get you into trouble," he said.

Zeb left the merchant to wrapping up the furs and readying them for proper tanning and wandered into the market. His stomach growled, so he found someone selling hot food and bought himself something to eat. As he ate his bread and cheese, a big man came up to him.

"Sheriff wants to see ya," the man said. He moved to grab Zeb's arm and Zeb swung his staff to the ready.

"Easy, boys," another man said coming up behind the big man. "Bailey, how many times have I told you that politeness is easier than fighting?"

"He ain't no problem," Bailey said flexing his muscles.

"He has killed at least six wolves with that stick, according to Joseph. He might surprise you. Size isn't everything."

"Well...." Bailey looked doubtfully at Zeb.

"Would you like another wrestling match?"

"Uh, no, Sheriff," Bailey said, "I be going over to check the horse stalls now."

The sheriff chuckled and slapped the big man on the shoulder.

"He's a good enough man, just a little...thick on occasion." He offered his hand to Zeb, "Sheriff Jones, at your service."

Zeb looked doubtfully at him then shook his hand.

"I don't know my name," he said, "never thought about it."

"Bump on the head?" the sheriff asked.

"Several," Zeb said.

"I've heard of that," the sheriff said. "How long can you remember back?"

"To last summer," Zeb said. "People would just yell at me. I never thought much about names."

"Names are important, and not just for letting people call you for supper." The sheriff began walking through the market. Zeb followed him.

"Since you remember the summer, you'd remember if you were a bandit."

"Do I look like a bandit?" Zeb asked.

"No, you don't," the sheriff admitted, "but then that weasel Chancy looks more like a monk than a bandit and he is one of the worst."

"The shepherd warned me about him," Zeb said. "He told me to stay west until I was past the forest. I didn't see Chancy or his men."

"Shepherd?"

"I spent the winter with an old shepherd, then went to the high pasture with him and his flock. We had some wolf problems."

"I see; they were after the ewes?"

"No, they went for the lambs, mostly."

The sheriff nodded and they walked in silence for a bit. People waved at the sheriff and mostly he just nodded at them. Once or twice, he stopped to talk quietly with people.

"I think you are okay," he said finally. "You did come from the north and west, not from the east like someone from the forest would have, and you have worked the sheep. You still have that watchful look about you. Where are you going next?"

"I have some business in the city," Zeb said.

"You might want to get some different clothes, then," the sheriff said. "Those are warm, but they will make you stand out in the city, and that can cause trouble." He introduced Zeb to a couple of merchants that sold good used clothing. "You might want to pick a name for yourself too. It makes folks more comfortable with you. I won't take any more of your time, but if you run into problems, don't hesitate to find me. Anyone can tell you where." The sheriff shook his hand again and wandered off into the market.

Zeb bought some clothes that the merchants recommended as 'good enough for the city', then, after getting some more food for the journey, started south on the road toward Bellpolis. He didn't change his clothes yet, but added the new ones to his bundle. Bailey saw him leaving the town and waved at him. Zeb waved back then forgot him.

Every step that Zeb took toward the city faded the ache in his bones. He hadn't noticed it much in the mountains, but south of Westfale, it was like time ran backward as the pain vanished. Zeb grinned. The mage was going to find Zeb wasn't easy to lead around, but, in the meantime, he enjoyed the new freedom. Another bonus was the weather. No rain, and the nights were warm enough that Zeb wrapped himself in his blanket and slept under a tree beside the road.

Five days after leaving Westfale, two men tried to rob Zeb while he slept. They crept up on him and one had a knife at Zeb's throat before he was fully awake. The other pulled on the bundle Zeb was using as a pillow. Zeb took hold of the blade and twisted the knife out of the first man's hand, then punched the other man with the hilt of the knife. In a second, he was on his feet, with his staff at the ready, but the men cursed and ran off. After that, Zeb took care to choose more hidden places to sleep. He put the knife in the center of his bedroll where it wasn't visible, but was handy at need. It was a better knife than what the shepherd could spare.

There were no other incidents with thieves, but several times he was offered work in exchange for food and shelter. Zeb didn't mind the work, usually splitting wood or cleaning barns, and the food was better than what he carried. It did puzzle him that people were so trusting.

"We don't have much problem here, being so close to the city," said one farmer when he asked. "We have more problems with the young people going to the city and leaving us short of workers."

As Zeb worked his way toward the city, he observed the people around him trying to imitate how they acted and talked, pretending to the emotional responses these people had to everything from sunsets to babies. He traded his warm sheepskins for cooler clothes that 'fit in' better.

At first it wore him out, but as he got used to how the different expressions felt on his face he found he wasn't pretending anymore, but feeling physical responses to his environment. He was more likely to get work if he smiled, so he practiced smiling. Soon, a smile was as natural to him as the flat stare that he had used on the farmers while he was a bandit.

While he was learning all these new things about being human, Zeb gave some careful thought to what he was going to do about the mage and his demand. Zeb felt no particular qualm about killing the king, but he didn't like the idea because the mage had ordered him to. Underneath all the changes he was making in himself, there was a part of him still whispering he would not willingly serve any other being.

His route to the city became a broad meandering walk. As long as he was making even the slightest progress to the city, the pain was held at bay. While he walked, he learned and planned.

Eventually, even his slow progress brought him within sight of the city. He had new muscles from helping with the early harvest. He looked and sounded like a farmer. His bundle had been replaced by a backpack, his small store of coins sat in the bottom of the pack. The only thing that continued to set him apart from the other young men who were heading to the city was the wariness in his eyes. The most dangerous of wolves were still about: the human ones.

On the first day of fall, Zeb gave in to the inevitable, and walked across the boundary of the city of Bellpolis. It was getting late in the evening, so he stopped in at an inn and tavern called the Broken Dog.

THE EMPRESS

Marriette rode home from the ball in blissful exhaustion. Soon after they came home from Northdale, an invitation to a royal ball had arrived. They had too little time for Marriette to get a new gown, so she wore the gold one from the Summer Ball. The king himself complimented her on her dress, silencing the women who whispered about the poor taste of wearing the same dress twice. Torrance danced with her three times. She looked over at her husband whose expression was a fair match for her own. The only sour note had been her father's glare from across the room.

Anna met them at the door and welcomed them home. Marriette put her arm around Torrance and walked with him to the bedroom, though he didn't truly need the help. She let her dress fall to the floor and made Torrance lie on the bed. She slipped his pants off and massaged the muscles of his bad leg. Though they were much stronger than before they would never match the strength of his other leg. She worked up his leg making him groan with a mixture of pain and relief. He rolled to his back and she continued to knead the muscles of his thigh. Now his groans had little to do with the knotted muscles she was untying. When he sat up and kissed her she kissed him back with as much passion and need. Their sharing that night was the deepest yet.

In the morning she woke and trailed her fingers along her husband's ribs.

"So," she said, "this is the life of a noble lady. Days of idle ease, evenings of dance, and nights of passion?"

"Well, mostly." He caught her hand and kissing it, "what more do you want?"

"I want to make a difference. What good is it to be noble and rich if you don't accomplish something worthwhile?"

"What did you have in mind, my love?"

"I don't know yet, but it will be more important than what dress to wear next."

"When you know what you want to do, let me know, and all my resources will be yours to use."

"All of them?"

"All. I would rather be the penniless husband of the woman who changed the world for the better than the richest man in the city with an empty headed wife."

"Well, then, we had better get up and look at the accounts," she said, "I want to know how much I have to spend."

"Maybe the accounts could wait a while?" He let his hands wander.

"Maybe a while."

After the noon meal, Torrance sat Marriette down in his office and began showing her the books of his accounts.

"Good grief." She rubbed her head, "I can see why Giuseppe uses his system. I can't keep track of what is going in and out."

"Giuseppe's system?" Torrance said.

"Let me show you." She took an empty book and drew quick columns. She picked up the most recent book and began making entries for expense and income. Soon she was so involved that she didn't notice Torrance leave and come back with a tea tray. Marriette drank absently of the tea and went back to her work. In the end, it took several days for her to complete the entries for the one ledger.

"Now," she said, "here is where your money is coming in, and where it is coming from. Here is how the money is being spent and where it is going. The difference is how much extra is available. If I add the income to how much you had at the beginning of the book and subtract the expenses, it should equal the amount that you have on hand now."

"That seems like a very complicated way of doing things."

"It is at first, but it lets you track just how much you spend on repairs on the estate, or here, or whether a vineyard is producing as much as it did in past years, or even whether one of your people is stealing from you."

"Stealing?"

"I think so." Marriette rubbed the back of her head. "See, here are the values of the shipments from your estate. Here are the values as recorded by your secretary here. They are different. Not a lot different, just enough to make me think that something isn't right."

"So, you think Harold is stealing from me?" Torrance was outraged.

"I don't think it's Harold, or the numbers would match."

"So, who?"

"I don't know yet. Giuseppe would be able to help me, but I think I can at least eliminate most of the possibilities. Give me some time and don't say anything yet."

Torrance reluctantly agreed. Marriette spent her afternoons in Torrance's office. What she had thought, once, to be wonderfully well organized was revealed as a labyrinth of paper. She persevered and gradually built up a picture of what was happening. The wagons were leaving the south with one load. They were arriving with a slightly different load. What she didn't know was whether the extra goods had ever been put on the wagons or whether they were dropped off on the way and bill of lading changed. She needed someone to go with the wagons and watch.

"I think I know what is happening, but I need to catch the thief in the act."

"I hope you don't mean in person," Torrance said, "I value you more than the small amount this thief is taking."

"I was thinking more along the lines of having someone accompany the wagons and watch."

"You have someone in mind?"

"I have someone I can ask," Marriette said. "I need to talk to Joan anyway. I think she is avoiding me."

"Let's go talk to Joan, then."

Torrance called the carriage and soon he and Marriette rode down toward the market. The late afternoon sun gilded the market when they arrived. Joan stood with her board as the wagons were loaded. When she saw Marriette and Torrance, her face lit up, and she ran up and hugged her friends.

"I wasn't sure you would want to talk to me again," Joan said.

"Nonsense," Torrance said, "without you we would still be making each other miserable."

"Now we need your help again," Marriette said.

Joan sent them inside while she finished the wagon. Marriette found Master Candler sitting at his desk.

"Giuseppe didn't work out?" he asked after he recovered from the shock of learning Marriette was a noblewoman.

"He was wonderful, but life took me other places. He is training his daughter now."

"I remember when I took him and his wife in. They had a young daughter and nothing else. He was honest and smart, a rarer combination than you might think. He worked here until Joan was old enough to help. I remember her following him around with a little board imitating everything he did. Agathia was like a mother to Joan."

"He is doing well, with three beautiful girls now."

"Yes, he sends me letters now and again. I asked him to watch for Arthur." The old man peered at Marriette sharply. "You didn't see him while you were there, did you?"

"Sadly, no," Marriette said.

"You want to keep this one, son," Candler said to Torrance. Marriette held her breath, afraid that he might take offense, but Torrance just smiled.

"Yes, Sir," he said, "I most certainly do."

Joan came in and Marriette explained the problem and what she wanted from Joan and her father.

"Look at the bottom of the page," Master Candler said, "if the last line is squeezed in, I always check it twice; especially if the writing is different. That's how people will sneak something onto a load, or make the drover sign for it then complain when it never arrives."

"So, do you have someone you trust who could take a few loads back and forth? Perhaps we can catch the thief now that we know what to look for."

"Send George, Father," Joan said, "he's smart enough, but everyone underestimates him."

Before they went home, it had all been arranged. Joan thanked them as they climbed into the carriage.

"I haven't seen him take this much interest in life since Arthur disappeared."

"I hope it lasts, then," Marriette said.

The ride home was quiet as Marriette was deep in thought. When they arrived at their home, Duke deLanguiers' carriage waited in the yard. At first, Marriette wanted to drive right past, but it was far past time that she faced her father and freed herself from her fear. She straightened in the seat, and when their carriage stopped she allowed Torrance to help her out as if she were the queen herself.

The duke waited in the sitting room, pacing back and forth as if he had been there for hours. Anna whispered as she took her mistress's cloak that he had just arrived. Marriette walked in on Torrance's arm.

"Father," she said.

"Is that all the welcome you give your father?" the duke said.

"It is enough," she said.

"How dare you be rude to me," the duke stepped forward with his arm raised. Torrance stepped in front of his wife.

"What is your business here, Sir, other than threatening my wife?"

"My daughter."

"You gave her to me at the altar," Torrance said. "It is too late to change that."

The duke ground his teeth and his face turned deep red.

"The reason for your visit, Father," Marriette said.

"Can a father not visit his daughter for no reason?"

"Not if you are the father and I the daughter."

The duke stomped out of the room without another word. When she heard the carriage pull away, Marriette began shaking.

"Forgive me, Torrance," she said, "but I cannot bring myself to be civil with him."

"And here I was thinking you were remarkably civil."

Torrance led her to a settee and held her until she stopped shaking.

The next morning she announced that she knew what she wanted to do.

"There are many people like Giuseppe. They arrive here with no money for whatever reason. Some of them have children. What happens to them?"

"Most end up in the poor quarters. They don't speak well enough to hold any but the most menial jobs. Some have special skills and do better, like Giuseppe, and the man I have managing the vineyards."

"So what if we made it possible for them to learn our language faster? Helped them to find jobs that they could do?"

"I think the church does some work in the poor quarters," Torrance said. "It would be better to ask them."

Marriette would have set off immediately for the cathedral, but Torrance asked her to wait.

"Even archbishops need to eat breakfast," he said. "You have made a connection there, but it doesn't hurt to be polite."

Marriette sent a note to the cathedral with one of the servants then waited impatiently for a reply.

A note came back that afternoon inviting her to join the archbishop after Mass the next morning.

Marriette asked Anna to choose something appropriate to wear to Mass, since she had never been to the church other than her wedding. She was sure it was nothing like the simple chapel she had attended with the monks through the winter.

Early the next morning, she and Torrance rode to the cathedral. Marriette was astonished the deep green gown that she thought too rich for church was the plainest dress in the building. Mass was a complex ritual of incense, music and word. Most was spoken in the sonorous Latin language. Amidst the pomp she caught glimpses of what she had seen at the monastery. She had been neglecting her prayers and contemplation since she and Torrance had reunited. She blushed at what she did instead of her spiritual exercises. Marriette took a deep breath and lost herself in the grandeur and mystery of the mass.

Too soon it finished, and a young priest came and invited them to follow him to the back. He led them to a sparsely furnished room. Marriette held tight to Torrance's hand. The archbishop came in dressed in far simpler robes than what he'd worn for Mass.

"Welcome, child," the archbishop said. "I see time and God have healed your marriage."

"The advice you gave was good, Your Excellency, but it took some time for me to put it to use."

"Never mind," he said, "you did, and the world is richer for your love."

He poured tea for them.

"Now, why did you want to see me?"

"I have met a few foreigners to our land, and it seems to me that their fate rests as much on chance as anything else. If they meet someone who sees their value, they may do well, but too many are lost to poverty and their children with them."

"The church has missions, we preach the good gospel to them and help them as we can."

"What good is the gospel if they are hungry? Even the monks had sufficient food, if plain."

"What do you think?" the archbishop asked Torrance.

"I think my wife is wiser and more generous than I," Torrance answered.

"So, child, what would you have me do?"

"How can I help?" Marriette leaned forward. "There must be some way that I can help make their lives better?"

"I will think upon it, and we will talk again," the archbishop said. "Now, tell me about your stay at the monastery. The abbot sent me a letter, but I want to hear from you."

So Marriette spent the rest of the morning talking about the abbot and Brother Stephen. Torrance listened with obvious interest as well. She hadn't spoken much of the winter to him. They had talked more about their own relationship.

"So, now I realize that I have been neglecting my prayers for...other things," Marriette concluded, blushing again.

"Those 'other things' are also precious to God, my dear," the archbishop said, "but perhaps it is time for you to attend to your spiritual life again; especially if you are going to undertake something like the work with the foreigners. You will need God's guidance and strength. I will look to see you at Mass again soon."

They left soon after that, but Marriette and Torrance agreed that more visits to Mass at the great cathedral would not be a bad thing.

THE EMPEROR

"He is almost here," the mage said to his co-conspirator. "He imagines that he is successfully avoiding my magic, but it is drawing him in. There is no escape for him."

"It is well past time," the other said, "you had promised would be sitting on the throne by now, and still I live in a drafty old house far from the power that I deserve."

"Say rather, the power you 'desire'. There are no secrets, no lies, between us."

"What does it matter? The important thing is that now we will see the end of our plotting and we will have our way."

"The end is closer, true, but many a fine plot has been ruined by impatience."

"I grow tired of this. Patience, you say, patience, again. I want what I deserve, yes, what I desire, and I do not want to wait any longer."

"Yet you must wait, or you will bring all our plans down about your ears."

The other man paced around the dim room on the edge of violence before flinging his hands in the air.

"Okay, we wait," he said finally, petulantly as a child.

The mage wisely said nothing, but let the other leave. He sat in the darkness turning plots over in his head. His partner in treason was growing harder to control and thus more dangerous. Still, he is needed, for now. He, too, left the room and walked back to his home secure in the knowledge that he was being followed. His co-conspirator was not completely a fool.

***

The mage received a message from the other that they needed to meet again. He walked inconspicuously through the streets and entered the tavern through the back door. The proprietors were used to such comings and goings and didn't care what the purpose was, as long as the coin was good. As usual, the mage arrived first. The other thought he showed dominance by making the mage wait. He didn't know how little the mage cared for such things. He could wait a season or longer for what he wanted. He had waited years already; a few minutes were paltry in comparison. The other arrived, barely schooling himself to be unnoticed.

"She's home," he burst out almost before the door closed behind him, "the wench is back and they are as giddy as newlyweds."

"The happier she is now the deeper the cut of betrayal will be later."

"Bah, she will believe nothing bad of the cripple, she is so besotted with him."

"That would be a problem if it really mattered what she believes. It is not her faith in him that we aim to shake."

"True, but it makes me sick to see them."

"You mean it enrages you that someone else has awakened the woman you tried to bury deep in pain and horror. That a cripple sleeps with her and has her love—"

"Enough!" yelled the duke. "She will return to me, whether she wills or not. She is mine! I will school her properly when she is back under my control."

"Take care," the mage said, "that she does not turn and destroy you."

"She is but a girl."

"Men have been destroyed by less."

"Enough, again. I will not be guided by your cautions and riddles."

"Without my caution, your head would be decorating the spikes on Traitor's Gate."

"Without your caution, I would be wearing the crown!"

"You will be happy, then, to hear that our pawn approaches ever closer to the city. I will let you know when best to play your trump and perhaps you will claim your crown and your daughter in the same move."

"Now that is a happy thought!" the duke said. "I will await your message." He swept out of the room without any further word. The mage who thought he had schooled himself out of any emotion or feeling discovered his hands were balled into fists of rage.

"I am beginning to think that the crown would sit very uneasily on that impetuous head, O Duke," he said to the empty room, "I think the plan must change to have it set on a calmer head." He left the room and walked home considering how to rid himself of a partner who had become a dangerous liability. The man was too full of petty angers, look at who he sent to the mage for their project.

Look indeed, his small vengeance may be exactly what I need to rid myself of the second most important man in the kingdom.

THE CRUX

KNIGHT OF SWORDS

The Broken Dog sat on a crossroads a little way from a bridge across the river defining the northern edge of old Bellpolis. Zeb looked at the sign showing a black and white dog in pieces as if it had been made of glass. It was no odder than the signs of other taverns he had seen in the past weeks. He pushed the door open and walked in.

"Arthur!" someone shouted. Zeb walked to the bar and ordered a drink. The man behind the bar looked like he had seen a ghost. At that moment, a large hand clapped down on Zeb's shoulder and spun him around.

"Arthur, you dog," the man said. "You're alive?"

"Who is Arthur?" Zeb asked.

"Who is Arthur? Who is Arthur?" the man said. "Are you putting me on? I would recognize you anywhere. Now stop playing games and come over and have a drink with an old friend."

Zeb picked up his drink and followed the big man to a table full of other men. They were dressed better than the farmers that Zeb had been working for. He guessed they were merchant's sons.

"Hey, look who I found!" the man said as if he had indeed gone out and dragged Zeb out of the mountains singlehandedly. In an instant Zeb was surrounded by a crowd of young men who whooped and shouted while they thumped his back. Zeb's drink was a lost cause, but every second person determined to buy him another. Finally, the maelstrom calmed enough for Zeb to take a drink from his glass.

"Where have you been?" the first big man asked, who, as the discoverer of Zeb, was tacitly appointed spokesman.

"Around," Zeb said. "Where was I supposed to be?" Most of the young men laughed, but a few looked concerned.

"Is something wrong?" the big man said. "You don't look like yourself."

"Not surprising, considering I have no idea who I am," Zeb said. Something the sheriff in Westfale said came to his mind. "I took a blow to the head, in the spring, and I have lost all memory from before that."

"No!" they shouted and immediately started demanding that he must remember them.

"Whoa! Give the man some space," shouted the big man. "Look, if you are Art, you will have a scar here on your ribs," he said pointing to his own ribs. "It is from a fight we were in the winter before last."

Zeb pulled up his shirt and looked at his ribcage and sure enough there was a scar there. "I guess you can call me Art."

"What did people call you before?"

"Mostly 'hey you'," Zeb said.

"I'm Daniel," the big man said. "Whether you remember me or not, I have your back."

"John."

"Fredrick."

"Hal."

The names came thick and fast. Zeb struggled to attach the names to the faces. These weren't bandits in the forest, they could be invaluable to him, and he was glad enough to have a name for people to call him.

The reunion party went on all night with the men taking turns telling stories about Art's escapades. I already have a reputation for troublemaking; that could be useful, if the mage doesn't know or care too much about my background.

The stories ran out at about the same time that the sun came up.

"So, Art," Daniel said, "what can you tell us about the past year."

Zeb didn't think telling them about being a bandit would go over well, even in this crowd. "I found myself a good way north of here. I mostly wandered about doing odd jobs. I spent most of the winter and part of the spring with a shepherd up in the mountains."

"A shepherd," Hal said, "you mean like watching sheep?"

"Yes, and killing wolves," Zeb said.

"Wolves!" they said, so Zeb told them about the wolves while they ate the coarse bread the tavern served for breaking their fast.

"Look, fellows," the bar man said when they had finished breakfast, "I know you just found your friend, but you really need to move on."

"Sure thing, Jack," Daniel said, "we're just going."

Zeb picked up his pack and his staff and followed Daniel and the others out.

"The owner doesn't mind our money, but she really doesn't like to see our faces," Daniel explained to Zeb.

"That might have something to do with you trying to seduce her one too many times," John said, nudging Daniel. They continued jostling and joking with each other like the young men Zeb had met heading to the big city to find their fortune. Zeb guessed that it wasn't much easier to be a merchant's son.

They reached the bridge, and as Zeb's boots sounded on the wooden planks a vast pit of terror opened up inside of him. The others stopped as they noticed that Zeb had frozen at the edge of the bridge.

"What's wrong?" asked Daniel.

"I don't know," Zeb said, "but I can't make my feet cross the bridge."

"Weren't you supposed to meet that noble's girl on the bridge? That was the night you disappeared."

"Yeah, you were all ready to get you some noble loving."

"Maybe you fell off the bridge that night and that's how you ended up in the north."

"Perhaps. I don't remember."

"There is a ford a little way downstream," Daniel said. "We can cross there. We'll meet at the Unkissed Prince tonight."

"Their beer isn't as good as the Broken Dog's."

"And the girls aren't as cute."

"You are going to wade back and forth across the river every night?"

"Okay, okay, the Unkissed Prince at sunset."

The other men walked off across the bridge.

"This way," Daniel said. "It is just as well, I need to talk to you about some stuff without them jawing in at every sentence."

"Lead on," Zeb said, shaken more by his body's rebellion than by the fear. What else have I inherited with this flesh?

"That noble girl you were after got herself married to a Baron leBraun just after you vanished; by all accounts, she is happy too.

You'll want to stay away from her. Her husband won't appreciate you showing up at the door."

Zeb agreed silently. The last thing he wanted was more complications.

"You are going to have to see your dad and your sister, Joan. He never figured you for dead. I guess he was right." They arrived at the ford. The water was low enough they were able to cross without getting their feet more than damp.

"The last thing is that you have a running feud with this Count laFreeid's son. That is where you got that scar of yours. You were just plain lucky that it wasn't worse. I will try to point him out to you so you can avoid him. He and his cronies are bad news, and they hate you like poison. I don't know why."

"I don't remember either," Zeb said, not having to work at sounding frustrated. Bad enough the mage had him tangled in chains of magic without needing to deal with old enemies of this flesh.

"You'd better go and see your dad before some clown lets him know you're back." Daniel shook his head. "You two are worse than my old man and me, so you needn't pretend to any great liking. You will want to try to be a little bit contrite. If you keep him happy, he won't be on your back all the time."

Daniel and Zeb planned out the coming reunion as they walked through the city. They came to the market. Zeb saw a young girl with a small board in her hand watching men unload a wagon. She saw Zeb and dropped the board. A moment later, she had launched herself at Zeb. He braced himself, but instead of the embrace he expected, she pounded on him with her fists while swearing with a facility that was making the watching crowd of men grin in appreciation.

"Arthur," Daniel effortlessly lifted the girl off of Zeb, "meet your sister Joan."

"What do you mean, 'meet your sister'?" Joan said. "You know me, don't you, you reprobate.... Don't you?"

"Arthur took a bang to his head, Joan," Daniel said. "He doesn't remember anything at all."

She launched herself again, but this time to hug instead of attack. Zeb knew from the summer he was expected to hug her back, so he wrapped his arms around her while she wept on his shoulder.

"It must be terrible for you, not to remember anything," she said finally. "I imagine that it would be terrifying, never knowing if you know the person you are talking to or not."

"It is unnerving," Zeb said.

"What is going on?" An older man stood in the doorway of the building beside the yard.

"Father...." began Joan and she started crying again.

"Well, it is about time you got home," Arthur's father said, "I've been waiting for you."

"That is not what I expected," Daniel said. "I had better get on or my own father will be saying the same to me." The big man waved casually at Zeb and walked away. Joan took Zeb's hand and pulled him into the building.

"Father," Joan said, "Arthur was injured and lost his memory. That is why he took so long to come home."

"Nonsense," her father said, "it is just more of his foolery." He looked at Zeb. "What was it this time? A bet, another fight, another woman? Do you know how hard it is to hold up my head in this town with a son who has caused as much trouble as you?"

"I have been told that I was not a good son," Zeb said, "I don't know what to say, since I don't know what I have done to distress you."

"You lie," Arthur's father shouted, "this is just another one of your tricks."

"Look at his eyes, Father," Joan said. "He really doesn't remember."

"Bah," her father said, "the wagons need unloading. I don't have time for this." He picked up some papers and started working.

Zeb walked back outside. The men were standing around.

"Well, this thing won't unload itself." Zeb picked up a box off the wagon. Joan retrieved her board and stared at him.

"Now I know you lost your memory," she said. "Put it over there with the rest."

Zeb helped with that wagon and a dozen others through the day. Several times, he caught Joan watching him doubtfully. At sunset, the last wagon rolled out, and Daniel came by to see them. He laughed when he saw Zeb covered with sweat and dust.

"Now that is proof that you lost your mind, Arthur," he said.

"Joan said the same thing," Zeb said.

"Oh, Arthur, do you have to go out?" Joan said. "I have so much to tell you."

Zeb looked at Daniel who just placidly stared back at him.

"I will be back by moonrise," Zeb said.

"That's the Arthur I know," Daniel said laughing. Joan just nodded her head and went inside.

The evening was spent telling and retelling the stories of Arthur's doings. Zeb was sure they had grown since the night before. He didn't drink much. Zeb didn't like how the beer lowered his barriers. The others, except maybe Daniel, never noticed. When Zeb saw the moon above the houses across the street, he stood up.

"Time for me to get back."

The other young men just stared at him in disbelief. Zeb shrugged and left. He found when he got home that Joan and her father had already gone to bed. Without anyone to tell him where he should sleep he lay down on the floor with his backpack under his head and slept.

Zeb hadn't dreamt much since he left the monastery, but this night his dreams were replays of the death and despair he had left in his wake. He saw the wolves tear Lamb apart, but then they turned and attacked Joan and her father. The soldiers from the forest came, and, still bleeding from their death wounds, began hacking at Arthur's friends. Zeb could hear the mage's laughter through it all.

"You can't escape me, demon. Though you won't surrender, you will do as I ask, or these others you claim will also be destroyed."

Zeb woke in the morning shaking.

Joan came down and looked at him with a frown.

"What time did you get home?" she asked.

"At moonrise, as I said."

"So, why aren't you in bed like a civilized person?"

"I don't know where my bed is."

Joan's eyes filled up with tears again.

"Forgive me, brother," she said, "I had assumed that you had returned to your old habits."

"I used to sleep on the floor?" Zeb asked.

"The floors of the taverns," Joan said. "Come, I will show you your room."

Arthur's room was small but comfortable. The wardrobe was filled with clothes that were very much like what Arthur's friends wore. Zeb left them there, for now, and put on clothes from his backpack. They were better for the work he was doing.

He spent the day working with the men on the wagons. Arthur's father came out and watched for a while, then went back inside without saying a word.

Daniel, again, came by at sunset and Zeb went with him to the tavern. The Unkissed Prince showed a frog with a prince's crown slipping down over one eye. Zeb thought it looked more than a little drunk. He left at moonrise again, to the astonishment of the rest of the group. Conversation had turned to other subjects and Zeb was finding it hard to keep track of who and what they were talking about. This time Daniel left with Zeb.

"Maybe it is time I learned responsibility," he said, "though, my father would die of astonishment if he knew I was learning it from

Arthur Candler. It is good to have you back." He slapped Zeb on the shoulder and headed off toward his own home.

This time Joan had waited up for him.

"What is it like?" she asked him. "Not to remember the people you love?"

"It is confusing to have people who know me and treat me like their friend," Zeb said, "especially since I know nothing of them."

"So, there is nothing at all? No indication that you once loved this person?"

"I don't know anything about love. Just loss. It seems to me that love is a dangerous thing."

"Yes, I suppose it is, but it is wonderful too."

"I don't see the wonder."

"No, I guess you don't." Joan sighed deeply. "Did Daniel tell you about Marriette?"

"Marriette is the girl who is married now?"

"Yes, we are friends, strange as that may seem. I don't want to see her get hurt anymore."

"I will stay away from her. Daniel thought so as well. I don't want the...confusion of trying to resolve something I don't recall."

"Thanks, brother." Joan stood up and yawned. "Time for me to go to bed."

"Don't do that," Zeb said.

"What, go to bed?"

"No, call me 'brother'. I don't remember being a brother. I don't know how."

"It isn't something you do. You just are, memory or not." Joan hugged him and left him alone to his thoughts.

KNIGHT OF CUPS

Marriette held on tight to Torrance's arm. They walked with a young priest who was showing them through the poor quarters of the city. Marriette had thought she was living dangerously when she had visited the market by herself. What she was seeing now was beyond her imagining. People stared at them from doorways of buildings that leaned crazily against each other. Clothes that Marriette wouldn't have used as rags hung haphazardly from lines strung wherever there was space. The children were the worst. They either ran with frenetic energy, screaming and fighting, or sat listless on the side of the road.

The horrific smell wasn't all from the butcher yard upwind. She hated to think of what she was walking through.

"Almost there now," Father Thom said, though Marriette found it hard to call a man younger than her 'Father'. "This is one of the better sections—"

"Better!" Marriette said. "How can it be worse than this?"

"The people here still care, a little anyway," Father Thom said. "There are neighbourhoods where all hope is gone. We don't go there."

"Why not?"

"Because the people who go…don't come back," he said sadly. "Here we are." He led them up the steps of a building that looked identical to all the others. Inside, there were monks and nuns tending the sick. Marriette saw a room full of children listening to a nun. Another room had a burly monk standing by the door while a smaller monk handed out tiny sacks of food.

"How many of these missions are there, Father Thom?" asked Torrance.

"This is it, and we can barely afford this."

"Surely, this doesn't cost that much," Marriette said.

"We can only spend the money we are given," Father Thom said, "most people would rather give to a stained glass window their friends will see."

"I see," Torrance said, "even in charity, status is important."

"Oh, yes, most of the gifts for this work come from labourers and poorer merchants; people who have reason to know what it is like to live this way."

"So what can we do?"

"Money is always helpful, but it won't solve the problem. What we really need is to change the way we do things, so that a labourer or a farmer has as much respect as a noble. We could get along fine without the nobility, but without farmers we would all be in trouble."

"There needs to be someone who co-ordinates effort."

"Co-ordinates, yes, the nobility siphons off as much wealth as they can and leave the people barely enough to live on." Father Thom reddened. "Forgive me. I get carried away."

"No forgiveness necessary, Father," Torrance said. "Sadly, your words are too true, most of the nobility have stopped caring about any needs but their own."

"Thank you for showing us your work, Father Thom, but I need to go home and consider this."

"I will walk you back to your carriage."

They were all silent on the long walk back. Marriette continued to be silent on the ride home. Even at their home over dinner she hardly spoke at all. After supper, she went into the garden, and sat until the moon was high in the night sky. Torrance came out and sat with her. She looked at the moon, and even it seemed stained by the poverty she had seen.

"It isn't enough to just throw money at the problem," she said just as the moon touched the wall around the garden. "We could give every penny we have and not make a difference in how those poor people live. I thought it was just newcomers, but our own people are just as destitute."

"What are you thinking?"

"Schools."

"Hmmm," Torrance said.

"What kind of people do you need to work your estate?"

"Trustworthy, dedicated workers who know what they are doing."

"Are they easy to find?"

"Heavens no," Torrance said, "I have a person whose only job is finding people who fit."

"So...what if we create them?" asked Marriette. "We train people for the jobs that you need done. They get work. We have people we can trust."

"Can we trust them?"

"As much as any other stranger."

"True." They sat in silence a long time. "So, where do we put this school?"

"I am thinking near the market. Not in the poor quarters themselves, or we won't be able to find people to teach. It needs to be close enough to the people for them to walk there."

"So, do you want to go and look now?"

"No," Marriette said, "I think tomorrow will be soon enough."

The next day, it poured rain, and Marriette agreed that it was better to stay inside. Instead, she busied herself with the accounts.

"We will need more money," she told Torrance as they ate their supper. "I wonder if a school could be as fashionable as a stain glass window. After all, they must be running out of room for new windows."

"What are you plotting?"

"All those women who never wear the same dress twice. What do they do with the dresses?"

"Store them in rooms?" Torrance guessed. "I don't know. Let's ask Anna."

Anna was a fountain of information.

"Some ladies do store the dresses and never look at them again. Others have them remade for other events that aren't as important as the royal balls. Some sell them so they have money that their husbands don't know about."

"Ah," Marriette said, "when is the next royal ball?"

"I believe the Summer Ball is coming up soon, you have a fitting for a dress tomorrow."

"Perfect."

The next day, Marriette went to her fitting for a dress that was the colour of autumn leaves. She endured all the usual fussing about trim and neckline and who was wearing what. When they were finished, she sat down with the seamstress.

"How much could you sell my green dress for?" Marriette asked with a twinge of guilt. She knew the gold dress was more valuable, but she couldn't imagine letting it go.

"You aren't running out of money, are you?" The seamstress looked as if she was ready to jump up and cancel the autumn leaf gown.

"No, I am raising money for a school to teach trades."

"Oh, my!" the seamstress' eyes widened. "Wait here."

Marriette wondered what horrible thing she had done, but in a couple of minutes the seamstress returned with Madame Gauliur chattering in a language Marriette didn't recognize.

"When do you plan to open this school?" Madame asked.

"We are looking for a good place to hold it, then we need teachers, and money—"

"We will help. I will sell your dress with no commission. You must promise to let me send a teacher. We need more women to sew. Men too."

"I will send the dress down with Anna tomorrow."

"My Lady," the seamstress said, "excuse me, but my brother has said there are empty warehouses by the river."

"Thank you, both," Marriette said.

The dress was sent with Anna, who approved of the scheme. Torrance went looking for someone who had empty warehouses, who could be persuaded to let one become a school.

The night of the Summer Ball came and Marriette rode in the carriage with Torrance. Even with his approval, she was more afraid than she had been since she left her father's house. Her father wouldn't like what she was going to do. That thought helped her to settle her nerves. If the Duke deLanguiers disapproved then she could be certain it was the right thing to do.

Their carriage pulled up and the footmen met them and ushered them into the ballroom. It loomed huge and unwelcoming. How was she going to convince these self-satisfied people that giving to her school was a good idea? She smiled, one person at a time of course. Marriette swept into the room and wandered from conversation to conversation. She found one that was perfect.

"I wanted to donate a font to the church in memory of my father, but they don't need any more fonts. What is a font anyway?" the speaker asked. "I am sure they could use a spare."

"It is so hard making meaningful memorial gifts these days," Marriette said, "all the good places are taken, so your contribution is hidden away in a corner."

"Oh," said the woman, "and what would you know about it?"

"There's a new school being dedicated; it will probably be located between the market and the river. The archbishop is very excited about it."

"A school?" the woman's voice dripped with scorn.

"Well, at least I know what a classroom is," Marriette said.

The woman walked off in a huff, but one of the others stayed to talk about it.

"So, how much do you think it will take to sponsor this school?"

"I don't know yet. The project is just getting off the ground," Marriette said, "but I am sure you could make a significant contribution for the cost of a good dress."

"I hate to say this," the woman said in Marriette's ear, "but I have been buying my dresses secondhand for the last year. Our estate is just not bringing in money like it used to."

"Every bit counts," Marriette said. "Call on me next week and I will introduce you to my dressmaker; she is very discreet."

Marriette started similar conversations throughout the night. She was surprised how many of her peers were hiding financial difficulties. Curiously, the harder up the person was, the more they seemed interested in the project.

When the archbishop arrived, Marriette arranged to bump into him.

"I didn't get a chance to warn you, but you are very excited about the project to start a school for the poor quarters."

"I would be, if I knew it was true."

"Torrance and I are setting it up. I'm raising money for it. I must confess, I may have persuaded someone to put money into the school instead of a font."

"No loss," the archbishop said laughing, "I don't know why everyone wants to donate fonts these days. One year, it was chasubles. I would be very happy to encourage support of a school."

The evening progressed and Marriette found that as often as not the women were already discussing the school project even before she joined them. She had the unusual experience of having a great many women asking her to stop in for tea, and an equal number snub her. Her father made his entrance; from the look he shot at her, he'd already heard about the school. The king and queen made their appearance and circuit through the room. The queen stopped in front of Marriette.

"Good evening, my dear. Marriette, is it not?"

"Yes, Your Majesty." Marriette curtsied deeply.

"My husband wished me to remind you that you need a royal fiat to start a school within the city." She looked at Marriette and tilted her head. "He also asked me to invite you to the palace tomorrow so you may enlighten us further that we may properly support your endeavour." The queen leaned in close to Marriette. "I think it is a perfectly marvelous idea. I will give you a sizable donation, and you will invite me to open the school." She rapped Marriette on the shoulder with her fan and moved on into the crowd.

Marriette could hardly breathe for excitement. She had the queen's public approval, and an 'invitation' to appear at the palace tomorrow. Marriette could hear the buzz of conversation as word spread that the queen had spoken to Marriette and granted her a touch. The royal couple didn't make physical contact with anyone not part of their inner circle. Marriette and Torrance had just been given a huge boost in social standing.

Marriette didn't remember the rest of the evening. She might have danced with Torrance once or twice. She knew she danced with the king's cousin, Kris vonFromme because he had handed her a note for an amount which almost made her faint. It was more than the leBraun estates made in half a year.

"I know other people will give more," he had said, "but I want you to remember that I gave first."

She tucked the note away and concentrated on not stepping on his feet.

Anna was flabbergasted when she heard Marriette had an invitation to the palace. She went out immediately to wake Madame Gauliur.

"She will want to fit you first thing in the morning," Anna said as she left. "You won't be sleeping in."

Torrance shrugged. "Don't look at me. I have never been to the palace, except for the Hall of Judgment." He swung her around the room, "With the king's support, we can open in a few months."

Anna kept to her word and dragged Marriette out of bed while the sun was still touching the horizon.

"Time to go."

The dressmaker's shop was a hive of activity. A dress that looked like it was woven from sapphires was the center of attention. Since Madame had Marriette's measurements from the autumn leaves gown, Marriette wasn't surprised it fit perfectly. That didn't stop Madame from fussing over it for the rest of the morning. When it was done, she took Marriette aside.

"When the queen asks where you got your dress, you will tell her that I designed it just for you. You may let it slip where my shop is."

"Won't the queen expect you to give her a gown as a gift?"

"Of course," said Madame, "and I will be honoured to do so, even if it didn't mean every lady in the city will want one of my gowns."

Marriette grinned at her.

"I will be sure to do you proud, then."

Anna decided by some process known only to her that Marriette should appear at the palace just after the noon meal. Marriette had no better idea, so she ate a light meal then was whisked away in the carriage. She had expected Torrance to accompany her, but he said that the invitation didn't mention him, so he was going down to the warehouses to look at prospects.

By the time the carriage pulled up in front of the palace gates, Marriette had herself convinced that it was all a mistake. She would be thrown in prison for presuming to arrive without a written invitation. The guard simply waved the carriage through. At the steps of the palace, a man in royal livery waited for her. He gave her his hand to step down from the carriage, and gave her a discrete inspection. After the slightest of nods, he led her up the steps and into the palace.

Marriette thought her father's house was big and ostentatious. The palace made it look like a farmer's cottage. Everywhere she looked, there was the gleam of gold. Sculptures stood in corners while paintings and tapestries covered the walls. After walking for ages through hallway after hallway, they arrived at a pair of doors flanked by two guards.

"The queen's guest," the servant said, and the guards opened the doors.

"Lady Marriette leBraun," announced the servant, who then bowed and backed out of the doors as they closed behind him.

"Come in, Marriette," the king said, and nodded as Marriette curtsied. "We will not be very formal today. We were most curious about this school that you have been talking about."

"It's alright, dear," the queen said, "please, sit. We have finished luncheon, but would be glad to share a cup of tea with you." She poured out a cup for Marriette. "I love your dress, it isn't by a dressmaker that I am familiar with."

"Madame Gauliur has a shop not far from our city home, Your Majesty. I would be delighted to introduce her to you."

"Gauliur," the king said, "that is a foreign name."

"My husband tells me that they need to bring new vines in occasionally to strengthen the stock. I imagine that foreigners do the same for your kingdom, Your Majesty."

The queen laughed and pointed at the king.

"I told you she was smart. She had all those vicious women doing exactly as she had planned. They didn't even know it."

The king shook his head.

"You were right. I should know better than to bet against you." He handed Marriette a tiny scroll. "Your royal fiat. You now have our blessing to raise money for your school, and the queen shall make a grand appearance and open it. I believe my cousin made a donation to your cause already. I will match his contribution today, and again when the school opens."

"What have you considered for an opening date?"

"I am afraid that we haven't got that far yet. Torrance is looking at venues as we speak. We will need to find teachers and furnishings—"

"The Vandelusians are sending an embassy in a month's time," the queen said as she looked up into a corner of the room, "I would dearly love to show him how well we educate our people."

Marriette was sure there was a great deal behind the queen's statement, but her heart pounded so hard she could barely think. A month!

"I will do everything in my power to impress the ambassador," she said.

It was the king's turn to laugh. The queen shook her head and pulled a hairpin with a tiny, beautifully crafted butterfly as its end from the complex arrangement on her head.

"Wear this, Marriette," she handed it to Marriette. "I guarantee you will find plenty of sponsors."

The servant appeared at Marriette's shoulder. "Your carriage is waiting, my Lady." Marriette put the pin in her hair and made sure she had the scroll. Curtsying again, she let the servant lead her out of the palace.

"Do come again," the queen said as the door closed. Between terror and elation, Marriette didn't think her feet touched the floor at all the whole walk back.

KING OF WANDS

King Harald of Belandria watched the young woman as she floated out of the room.

"Were we ever that young?"

"There is nothing wrong with wanting to change the world," Sarandia said. She winked at him and Harald felt the rush of desire he always did in her presence. It didn't matter that she was several years his senior, or that they were a political match, after five years, he was still crazy in love with his queen.

"Change is dangerous." He picked up another sweet from the tray he had forgotten to put out for their guest. Sarandia would make him pay for it later. She was a stickler for hospitality. Harald imagined Marriette eating the sweets as obliviously as she drank the tea. He thought of something Sarandia told him once and choked on the sweet.

"Serves you right," the queen said, "you should have put the tray out for Marrisa."

"Marriette, my dear," the king said when he could speak. "I just had the thought we could have put out candied grasshoppers and she wouldn't have noticed."

"I will have to try that and see if you notice."

"Where do you get candied grasshoppers?"

"There is a country, south of my home, where the people eat locusts. I'm sure I could get father to send me some."

"What do I get if I eat one?"

"A delicious snack, according to my chief maid when I was young—I never had the nerve to try one."

"That isn't what I meant."

"I'm sure I can come up with a proper reward for such a courageous endeavour." She walked over and sat on Harald's knee. "Yet, there is still the small matter of a bet that you must pay." She nipped at his nose. Harald gripped her tight and kissed her. He let her intoxicating scent overwhelm his senses. He let practiced fingers deal with her dress while they embraced.

"I don't know why you need to fling my clothes to all points of the room," Harald said as he walked around picking up a bit here and a bit there.

"There is something delicious in watching a king stalk about dressed only in a single sock." Sarandia made the last few adjustments to her hair looked as immaculate as ever. Harald knew he'd feel rumpled for the rest of the day wondering how many people were seeing his disarray and snickering at their king's desire. He loved his queen dearly, but he didn't want to appear that he was led about by his lust.

Sarandia came and helped him dress.

"Fear not," she said, "you are not in such disarray as to be an insult to the people you meet. They will take comfort in the thought that you are striving for an heir."

"My cousin is restless in the role of heir," Harald said as he adjusted his jacket. "He would be most grateful for news of his release."

"The time isn't right yet," Sarandia said, and motioned for him to turn. She fixed his jacket. Harald could feel the difference even as he had no idea what she did.

"How is your father?" he asked. Sarandia's hand paused on his shoulder before brushing his face.

"He is comfortable," she said, "but my brother fears he will be king before another year passes. The Vandelusians sniff at the borders like hungry dogs."

"If you wish to travel to see him—"

"No, my King," Sarandia said as she walked around to face him. "My place is here by your side. As you said earlier, change is dangerous, but it is also necessary. My heart tells me that there are deadly times ahead."

"Aren't there always?" Harald reached for her again, but she put him off with a finger on his lips.

"As delightful as our dalliance is," she said, "there are things that need your attention.

Harald sighed and rapped on the door. His marshal opened the door. Harald imagined the marshal listening to them through the door, but he pushed the thought out of his head. The door was heavy, and of all the people in the kingdom the marshal was the most loyal. The church pretended the Liturgy of Binding was what made the marshal loyal to the throne, but Harald knew there was magic on the sword created by the Wagoners centuries ago which made the man absolutely trustworthy.

"You are late for the report from Master Tiron," Marshal said.

Harald walked quickly behind the marshal. Reflected loyalty didn't mean that the man couldn't be irritating too. Like Sarandia so often was, he was also right. Those stolen moments would mean that his entire day would be off schedule. That meant ruffled dignities to smooth. Master Tiron wasn't bad, but Tamas was a stickler for punctuality. He wouldn't go as far as to complain, but his manner communicated clearly his disappointment in the king's tardiness.

"Your Majesty," Master Tiron said, when the marshal entered the room and stepped aside for the king. "I believe you met with a most interesting young woman over tea." The lifted eyebrow let Harald know that the master also knew when the girl had left.

"What can you tell me about her?" he said and sat on a chair the marshal slid over for him.

"She's the only daughter of Duke deLanguiers. Oddly enough, given the duke's conservatism, she is also his heir. He is healthy enough for the moment, so no one on the council has raised any concerns. Not that the duke would care. You know what he's like. She was a poor, meek thing until she was married to leBraun. There was some scandal involved, but leBraun was desperate enough to overlook it. She went running off north and spent the winter in a monastery of all places. leBraun spent the winter waiting for her in some little town on the edge of the northern forest. Seems to have done him good, the limp is almost gone. Religion has lit a fire in the girl and she, as you well know, is looking to raise money for a school to educate the poor to make them better workers. I'm sure I saw a token in her hair, so she would also have your royal permission to pursue her hobby."

"Is she the kind to upset people?" Harald asked. "I don't want the council complaining."

"I expect she will be very circumspect and proper. I give her better than even odds of having the school ready by your deadline."

"Deadline?"

"The Vandelusian ambassador is expected within the month. I'm sure you will want to show what a progressive kingdom you have." The master's mouth twitched in what might have been a smile. "If you don't, I know that your queen would be most eager to." Master Tiron leaned back. "I would be a poor spymaster if I didn't understand the political importance of that worthy ambassador's visit. But enough, I'm delaying you. You most certainly don't want to keep Tamas waiting. He doesn't have the same patience as Marshal. He gave another almost smile and Harald followed Marshal out of the room. If he went back in, the spymaster would no longer be in the room. It delighted the man to travel through the semi-secret passages in the walls.

Harald could hear Tamas speaking firmly to someone in his office.

"I don't want to hear of any more people being punished based on your gut feelings. You need witnesses or other proof. If you don't have it, look for it. What you do reflects on your king." Marshal knocked on the door. Tamas dismissed the guard. Harald waited until the other door closed before he let Marshal open the door and usher him in.

"Majesty," Tamas bowed, "how may I serve you today?"

"There is a young woman raising funds to start a school in the poor quarters of the city. If anyone questions it, let it be known she has my permission."

"It sounds like a great idea," Tamas said but his voice carried a contrasting message.

"You aren't sure?"

"I imagine that some of your council will be concerned that too much learning on the part of the poor will render them less malleable."

"The poor are my subjects too, Tamas."

"It does you credit that you see it that way, and there are great advantages to having more skilled people. I'm just saying that some of your council will see it as a threat."

"Some of my council see everything as a threat," Harald said.

"True enough," Tamas said, "but a threatened council is hard to manage."

"I'm sure that you will go out of your way to soothe any concerns," Harald said.

"As you wish, Your Majesty."

Harald nodded and left the office.

"Why does that man always leave me feeling that I'm not half the king that my father was?"

"Because that is how he wants you to feel," Marshal said, "I can't challenge him for being stuffy, and he did run much of the kingdom in your father's later years."

"I know all that, but I still feel that I've failed a test every time I talk to the man."

"You have, as long as you try to pass his test," Marshal said. "Don't worry about gaining his favour. As long as he does his job, you don't need to worry about what he thinks of you."

***

Harald kept up with Marriette's work on the school through Master Tiron. She made astonishing progress. It helped that she had royal favour, but she also showed an ability to approach different people in ways that made each of them think that they were the most important contributor to the school.

The council wasn't as enthusiastic as Harald.

"She is an embarrassment to my House," Duke deLanguiers said to Count duSarche on his right. The poor man had the look of a trapped rabbit.

"I'm sure it will be very useful to have people who know what they are doing," the count said.

"Nonsense," the duke said, "they will start thinking they are here for more than doing the work of our estates."

"Are they not?" the archbishop said. "They are made in God's image as much as you or I."

The duke just glared at the archbishop, but the old man looked back with a gentle smile. Harald had been tutored by the archbishop, and he recognized the steel running below the surface. Oddly, as the oldest member of the council, the archbishop was the one who made Harald feel most like the king.

"Enough squabbling," Tamas said and rapped the table with the wooden gavel, "the king has given royal approval for the project and none of you are being taxed to build it."

"Taxed?" the count said. "It must be the only thing that we aren't being taxed for."

"Taxes are a necessary evil of an organized country," leBraun said as he slipped into the chamber and sat down.

"So, you enjoy paying taxes, do you?" the duke said.

"I must admit that I don't find the loss of money pleasurable," leBraun said, "but I had the opportunity to see how some of those taxes were being spent on the roads, and I approve."

"So, you can pay my taxes, then," Duke seGraine said. He was in the city on a rare excursion from his southern estate.

"Only if I then get the benefit of the improved roads in my holdings."

"We were never taxed so under the old king," Count reTaggin said. Harald was reasonably sure he wasn't meant to hear the comment. The count was going deaf and got louder each month.

"No," Tamas said, "the old king taxed you at need and you complained just as bitterly. If you looked at your accounts you would see that you are likely paying less in tax now than you were then."

"So, if we're paying less tax, why do we have less money?"

"We are taxed according to our holdings," leBraun said, "not our incomes. If you make less money, you will feel the bite of the taxes more."

"Who says I'm making less income?"

"I believe you just did."

Count reTaggin stood up as if he planned to challenge leBraun, but Marshal cleared his throat and the count thought better of it.

They wrangled a little longer, but without any fixed plan, it was just complaining. Harald remembered the early days of his reign when they came with the clear agenda of bending a young and inexperienced king to their will. Harald gave thanks again that his father's last act as king was Harald's betrothal and marriage to Sarandia. The council hadn't liked it, they all had daughters or nieces they had in mind for the role of queen, but his father had ruled the council with an iron hand and no one had dared to do more than mutter.

Harald didn't mind the griping. Sarandia told him that public griping was probably a good outlet. They felt that the king listened and so they went along with him. He looked at reTaggin and leBraun staring coldly at each other and hoped that she was right.

WHEEL OF FORTUNE

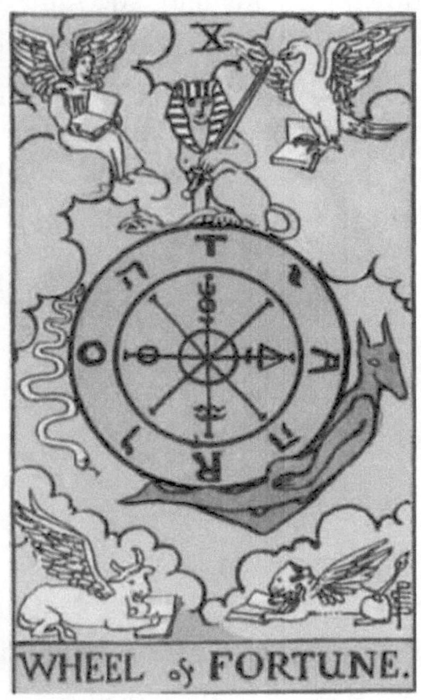

Life became a whirl of social events, planning and challenges. Torrance found a suitable warehouse. It had a large empty space for workshops to teach trades, and offices that would be used as classrooms. The biggest problem with the warehouse was its owner. It belonged to Marriette's father.

Marriette had sworn never to set foot in her father's house while he was alive, but a week of their month had already vanished. People beyond number depended on her to deliver on her promises. So she got in the carriage and went to visit her father. The only concession she made to her fear was taking along Giles, the young man t Torrance had hired to be her secretary. She wore the sapphire gown she had worn for the royal audience, and the butterfly pin in her hair.

The servant who opened the door was vaguely familiar. Probably one who had been given the duty of dragging the duke's daughter up and down the halls until she started to walk on her own. Marriette couldn't understand how she possibly could ever have been afraid of him. He lowered his eyes and stepped back.

"Please inform the duke that his daughter is here to see him." She walked past him into the foyer. What had looked like great wealth now just looked pretentious. Gilt in place of gold, art that had no emotion.

"Daughter," her father said, "I knew you would come back to me."

"Business, Father," she said. "It appears you own the warehouse that is best suited for the school."

"Education for the poor?" He stalked up to her. "You might as well toss pearls to swine."

"The queen doesn't agree. Neither does the king." Marriette looked her father in the eyes, and it was as if he changed in front of her. She had always seen him as powerful, ageless, an elemental force, but this man was growing old and heavy. His hair showed grey and the frown lines around his mouth were set deep. He wasn't someone to be feared, but pitied.

"It is something to pass the time," the duke said. "One of their endless wagers." He walked around the hall and straightened a couple of pieces of sculpture. "So, you need my help. Without my warehouse, you will fail, and your fall will be even faster than your rise."

"No, Father," she said, "I would like your warehouse, but there is another down the street. It is not as well suited, but it will do. The school will open, the only question is whether it will be known that the Duke deLanguiers donated the building or was the only noble in the city to refuse to aid the effort."

"You expect me to just give you the building?"

"Of course." She smiled at him. "You are the most important man in the kingdom next to the king; your contribution must be as grand. Besides, the building stands empty because the business it held has moved on and you can't find someone else who wants to set up in an area growing poorer and rougher by the day. It is costing you thousands in taxes and maintenance. You will turn a profit by giving it away."

"I have money, I don't need more." She duke stepped close to Marriette again. "I want you. I will give you the building, and you will do as I say when I say. You will leave that cripple and come back to me."

Marriette turned to her secretary.

"Come, Giles, we will go to Count vonFromme. He will be delighted to be known as the one who gave the building for the school—"

"Wait!" The Duke deLanguiers ground his teeth. "I will give you the building, but you must put the deLanguiers name on it."

"Of course, Father," she said, "please send the deed to me at my home."

"You have learned to play the game well, daughter."

"You taught me that people are only to be used, Father," Marriette said. "Do you regret it now?"

"It is the way the world works."

"No, Father, it doesn't have to be." Marriette left with Giles following behind. She didn't turn around to see the frustrated rage and malevolence she knew would be on her father's face.

Their next stop wasn't the king's cousin, but rather the wagon yard. She wanted to see about getting the warehouse cleared of the rubble piled up in it. Joan stared open-mouthed at the noblewoman in the deep blue gown who stepped out of the carriage. Marriette had been too busy to stop by since the school had taken off like a bolting horse. One of the men unloading the wagon looked familiar, but he didn't look at Marriette with any recognition so she put it out of her mind.

"I would like to talk to your father, Joan," Marriette said.

"Marriette?" Joan looked at her again. "I had heard that you were on the rise, but this...." She walked around her friend and admired the gown from every angle. "What I would give to wear a dress like that just once."

"When all this business with the school opening is done, I will see that you get the chance," Marriette said.

"Really?" For the first time Marriette could remember, Joan looked like a young girl.

"Let's go see your father," Marriette said. "Giles, would you mind taking over from Joan for a minute?" The young man nodded and had Joan show him briefly what she was doing with the board and wax pencil.

The house was the same as Marriette remembered. Master Candler was at the same desk. He stood and bowed when he saw Marriette.

"Lady," he said, "what may I do for you?"

"Have you heard of the school that is being opened between the market and the river?"

"Yes," he said, "many of the drovers and their families live in that quarter. They are very excited."

"Do you think they would be willing to help out?" Marriette asked. "I need the building to be emptied and cleaned before we can turn it into a school. It is an old warehouse that Duke deLanguiers has donated for the school."

"They would be delighted," the old man said. "The problem will be getting them to work for me while they are helping out. I still have a business to run."

"You could schedule them to work on the school in shifts. We will need wagons to haul rubble away. I can pay for the wagons and their time."

"Take money away from the school?" Master Candler looked shocked. "I wouldn't dream of it. I may not be noble, but this is my city too. We will get your warehouse ready for you."

Marriette was amazed at Master Candler's passion. She'd concentrated on the noble families so much she had forgotten that other people were a part of this too.

"Forgive me," she said, "I didn't intend to doubt your generosity."

The old man just nodded, then strode to the door.

"Arthur!" he bellowed. Marriette's knees went weak.

"I didn't get a chance to tell you," whispered Joan. "He came back a week ago." Tears filled Joan's eyes, "He was injured, and remembers nothing of who he is. It's like he is a stranger in Arthur's body."

"If he doesn't remember me," Marriette said, "we will let him forget." Joan just nodded.

Arthur came in at that moment. He looked at Marriette for a long moment.

"Forgive the dust and dirt, my Lady," he said. "What can I do for you, Father?"

"This noble lady is opening a school in a warehouse down in the river quarter. Her secretary will show you. I would like you to organize the men to clean it out and make it ready."

"Daniel and the others may want to help as well."

"As long as they help, not drink. Ask them, certainly. The more people we have on this the quicker it will go."

"Lady," Arthur said, "if you give me a minute to wash, I will follow you down to this building with a wagon and look at what needs to be done."

Joan took over from Giles again while Arthur recruited a couple of the men to ride with him down to the school. They took a roundabout route to the warehouse to avoid taking the wagon on crowded streets.

The warehouse was brick with heavy shutters on the windows. The door stood half open, jammed on heaved paving stones. Inside the long, low building it was dim and filthy. Trash was piled in corners. Heavy stairs led up to the next floor.

"All this needs to be emptied, cleaned, and repaired in two weeks," Giles said. "Then we will be bringing in fixtures and such to turn it into a school."

"What about us?" a truculent voice asked from behind a broken crate. A man came out with two young children peering around his legs. "We live 'ere, and nobody asked us about building no school 'ere."

"Since you live here already," Marriette said, "you must know the building very well."

"That I do," the man said, "there's an old couple who flop over there, and some kids who live in one of the rooms upstairs."

"I will need your help, then."

"Help to move us out of our own home?" One of the children began to cry.

"My name is Marriette, I am going to open a school here to help people learn what they need to get work. A school needs people to look after it. Maybe you and your friends could be those people?"

"You mean, you won't put us out on the street?"

"No. I won't, but you can't live in a crate. You must have a proper room."

"Lady," the man said as he picked up the crying child, "my name is Bill, this is Cassie, t'other girl is Lindie. If I can 'elp you I will."

Marriette arrived home exhausted but pleased with her day's work. She'd left Giles with Arthur and Bill to talk to the other tenants of the warehouse and make some accommodation for them. She had no intention of starting her school by putting anybody out on the street.

When time permitted, over the next couple of weeks, she visited the warehouse. Each time, it was alive with activity. People of all ages were hard at work, from children who scrubbed floors to oldsters who pushed brooms. Giles told her the challenge wasn't finding enough people, but finding enough work for everyone who showed up. Word had spread like fire through the neigbourhood and every day more people came to help.

George found her at the warehouse one day, helping to scrub floors. She wanted to show the people that she didn't think she was above them. She was glad enough to straighten and talk to her drover friend.

"Hi, lass, Joan told me you would be here. We caught your thief slick enough. He was rushing in at the last minute with the bills of lading; the lads were in such a hurry they didn't notice the extra lines squeezed on the bottom of the middle pages. He was a clever enough lad."

"What will happen to him?"

"We left him with the sheriff," George said, "I expect he'll be doing heavy labour until he pays back what he stole. Now, milady, how about you give me a tour of this fancy building of yours."

By the end of the two weeks, the building was hardly recognizable. The bricks glowed in the light of the sun pouring through the windows. Wood was sanded and oiled. Bill and his family had found a room at the back that had probably been the night watchman's. It had a door that let out into a tiny courtyard. The older couple had an office next to them, and the families had become fast friends. The young teens who'd been living in one of the upstairs rooms moved themselves into a tiny house which formed one of the other faces of the courtyard. They'd appointed themselves the security for the school and took turns watching over their transformed home.

The teens were from the country, as was the older couple, Tedward and Licia. They had come to the city to find their fortune, and, as Tedward observed, lost themselves.

People and equipment poured into the building. Giles and Arthur organized and placed everything from a blacksmith's forge to a potter's wheel. Marriette quickly forgot Arthur was once almost her lover. As Joan said, he wasn't the same at all. He was never anything but proper around her and, according to Joan, no longer caroused and drank all night with his friends.

The Vandelusian embassy arrived. With one last paroxysm of preparation, the school was ready to open. Marriette had given up the idea of planning the opening herself. She asked Kris vonFromme to plan the event, suggesting it include as many common people of the neighbourhood as possible. Tamas, the Justicar, was by several times admiring the work and checking the layout. It was his job to keep the king and queen safe when they left the palace. Having them visit this rough and tumble quarter of the city was a major undertaking.

The date had been set. The plans made. Marriette had succeeded beyond anything she'd imagined. She went to sleep the night before the dedication exhausted but happy, with Torrance warm and strong beside her.

In the middle of the night, Marriette woke screaming in terror.

"What is it?" asked Torrance sleepily.

"A terrible dream," Marriette said through her sobs, "I don't remember it now, except that you were gone."

"I will never leave you," Torrance said, "not in this life, or the next."

The sun shone bright in the morning and drove the last dark wisps of her dream from her mind. Marriette was dressed by a frantic Anna, who was determined if her mistress didn't outshine the queen she would be a very close second. Marriette put the butterfly pin in her hair then went out to the coach with Torrance.

At the school, Giles and Arthur were already hard at work. They had found matching clothes for the young people and set them to giving tours and answering questions. Bill and Tedward directed traffic while Licia watched the girls. A wooded stage had been built outside the building and a sign hung on the wall over the door and covered with a cloth. The street was already full of people who had come to catch a glimpse of royalty. Nobility filled the stage as they came to see how their money had been spent. Soon the only spaces left were the seats for the embassy and the royal couple.

Trumpets blared up the road, hats were removed and heads bowed as the royal coach pulled up. Guards formed up and escorted the Vandelusian ambassador and the king and queen to their seats. Marshal took his place behind them.

The speeches were interminable. Everyone had something to say, and took as much time as they could to say it. Finally, the archbishop was asked to bring God's blessing to the school, which he did with merciful brevity. It was time for the queen to make the dedication and open the school.

"Friends and subjects, we are only strong as a country when we are all strong. There are too many of us who lack what we need to fully contribute. This school is a chance to correct that. You will learn what you need to work well and hard. You will learn what you need to create opportunities for yourselves. By making yourselves stronger, you will make all of us stronger..." she continued to speak for at least half an hour; each person straining to hear, as if she were speaking only to them. "...and finally, I would like to thank Lady Marriette for her tireless efforts to make our city, and our country, a place that has a place for everyone. I dedicate for you, my people, the deLanguiers School for the Trades." She pulled the cloth off the sign to reveal the duke's family crest with the symbols of different trades beneath it. Deafening cheers went on and on. Marriette, in the only part she had in the opening, invited the queen and her guests to tour the building. They walked through and admired the workrooms and the classrooms - every corner ready for the great work to begin the next week.

"You have done well, dear," the queen said. "We are very pleased." She gathered her retinue and drew them back out to the coach. With another blast of trumpets they were gone. Then the nobility had their tour, guided by the young people in their uniforms. They stood around and admired the plaques over the classroom doors or set into the floor that detailed their generosity. They nibbled at the buffet tables that had been set out for them, then they, too, went back to their homes, knowing all was right with the world.

Now, the people for whom the school was built poured in through the doors. They oohed and awed at the work areas and imagined what it would be like to come and learn. Excited groups looked through the classrooms. They admired the plaques, but it was the potential for a better life they talked about. Finally, even those people started to go home, carrying with them the promise that Giles and others would be at the school the next day and every day after, to accept students.

Marriette looked around her and grinned. The easy part was done.

"Well, Torrance." She leaned back into his strong arms. "We did it. We got it started. Now we just need to make it work."

"That's him," a strident voice cried.

Marriette looked up to see a woman she had hoped never to see again. Sylvie had the same self-satisfied smirk as she did coming out of Torrance's room the night that Marriette left.

"That's my husband," Sylvie said as she waved a piece of paper. "You didn't think you could just send me away, did you?" She sneered in Torrance's shocked face.

Behind Sylvie stood Tamas, the Justicar, and Marriette's father glaring in triumph.

"I'm afraid, Sir," Tamas said, "that you will have to come with me."

"This is nonsense, Tamas," Torrance protested, "I am not married to this woman."

"She has a marriage certificate that says you are. The Duke deLanguiers is requesting I treat this as fraud." Tamas sighed and waved over a couple of guards. "Please, come with me."

The Justicar led Torrance out of the building, followed by Sylvie, still shouting imprecations.

"So, you are mine again," Marriette's father said.

"No, Father. I am not."

Her father shrugged. "You will see." He followed Tamas out of the building.

Marriette collapsed on the floor weeping.

"Take her home, Giles," Arthur helped Marriette from the floor. "I have been told that we were once...friends. For the sake of that friendship, if there is anything that I can do, I will do it."

Marriette looked at Arthur and tried to smile, but what she saw in his eyes wasn't friendship, but raging anger. She let Giles lead her out of the school.

Without Torrance, her triumph had become dust.

JUSTICE

Zeb watched the young woman being led from the school. His fists clenched and he burned so hot he was surprised the stones didn't melt under his feet. Here was another caught all unawares in the mage's trap. He'd worked with the people all week getting the building ready for this day. Giles had talked on and on about how Lady Marriette was going to change the city for the better. After some prodding, Daniel had confirmed that this Marriette was the noble girl that Arthur had been seeing.

Zeb didn't feel anything different around her. He still didn't understand this love people kept talking about. Hal seemed to fall in love with a different barmaid every night. Joan declared that he was her brother whether he knew how or not. Love or not, Zeb found some people were more pleasant to be around than others. He looked forward to Daniel's company and to Joan's. They made him feel...comfortable. He hadn't talked much to Marriette, but her reaction to Torrance being led away reminded him uncomfortably of his own pain when Lamb had been killed by the wolves.

The wolves are circling. It's time to go hunting again. The look of satisfaction on the mage's face as Marriette's life was destroyed added to the flames in Zeb. The mage was far too confident everything was going his way. So Zeb took charge and made sure that Marriette would be taken home. Then he went back to his room to think about what he should do next.

Joan knocked on his door in tears, so he sat and listened to her talk. Though it reminded him of the wolves attacking the flock, this wasn't an animal feeding its pack. This was one man's obsession with power grinding lesser beings into shards. Zeb knew that, but every time he thought about going against the mage pain shot up his spine into his skull. He was too close to play games and pretend he was free of the mage's chains.

Yet, if he couldn't actively go against the mage, his friends were under no such compulsion. Maybe all it would take was a word or two in the right place.

"So, who is this Sylvie person anyway?" Zeb asked.

"Marriette said that she was a maid that Torrance had an affair with before they were married. Torrance sent her away."

"Marriette knew about her?"

"She and Torrance did a lot of talking while they were up north. She told Torrance about you."

"So, Torrance knows who I am?"

"Probably. He trusts Marriette, so it isn't an issue."

"Let me get this straight. Marriette and Torrance told each other all the truths about what they had been doing before they were married. Why?"

"I think, so there wouldn't be any secrets between them. That is why this is such a shock to Marriette."

"What would it take to fake this?"

"I don't know," Joan said, "they would need a priest who would swear to the marriage, a certificate, an entry in the register."

"Who would have the power to do that?"

"Marriette's father would," Joan said. "He has an obsession about Marriette being his. He married her to Torrance, but then has been trying to get her back."

"So, what are you going to do about it?"

"Me?"

"Well, I'm her ex-'lover'. It wouldn't look good me asking questions about the whole thing."

"I guess you're right, brother." Joan sighed and stood up. "I'll go up to the house tomorrow and talk with the servants. They'll know the truth."

She went off to bed and Zeb nursed his head. While Joan was talking to servants, it wouldn't hurt for Zeb to keep his ears open too. He wanted to know more about this king.

In the morning, he went down to the school like he had for the past three weeks. He discovered a disconsolate mob rehashing the events of the evening.

"I should have stopped her," said one of the young 'guards', "I knew that woman was trouble."

"Yeah, but she had already talked to the Justicar," Tedward said. "It was going to happen regardless."

"So, he gets arrested for *maybe* having two wives?" one of the other young men said.

"It is against the law, but there is more than that." Licia said, "The duke was claiming fraud. If he proves that Lord Torrance deliberately lied, then all the leBraun estates will be forfeit."

"So, it's a money grab?" Zeb asked.

"Not just money, everything. Land, buildings, people."

"So, if someone wanted to destroy Lord Torrance and take over the leBrauns, this would be a good way of doing it." Zeb found himself looking at a circle of staring eyes.

"Of course, Arthur," Tedward said, "they do it all the time to us, now they are starting to eat each other. That's why Licia and I are here. Our lord raised our taxes so much we couldn't pay, so he seized our farm as payment. The choice we had was to work our own land as peasants, or come to the city and starve." He shrugged, "You know what choice we made."

"Are we going to let them do this to our lord and lady?" Bill said.

"It's between the nobility," Licia said. "The best we can do is stay out of it."

"There must be something we can do," Bill said.

"Find out about this Sylvie," Zeb said. "She's no noble blood."

"We can at least ask around," a young man said.

"Be quiet about it. If the nobles find out we have our fingers in their pot, there will be hell to pay," Tedward said.

The people at the school didn't find out anything of interest. All Joan could say was that Sylvie had come on after Torrance's first wife had died and had been sent off somewhere a month or so before the wedding. None of the servants would believe that Torrance had married her, but they also couldn't believe that a priest would lie. Marriette hadn't come out of her room at all while Joan was there.

There was nothing new from anyone, as if the woman had appeared from nowhere. The entire city buzzed over the scandal, and people were constantly coming by the school, not to become students but to get the newest gossip. If something didn't change then the school was going to fail before it started.

Zeb was frustrated. These people were important to him. He wanted to help them. If they knew what I am, they would destroy me in a second.

Out of desperation, Zeb went to see Marriette.

The old woman who answered the door didn't want to let Zeb in. Only when he said it was about the school did she relented. She left Zeb in the foyer and went to talk to Marriette.

"I am sorry, young man," she said, "but the mistress isn't seeing anyone today."

"Tell her I will give her five minutes, then I will go in and drag her out of bed." The old woman looked horrified, but walked off again.

Three minutes later, Marriette came out. She looked like she had just been pulled from the grave.

"How dare you come into my house—" she began.

"Do you trust Torrance or not?" Zeb said.

"Of course I do!"

"Then why are you acting as if it was all true?" Zeb said. "Everybody watching you is thinking you don't trust him. It's time you stopped feeling sorry for yourself and began acting like his wife again."

"How?" Marriette sat in a chair and put her head in her hands.

"The school needs you to be there," Zeb said. "That would be a start. You could go talk to the archbishop and find out what he knows. Anything but lying around and letting people think that your father's beat you."

"Get out, get out!" Marriette jumped out of the chair and started pushing Zeb to the door. "I never want to see you again."

Zeb left, shaking his head. At least he tried.

The next day Marriette showed up at the school. Still pale and refusing to look at Zeb.

"It is long past time that we got classes started. We will start with what teachers we have and what students. Others will join us as we go. I am not going to let all our hard work fall apart. Torrance will be counting on us."

People started moving with purpose again. One of the young teens ran to find Giles, the others to start rounding up the people they knew who were going to become students.

"Arthur," she said, "you were right. Thank you." Marriette gave him a quick hug. A heat bloomed that was new to him. He hugged her back, but made himself scarce when he could. Whatever was going on inside him was too dangerous. He didn't want to care, though if he was honest with himself, it was too late.

Students and teachers trickled in. Marriette greeted each new person herself. Most were soon deep into the sharing of new knowledge and didn't give it a second thought. Again, the school buzzed with excitement. Men and women stood in clusters talking, not about the latest in the scandal, but about what they had learned that day.

Marriette came to Zeb one morning.

"They are having a hearing at the Hall of Justice. I need to be there, but I would like you to come as well."

"I don't think it is a good idea for you to be seen with me."

"You don't need to sit with me, Arthur, but I want to have at least one true friend there."

"I will be there, and I will bring Joan and some others. There will be more than just one friend at your back."

"Thanks," Marriette said, "the hearing begins at noon."

"Then I had better get busy." Zeb left quickly before she could hug him again. He headed up to the wagon yard to talk to Joan first, then over to Daniel's. Zeb bumped into Hal on the way and sent him to collect some of his other drinking buddies. Marriette would get her show of support.

Zeb, Daniel, and the others arrived early enough to get standing room about the area surrounding the throne. They pointed and gawked at the guards with crossbows and long spears.

The justice hall was a long room with seats for the nobility and places for people like Zeb and his friends to stand. Rails separated them from the open space Zeb assumed would be the site of whatever drama would unfold today. High balconies surrounded the hall on all sides and guards with crossbows stood at intervals around the hall. Large windows let in light making it possible to see clearly. The throne sat on a raised dais at one end of the hall. There were other enclosures in front of the throne to hold the accused.

"This is nothing," an old man standing nearby said. "You should see when the king is sitting on the Justice Seat. The place is thick with guards. You wouldn't get anywhere near this close. It's better when the Justicar sits. You can get right up close."

"So, what is going to happen?" Hal asked.

"They will ask questions and make speeches, and whoever puts on the most impressive display wins. It's just fraud, so they probably won't use the Questioners."

"Questioners?"

"Yup, those fellows over there. If a witness isn't answering fast enough, or they don't like the answer..." he shrugged, "they don't use them much anymore. It's too bad."

At that moment the Justicar walked in, followed by Kris vonFromme, the king's cousin.

"He plays the prosecutor when the Justicar is on the chair," the old man said, but he backed away when he saw Zeb's eyes.

Zeb clutched the railing and forced himself to breathe. The mage wasn't looking at him, but Zeb could feel the web of power from his place at the rail.

"We are met to hear evidence in the case again Torrance leBraun, on the charges of bigamy and fraud." The Justicar sounded bored as he sat himself in the seat.

"First, we have the woman, Sylvie Figsdotter, who will testify how she and Lord Torrance were lovers, and then made husband and wife. She has the Certificate of Marriage to support her claim." Zeb started looking for Marriette. He saw her sitting off to his right beside Torrance. "Second, we have the priest who performed the ceremony, and who will swear to it. He has also brought the register to show their signatures. Third, we have the Duke deLanguiers, who will testify to the dowry that was paid."

"Begin," the Justicar said.

Sylvie took the stand and told her story in bitter tones. "He made me his lover, and then his wife. He swore he didn't care that I was but a servant girl. Then he was offered this wealthy noble's daughter and he said he must marry her. He told me that I would continue as his lover, but he sent me away."

The prosecutor handed the Justicar a piece of paper he said was the certificate.

A tall, cadaverous man who was sitting beside Torrance tried to shake her story with his questions, but every time he pushed her, Sylvie would burst into tears.

"Enough," the Justicar said, "next witness."

The priest's testimony was even shorter. He had married them. Here it was in the book. He pointed to the bottom of the page. The register was carried over to the Justicar who glanced at it and nodded. He too, could not be shaken in his testimony.

The duke had nothing to say about the marriage, but he detailed the conditions of Marriette's marriage to Lord Torrance. That he made it sound like a business deal instead of a marriage didn't change the gasps at the amount of money that had changed hands. Torrance's advocate had no questions for the duke.

"We would like to examine the evidence closer, Lord Justicar," he said.

"I think we have heard enough," the Justicar said. "It is clear to me that the marriage is a true marriage, and since I find it hard to imagine that Lord Torrance would forget that he was already married, the charges of fraud will stand as well." He stood up. "In the case between Duke deLanguiers and Lord Torrance, I find for Duke deLanguiers. All estates and chattels of the leBraun family are immediately forfeit to Duke deLanguiers. Lord Torrance will be stripped of his title and ordered to establish residence with his true wife, Sylvie Figsdotter. Any further contact with Marriette deLanguiers will be forbidden."

"This is a travesty!" Torrance shouted. "I have seen more care in the trial of a common thief."

"Silence!" the Justicar bellowed. "Guards, remove him from the court, and make sure that Duke deLanguiers' daughter remains."

The guards dragged Torrance away through the crowd, while Marriette wept bitterly.

"So, daughter," the duke said as he loomed over her, "now you will return to me."

"No." She lifted her head. "No! I will not return to you. I deny you as my father. You are a perverse and evil man. I will die before I go into your home and allow you to touch me as no man should touch his daughter."

There was a circle of shocked stillness around the pair, so the crack of the duke's slap sounded even louder.

"You are mine!" he shouted. "You will do as I say."

"I am not yours," she screamed from the floor, "I will never be yours."

Zeb leapt over the railing and put himself between the duke and his daughter. The duke's next blow landed on Zeb's face, but he refused to move. Daniel came up behind him. Guards ran toward them.

"Take her away somewhere safe," Zeb ordered his friends.

Daniel picked her up and carried her screaming through the crowd. The duke rained blows on Zeb, but he stood and stared at the old man, his fists clenched. The duke's face turned purple as he sputtered with rage. His blows, powerful against Marriette, didn't even rock Zeb on his feet. Suddenly, the purple became grey, and the duke collapsed at Zeb's feet. People who were watching and laughing started screaming. The Justicar and vonFromme pushed their way through the crowd just in time to see the duke fall. The abbot stood beside them. Guards surrounded Zeb.

"He may be demon possessed," the abbot said.

"Arrest him," the Justicar ordered. Guards hammered at Zeb with the butts of their spears.

The last thing Zeb saw before he lost consciousness was the satisfied face of the mage.

SEVEN OF WANDS

Marriette finally forced Daniel to put her down when they were out on the street. He took her hand and walked so fast that she had to run to keep up. Hal and some of Art's other friends surrounded them.

"He said to take her somewhere safe," Hal said. "Where should we go?"

"We could go to the school," John suggested.

"No, they will look for her there."

"Well, it is better than her home."

"She doesn't have a home, remember?"

Marriette didn't pay attention to the argument. She replayed that awful moment when Torrance's shoulders had slumped in defeat and he'd withdrawn his hand from hers. He'd lost everything because of her. It was her fault. She should have known she wasn't supposed to be happy. Now he would go and live with that horrible lying woman and would forget Marriette in time. Tears poured down her face.

"Take me to the convent," she said, "even the king himself cannot force me from there."

None of them knew where the convent was, so Marriette made them stop and ask at a church. "Behind the cathedral, it forms a wall of the cathedral grounds," the priest said pointing back the way they came. They needed to go back and around the Hall of Justice.

"I know a another way," John said. "Follow me."

The convent gate was closed and barred, but Daniel banged on the smaller door beside it.

"No man may enter here." A wizened old nun peered out through a slot in the door.

"I don't need to enter, but my friend needs sanctuary," Daniel said.

"Let her speak for herself."

"Please, Sister," Marriette said, "only God may help me, but I need peace to find him."

The sister sighed and looked compassionately at Marriette.

"Enter, then, and may you find what you seek. The rest of you, be off, we will take good care of your friend."

"Thank you, Sister," Daniel said.

A tremendous burden fell from her shoulders as Marriette walked through the open door.

"Come, you must see the mother superior." The old nun walked very quickly, so Marriette didn't get much more than a glimpse of the convent. It didn't look much different from the monastery.

The mother superior was a younger woman, who briskly dismissed the old nun and made Marriette sit on a bench in her office. Marriette gathered herself and began looking for the light that she had discovered within herself only months before. There was no revelation, but her breathing slowed and her fears subsided.

"Good, you know something of what we are about," the mother superior said. "You will be given a cell, and we shall see from there."

"Thank you, Mother Superior," Marriette said.

A novice appeared at the door.

"Show our sister here to a room, make sure she is fed, but otherwise she is to be left in peace."

"Yes, Mother," the girl said.

The cell could have been the duplicate of the one Marriette had spent the winter in. She fell to her knees beside the mat and closed her eyes.

For the next two days, Marriette tried to find the peace she had found in the winter. Though her fears ebbed, peace eluded her. She remembered the defeated slump of Torrance's shoulders, Art standing between her and her father. It wasn't the time for peace. Art had said she needed to look like she trusted Torrance.

Even if she never saw him again, she would not pretend to believe the horrible lies that were spoken in that trial.

On the third day, Marriette ate some of the food that was on the tray that had been left for her. She tried the door and found it was unlocked. The novice looked up at her sleepily.

"Oh, hi," she said, "Mother Superior asked me to add my prayers to your own."

"I thank you, then," said Marriette. "I need to make a confession."

"You will need to talk to Mother Superior, then," the girl said. "I will take you to her office. She is in prayers now, but you can wait."

"Thank you, again."

The novice left Marriette outside the mother superior's office and went off, Marriette hoped, to rest.

The mother superior returned and invited Marriette into her office.

"What may I do for you?"

"I feel the need for confession," Marriette said. "Would it be possible to meet with a priest?"

"Follow me."

She led Marriette to a tiny room with a fabric square in the far wall. The mother superior pulled a rope that hung from the same wall.

"A priest will be with you in time," she said. "You may return to your cell when you have completed your penance."

Marriette composed herself to wait until a voice spoke from the other side of the fabric. She confessed her doubts and fears and all the things poisoning her soul. The priest on the other side listened, and occasionally asked a question. Marriette couldn't tell if he was young or old, but either way he was an understanding ear.

After the priest had pronounced absolution, Marriette asked him to wait.

"Please, let the archbishop know that Marriette is safe here, but desires to hear from him."

"You know the archbishop?"

"We have talked."

"What do you look for from him?"

"Instruction."

"I will pass on the request, but I cannot speak for him."

"Thank you, Father," Marriette said.

She sat in her cell, eating and drinking sparingly, when the mother superior came and opened her door.

"The archbishop begs leave to meet with you." Something in her voice made Marriette suspect she had committed a trespass by her request.

"Forgive me, Mother Superior, I felt the sudden desire for instruction from an old friend."

"That he is asking for you is proof to your truthfulness." The mother superior admitted, "and since you are only partially under my authority, I cannot forbid it."

"If you wish to forbid it, Mother, I will not argue."

"Then you shall see your friend." The mother superior smiled. "I will not be so petty as to deny you instruction from a man as wise as our archbishop." She led Marriette to another room. "This is a room for visiting male relatives. We do not deny all access to family. The archbishop will be here in a moment."

Only minutes after Mother Superior left, the archbishop let himself into the room.

"I am pleased to find you well. The mother superior sent me word that you were here and safe, but little else."

"I had friends of Arthur's bring me here. It was the only place I could think of safe from my father."

"You need not worry about your father anymore, my child. His heart failed him while he was attacking your friend. You are safe from him now, and he is facing judgment for his life."

"I can't say that I regret his passing."

"I understand."

"What happened to Arthur? Did he get into trouble for helping me?"

"Yes, and no." The archbishop sighed. "A friend of yours is visiting the city to report and recognized Arthur as a young man he suspected of being possessed by a demon."

"Not Arthur!"

"We have become inclined to agree with you, child. There is a test we are administering tomorrow that should settle the matter. In the meantime, he is safe enough. What can you tell me about this young man?"

So Marriette told how she had met Arthur again. How he had helped with the school and then dragged her from her house after Torrance's arrest.

"He is a true friend."

"So it seems."

"I wanted to ask you about the trial. It wasn't what I expected."

"No," agreed the archbishop, "there was plenty of politics in that trial, but the register was there, and the marriage certificate."

"Could they not be forged?"

"The certificate, perhaps, but the register? No. The marriage was in place between others by the same priest."

"It was the last entry on the page, wasn't it?"

"Why, yes."

"Someone stole from us by squeezing an extra line at the bottom of the bills of lading. They were never loaded and he would sell the stuff later."

"Clever."

"A priest could squeeze an extra line into the register to make a wedding look legitimate."

"That is a serious accusation."

"I would more believe a priest be false than Torrance lie to me."

"I see." The archbishop closed his eyes briefly. "I will investigate, quietly. I hold out no promises."

"Thank you," she kissed his ring then went back to her cell with a lighter heart.

The next day the mother superior stood outside Marriette's room again.

"The Abbot of the Mountain Monastery has asked to see you," she said. "You have powerful friends, Marriette."

"I have powerful enemies too, Mother."

Marriette followed the mother superior to the same room that she met the archbishop, where the abbot waited for her.

"I came to make my annual report on the monastery, and to visit my old friend, the archbishop. Imagine my surprise when I learn that you have been turning the city on its head. A school for the common people. An idea revolutionary in its simplicity."

"We need to do something, and it seemed that education was a good start."

"I agree; though I wonder if we have wandered too far down the wrong road to make it back."

"Some of us might have, but there are plenty of good, solid people who just want to contribute to life. Some of the stories they tell are tragic; being forced off their land so nobles can expand their estates. Taxes have been increased to support the nobility, so there is less for the common person. Yet the support for the school suggests most people are ready to change."

"The nobility may not be," the abbot said.

"The nobility may not have a choice," Marriette said. "The whole system they have created depends on loyal, skilled workers. At the same time, they are forcing those very people into poverty. The entire thing will collapse under its own weight."

"I wouldn't be talking that way to the nobles, they might not like the idea that there are limits to their wealth and power." The abbot shook his head. "Now, tell me about this young Arthur."

Marriette filled the abbot in on how Arthur had returned with no memory, and got involved with the school.

"He isn't much like the Arthur I remember from last spring," she said, "but then, I hardly recognize myself from last spring either."

The abbot left soon after. Marriette returned to her room and thought about their conversation. It was the kind of discussion that she and Torrance had while they planned the school. What scared her was the abbot hadn't disagreed with her. Marriette didn't know that a school was going to make enough difference to keep everything from collapsing. Sighing deeply, she knelt in prayer and offered the fear to God. Right now, there was nothing else she could do.

The following day, the mother superior, again, interrupted Marriette's meditation.

"The king," she said, "wishes to speak with his ward."

"I am not the king's ward," Marriette said.

"The king thinks so."

As Marriette followed the mother superior to the meeting room, she tried to work out what the king wanted from her.

The mother superior ushered Marriette into the room then closed the door behind her.

"We are sorry to disturb you in your grief over your father's death," the king said, "but we find ourselves needing to resolve the issue of inheritance. Your father died with only you as heir, so you inherit all his estates, which now include those of the leBraun family. As a young woman, it would be most inappropriate for you to manage this burden on your own. Our counselors suggested you become my ward. The crown would be most happy to assist you in the management of your affairs."

"I appreciate your concern, Your Majesty, but I remain married to Torrance. The 'trial' at which he was convicted was a farce at best, and a deliberate conspiracy at worst."

"There was ample evidence to convince our Justicar," the king said, his voice considerably cooler.

"There wasn't ample evidence at all, Your Majesty, and none of it was examined."

"You are my ward," stated the king. "You are not married to leBraun because he is already married to that servant woman. There will be no more discussion."

"You sound a great deal like my father, Your Majesty."

"Your father was a great man. He will be sorely missed."

"My father raped me when I disobeyed him," Marriette said. "How do you plan to command my obedience?"

The king's face went white, then red. For a brief moment, Marriette thought he was going to hit her, but he stormed out of the room and slammed the door.

Marriette sat stunned. She couldn't believe she'd talked to the king that way. If the king was anything like her father, he wouldn't take it lightly. He would make her suffer. She lifted her head, no more suffering at the whim of others. She left the room and went to the mother superior's office.

"I am leaving," she said. "The king made me his ward to gain control of my father's estates. He expected more gratitude from me."

"I must admit," the mother superior said, "I worried who was going to show up next to talk to you. Where will you go?"

"I am going back to the school, I have work to do there," Marriette said, "if the king is going to arrest me, he knows where to send his men."

It only took her a few minutes to pack the little she had and walk out the gate of the convent. Marriette headed down the hill to the school—the last place she had left to her.

KING OF PENTACLES

"You wouldn't believe what she said to me!" Harald took another turn around the room and decided not to kick anything this time. His soft leather boots were no protection from heavy wood furniture.

"She's upset," Sarandia said. "She believes in her husband."

"She shouldn't," Harald said. "He's an opportunist. The other woman is a piece of work, but I saw that register myself, and a priest wouldn't lie."

"Priests are human too...." Sarandia was interrupted by a knock on the door.

"Enter," Harald said. He took a deep breath and forced his anger away.

"I apologize for intruding, Your Majesties," Tamas said, "but I wanted to report my findings as quickly as possible. I interviewed the servants at deLanguiers' estate in the city, discreetly of course.

205

The duke was a hard man, but he worked hard to bring his daughter back after her encounter with the Wagoners."

"I know only the rumours."

"She was assaulted by the Wagoners and treated by a doctor. That is why the marriage to leBraun was so rushed and thus how he got away with hiding his previous marriage. I have people going through leBraun's accounts. It appears that he was making a great deal more money from his holdings than most of the council."

"How was he doing that?" Harald forgot his anger for a second. "I thought the council were all struggling."

"It seems that he has a lot of foreign workers on his holding, many of them from the Vandelusian Empire. I'm suspicious, this school is using foreigners too."

"You think he's a traitor?"

"It is too soon to say, Your Majesty," he shrugged. "The Vandelusians are interested in expanding their borders, as you are well aware, but it may just be coincidence."

"I'm not fond of coincidence," Harald said. "Keep me informed."

Tamas bowed and left the room.

"A traitor," Harald said.

"There is no proof." Sarandia put her hand on his shoulder.

"It explains why she doesn't want to be my ward," Harald said. "If they are conspiring against me, she wouldn't want to be under my view."

"You are letting your anger cloud your judgement—"

"No!" Harald shrugged her hand off his shoulder. "I will do nothing until we have proof, but I will have them watched." He saw the hurt look on his queen's face and pulled her into his arms. "I will not risk my kingdom over sentimentality."

"Now you sound like your father," Sarandia said.

"I think I understand him better now," Harald kissed her briefly on the brow and left the room. She said something to him as the door closed, but he didn't catch it. No matter, he'd find out later.

Harald nodded at Marshal then headed toward his suite of offices. He didn't use them very often, but the people at the desks stood to welcome him as if he'd been there every day. A maid left a cup of tea on his desk when he sat down. He gave her a note to take to one of his staff and waved her away. She closed the door behind her as she left. A pile of papers beside him detailed the current situation with the council. Why had leBraun never mentioned how well he was doing? Curious.

The hidden door creaked open sometime later. He waved to an empty chair.

"If I'd been an assassin, you'd be dead," Master Tiron sat himself.

"If you'd been an assassin, Marshal would have killed you."

"You can't trust too much in what you don't understand," Master Tiron leaned back and crossed his legs. "The binding gives him some sense of danger to his king, but it is subtle and it may be possible to subvert."

"Pfah." Harald jumped and paced the room. "I didn't call you here for conversation."

"Then why did you call me?"

"leBraun," Harald said. "Is he a traitor?"

"I've seen no reason to believe so, Your Majesty." Master Tiron looked at him for a while. "You want me to put a watch on him."

"And on his wife."

"Ah," the master nodded. "What could a young woman like that do to so anger a king?"

"She refused to be my ward," Harald said. "The council is having fits that a girl is the head of the most powerful house apart from royalty. They were all demanding that I place her under their care or marry her to one of their sons. I'm doing her a favour and she just makes disgusting accusations against her father and compares me to him."

"Your father and the duke had some similarities, Your Majesty."

"Don't." Harald put up his hand. "I'm not in the mood for your mind games."

"I will put a watch on them both, Your Majesty, and I will make sure they don't interfere with the man that Tamas will have watching them." He stood and peered at Harald. "One thing for you to ponder: if the Wagoners had treated the girl as rumour suggests, why bring her back to her father?"

Harald watched the infuriating man leave through the hidden door. That last question rattled around in his head. If she had been telling the truth....

Harald pushed the idea away. It wasn't possible. But the image of how the duke had looked at her at the Balls came back to him. The man hadn't been quite right when it came to his daughter.

It would explain why she joined with leBraun in turning away from her country.

Harald flung open the door to his office and walked out without noticing his staff.

"Do I have any brothers?" Harald asked Marshal.

"You were your father's only heir," Marshal said.

"That doesn't answer the question," Harald walked as fast as he could without breaking into a run.

"Some questions you don't want answers to."

Harald stopped and faced Marshal.

"Yes, I do."

They stared at each other in the hall. Servants who needed to walk past turned to find other routes. A bubble of emptiness formed around them.

"You have at least one brother I am aware of," the marshal said. His voice was like steel scratching on stone. "Your father asked me to kill him. I refused." He glared at Harald as if Harald had also just demanded murder.

"Is he a danger to me?"

"No," Marshal said, "he doesn't know who his father is."

"Let's keep it that way." Harald started off down the hall again.

***

The duke's funeral was three days later. Everyone of noble blood packed the cathedral to hear the funeral Mass. Everyone but his daughter. The chief mourner's bench was empty. The archbishop didn't care as he went through the long liturgy, but the empty bench burned away in Harald's mind. He couldn't imagine not attending his father's funeral. He remembered sitting there with the disbelief still echoing in his head. Then, as now, Sarandia's hand on his was his only anchor against the waves of conflicting emotion.

Would he have felt differently, if he'd know that his father was an adulterer? Had his mother known? She'd never said anything in the few years between his father's death and hers, but how could she not have known? She only had to look at Harald to know what he'd been up to. He was sure she was a truth teller. Certainly he could never lie to her, not successfully at any rate. Marshal's statement came back to him. Some questions you don't want answers to. Maybe she'd never asked.

After the mass, the council surrounded him and peppered him with questions. Harald commandeered a room at the cathedral and they sat around a table. The chairs were a good deal less comfortable than at the palace.

"What are your plans for this girl?" Duke seGraine asked.

"She will remain my ward until I decide," Harald said.

"Sarandia will not be pleased at having a young woman to challenge her place," duSarche said.

"I am not my father!" Harald looked around at the men who sat at the table. They were all older than him, closer to his father than their new king. They all knew that. None of them cared. It wasn't their daughters the old king had despoiled. He wondered how many knew about the duke, how many of them cared.

"She will remain at the school for now. You will leave her alone. She is safe enough there." He didn't bother to explain she was safe from causing harm as well as receiving it. "If you have suggestions about the disposition of the estate, you may leave it with my staff."

"What about the leBraun holdings?" seGraine asked. "They were forfeit to the duke for fraud, but does he not have any family to carry on the name?"

"We are going to let the leBraun name die," Harald said. "It isn't the first house to vanish from history, it may not be the last." He glared at reTaggin. "Do I sound sufficiently like my father now?"

"A bit too much for my taste," the archbishop said as he walked into the room. "I heard that you had taken over one of our rooms, Your Majesty, and came to offer what hospitality I could."

"The meeting is over," Harald said.

The council stood and left muttering amongst themselves.

"I see your anger, Your Majesty," the archbishop said when they were alone in the room. "Perhaps you would like to talk?"

"No," Harald said, "I would not."

"Marriette asked me to look into the matter of the marriage a little deeper."

"If you must," Harald said, "but don't expect to find anything. Tamas is very thorough."

"I'm sure he is," the archbishop said. "Be careful that you don't let your emotions get in the way of what you need to be a good king."

"If I need advice on how to rule, I will ask." Harald left the room and Marshal fell into step with him.

"Your father didn't like the archbishop much either," he said.

"I think I'd like to go through the rest of the day without hearing anything more about my father." They walked in silence back to the carriage where Sarandia waited for him.

As they rode back to the palace, Harald hoped that Tamas had more information for him.

TWO OF SWORDS

Zeb woke in a small stone cell. There was a mat under him and a bucket in the corner. It reminded him irresistibly of the room in the monastery. He sat up and checked the door—very solidly made of oak and iron, also locked. A panel at the bottom looked like it swung out to allow a tray to be pushed into the room. At least he wasn't in chains. He sat down on his mat and tried to work through what was going on.

The abbot had to be in the city for a reason. Zeb doubted it had anything directly to do with him. The last the abbot knew, Zeb had vanished into the forest. There was little to connect that brutal bandit with the young man who had stood between the duke and his daughter without raising a hand in self-defense. Nothing except the fact they were the same person.

Zeb had a hard time understanding the constant hate and rage that had filled the bandit. Something changed him during the winter with the shepherd. Now, he experienced more than anger and fear, even if he didn't understand what he was feeling. He was beginning to think none of the rest of these mortals understood either.

Lamb's death opened the gates. That was the first time he felt anything for something outside of himself, as if his grief had torn a hole in the barrier between him and the world. Meeting his friends, Marriette, and especially Joan, had torn the hole bigger until the barrier hung in rags. He hadn't thought about helping Marriette. It wasn't like the other times when this body had rebelled against him either. He and his body had acted in concert to take him over that railing and into the place between his friend and the man who was her father.

I wonder what Joan would say about it.

There was a bang on the door.

"Prisoner, move to the back of the cell," someone outside the door yelled. Zeb stood and put his back to the wall of the cell. The door swung open and the abbot stood in the gap frowning at him.

"I will stay here," the guard that had opened the door said. "If he is as dangerous as you say, you may need me."

"What is your name?" asked the abbot.

"Gordie," the guard said.

"Thank you, Gordie, I appreciate your concern for my safety." The abbot looked at Zeb for a long time before speaking again. "Do you have a name?" he asked finally.

"I am told that my name is Arthur," Zeb said. "That will do."

"You are told?"

"I have no memory of anything before waking in the north this past spring."

"Do you have any memory before arriving at our monastery?"

Zeb opened his mouth and tried to speak, but nothing would come out.

"I am not...permitted to speak of it," he croaked finally. Even that sent shooting pains into his skull.

"I see, so you are under some kind of geas." The abbot waved off Zeb's attempt to talk. "You won't be able to speak, if it is true. Don't try or you could damage yourself."

Zeb sighed and nodded at the abbot.

"So...Arthur, are you a demon?"

"I am not sure what I am," Zeb admitted, rubbing his head, "I don't remember being anything but what you see in front of you."

"After the attack on the monastery, where did you go?"

"It is still very foggy," Zeb said, "I spent time in the woods like a wild animal."

"With the bandits?"

"I can't really say, Sir," Zeb said. "My clear memories begin with waking up in a shepherd's hut in late winter. He nursed me through a great weakness. I began helping as I grew stronger. He gave me a lamb to nurse." Zeb found his eyes were streaming tears. "The lamb was killed by wolves. I hunted the wolves, but the shepherd told me that I must choose to be either a man or a wolf. I chose man. That choice led me here."

"Hmmm, you aren't like any case of possession I have read about," the abbot said. "Though the Devil can play a deep game, I don't feel the same unease I did in your presence at the monastery. You may have been possessed, and for some reason have been freed. The weakness you describe could be the result of the demon leaving you. I will think on this, and pray for guidance." He nodded to Gordie. "I am done. Treat this man with kindness until you have some reason not to. He may be blameless in all this."

The door closed after them and Zeb sat down heavily on the mat. He told the truth as far as he dared, and the abbot believed him. The abbot sensed the same change Zeb felt. There was complexity where before there had been simple fear and hate for anything not himself.

Later, the guard brought Zeb his meal, opening the door to do so. Zeb ate mechanically, lost deep in thought. He thanked Gordie and handed the tray back to the guard.

As Zeb lay sleeping that night, the mage visited his dreams.

"You think by lying there you are safe from me?" the mage said, as pain ran through Zeb's body. "I have plans for you, and they don't include you rotting in that cell. Though, I must thank you for the chance to rid myself of the duke. He was getting out of control. His daughter should be much more amenable to my...suggestions." Even in his dream, Zeb felt a rising anger at the mage. Marriette hadn't been freed from her father to fall into bondage to this man who was infinitely worse. He was glad that she was safe.

"Why do you think she is safe? No one is safe from me." The mage sneered at him. "I know where she is, and when I am ready she will come to me. You would do well to prepare yourself for the task ahead of you. This foolish girl is not the only one I can hurt, and I don't need to remind you of the others you have gathered around you." The mage sent a final shooting pain through Zeb's body, bringing him awake and sitting bolt upright on the mat. He sat there the rest of the night staring into the darkness and trying not to think of the people he now realized he cared about.

The abbot visited again in the morning, this time accompanied by the archbishop.

"Good morning, Arthur, I am the Archbishop of Belandria. You may call me Archbishop or Your Excellency. Foolishness, but the forms must be met."

"Yes, Your Excellency," Zeb said.

The archbishop went through the same questions as the abbot, and Zeb answered them in the same manner.

"I hear that your sleep was disturbed," the abbot said.

"Evil dreams," Zeb said.

"You are a puzzle, my boy," the archbishop said. "My old friend came to me very uncertain of himself. He was sure that you had a demon this spring, and yet now you stand here politely and tell as much of the truth as you are able. It doesn't make sense. I am coming to the same conclusion." He looked at the abbot. "The Justicar has put this entire case in our hands. We may proceed with the full trials and exorcism or not, as we see fit. He is even leaving the secular question of this young man's possible involvement in banditry to us."

"Is there some trial we could undertake before putting him to the full test? If Arthur has returned to himself, it would not sit easily on my conscience if we tortured him."

The archbishop held out his hand to Arthur. "There is a cross inscribed on my ring. If you are able to kiss the ring without pain that would be a fair beginning to proving that you are man, not devil."

Zeb approached the archbishop and bent over the man's hand. He looked at the black stone in the ring and indeed there was a cross set in gold there.

It is just gold and stone, Zeb said to himself and kissed the ring. A flash of light went through him, but nothing else.

"Ah, very good." The archbishop looked at Zeb keenly. "That was easier than you thought. Evil would have us believe that there is only one choice, when, in reality, there are many. Remember that. I must apologize for leaving you here, but there is another test I would like you to undertake that involves a bit more preparation."

"As you wish, Your Excellency." Again, Zeb sat alone in the cell. Only when he experienced that brief flash of light did it hit Zeb he hadn't seen the light shining from either man. He didn't think the abbot would have changed so much as to stop glowing with the One's light, so it had to be Zeb was less sensitive to it. He didn't know what it meant other than it reinforced that something in him had changed. It appeared he was closer to being a man than a devil now, and it had something to do with the choice he made in the mountains.

Two days later, the guards came to Zeb's door.

"His Excellency has asked you to attend Mass in the prison chapel," Gordie told Zeb. "He said we didn't need to put the chains on if you agreed to behave."

Mass? Zeb's heart raced. *How can I go to Mass?* He took a deep breath and looked at the guards. "I will behave." They led him through the halls to a plain door with a cross set in it.

"The Justicar and the king's cousin, Duke vonFromme are here to bear witness," Gordie said, "so don't make us look bad."

If the mage can enter this room, then I have nothing to fear from it. He nodded and they opened the door and led him in.

Only the Justicar and vonFromme, along with the archbishop and a priest that Zeb didn't know waited for him.

"This is Father Bartholomew," the archbishop said. "He will be celebrating the mass. The abbot had to be elsewhere and sends his prayers. Sit down and we will begin."

For the next hour, Zeb watched in bewilderment as Father Bartholomew went through the mass. None of it made any sense to him. He didn't understand any of the words. Zeb followed the actions of the other men in the room. As a bell rang, light began emanating from the bread and wine on the table. As much as he told himself it was just bread and just wine, Zeb knew better.

At the moment when the men, including the guards, went forward to receive the bread, Zeb felt the pressure of the mage's magic pushing him to the front. The mage thought he was still just a devil trapped in flesh and bone. Zeb hid a smile and received the bread from the priest's hand. A great wave of light washed through him; it tried to speak to him, but he couldn't hear. It vanished as quickly as it had come, leaving Zeb calmer than he had ever been.

"I guess that proves it," the archbishop said. "No devil would be able to receive the Eucharist. I suspect that he was possessed, but something drove the devil from him leaving him in full control of himself. Since he appears to have lived as a law abiding man from the winter on, I would think that any crimes he may have committed can be laid at the feet of the devil."

The Justicar nodded and looked at vonFromme, who shrugged.

"You are free to go," the Justicar said, "and try not to let any more dukes die at your feet." He left the chapel followed by vonFromme. Zeb walked over to the archbishop.

"Thank you, Your Excellency, I hope you never have reason to regret this."

"As do I, young man. Go with God."

Gordie showed Zeb out of the prison complex.

"No hard feelings?" Gordie held out his hand.

Zeb took it and smiled.

"No hard feelings."

The long walk from the prison to the wagon yard gave Zeb plenty of time to consider what he would say when he got home.

One more time, Joan screamed and threw herself at Zeb. This time he caught her and swung her around in a bear hug.

"Glad to see me, sister?" he asked and watched how her eyes widened and her arm clutched him tighter.

"Do you remember now?" she asked.

"Sadly, no," Zeb said, "but I had plenty of time in prison to think. I think I am honoured to be your brother. I will just have to learn on the job."

Joan dragged Zeb into the house.

"Look, Father, he's back, again."

"Always work to be done," Master Candler said, but Zeb was sure there was glistening in the old man's eyes.

They stayed up late talking. Zeb had to tell the story of his testing over and over. Arthur's father had a hard time getting past the idea his son had been in the presence of three of the most important men in the realm.

Early the next morning, Zeb left a brief note on the desk and went out looking for Daniel. He found his friend at his father's business carefully shaping barrel staves.

"Hi," Daniel said, "it looks like you found out my secret. I am turning respectable. My father is even talking to me again."

"That's great," Zeb said. "I have a favour to ask of you. I want you to watch over Joan and my father. The Justicar may have released me, but I am sure there are others who would love to punish them in my absence."

"Absence?"

"I draw trouble wherever I go. I think I will disappear for a bit and let it blow over."

"That may not be such a bad idea," Daniel said. "Just protect that head of yours. I don't want to go through all the work of reminding you how important I am to you. Go. I will watch over your family." He nudged Zeb with his elbow, "and Marriette, she's single again, and rich."

"She isn't single. That whole thing was faked. Tell her to keep her chin up and keep pushing for real justice."

"I will," Daniel enveloped Zeb in a bear hug. "Take care of yourself."

Zeb hefted his staff and walked away down the road.

THE STAR

Zeb walked quickly toward the bridge to the north. Agony accompanied every step, but he refused to give in to the weakness of his flesh. The pain in his spirit was harder to ignore. He regretted leaving Joan after giving her such hope, but it was too dangerous. He thought of Lamb, and of Joan in Lamb's place, torn by the wolves. Just the image was enough to make him clench his hand on the staff. He was going to walk until the pain made him fall, then he would crawl; when he could no longer crawl, he would lie and wait for death to claim him.

Whether man or a devil, he was not the plaything of the mage. He would not willingly serve any such master. So deep was he in his thoughts that he didn't see the group of men in front of him.

"Merchant's son," called one, making him look around him. There were at least five, dressed in fine clothes. They carried swords like they knew what to do with them. "I tossed you off a bridge a year ago." The lead man casually waved his sword at Zeb. "Now I am here to teach you another lesson."

"Come on, then," Zeb said, "and try your blade."

The first speaker came in fast with a straight lunge to the heart, only Zeb side stepped and tripped him with the staff. He heard a movement behind him and whirled. His staff caught the sword blade at the hilt and snapped it off. Zeb continued his spin and pushed another man's sword high while he spun the staff to crack the man on the knee. Another spin and he hooked a man off his feet and tapped his head with the staff. There were more than he had thought. Others came out of the alleys. Zeb didn't care. They were wolves, and wolves were his prey. The staff spun and howled through the air. Swords snapped or hands broke under its blows. Other men felt its weight on their heads or shoulders or knees. They shouted with outrage, but Zeb simply howled.

Then it was over. Men in once fine clothing lay groaning on the street while others limped away helping their companions. Zeb had taken wounds too, more than he could count. His staff lay shattered on the road. Zeb fought to stay conscious, but the ground moved under him and he fell. A strong hand helped him up. He would have attacked but he had no strength left.

"Noble ruffians," a voice said, and Zeb focused on his helper - a city guard. "Committing assault and murder on my shift. I am tired of it."

"Then arrest them," Zeb croaked out.

"If only I could," the guard said, "but the likes of them are above us. Trying to arrest them, or even interfere with their 'fun', will get me fired." He helped Zeb walk away from the scene of the fight. "I don't think they would appreciate me writing them up in my report. So I will leave them to get home as best they can."

"Thank you."

"It looks like they did some major damage to you, friend," the guard said. "You need some fixing up. Where would you like me to take you?"

"Gordie the guard, at the king's prison," Zeb said. The guard shrugged and put Zeb down on a wagon.

"I need to use your wagon to transport this fellow to our guard house."

"I suppose you are going to take it whatever I say," the wagon's owner said. "Just try to get it back by sundown."

The wagon bumped and jostled through the streets until it reached the prison. The guard had a quick word with the person at the gate then drove the wagon up to a smaller building beside the prison.

"This is our surgery," the guard explained. "They will fix you up here. I've left a message for Gordie."

Zeb nodded though even that sent pain through his body. Two men in white came out and carried Zeb into the building. They put a rod between his teeth then began cleaning and sewing up the wounds. Mercifully, Zeb passed out halfway through their work.

When Zeb woke up it was in a bed in a white room. The smell made him sneeze. Looking around he saw that he lay in one of eight beds. The others were all empty. One of the men in white came in and nodded when he saw Zeb was awake.

"Hmmm." He felt Zeb's forehead. "No fever, good. You'll need to drink plenty of water to replace the blood you lost, but you are lucky." He poured a large mug of water and set it, and the pitcher, beside the bed. He pointed to a bell. "Ring if you need something. Someone will come."

Zeb drank the water, then went back to sleep. He was wakened by a hand shaking him. Gordie stepped away from his wild swing.

"Just like my brother. He was vicious when he woke up too." He poured another mug of water. "Price of admission. They want you to drink more water." He watched Zeb drink the water, then filled the mug again and set it beside the bed. "They tell me they brought you in all cut up from a fight with a noble with a sword."

"More than one," Zeb said, "at least five, maybe more."

"And you're still alive?" Gordie said. "You are one lucky man."

"Not lucky, stupid," Zeb said. "If I was smart, I would have let them kill me. It would have saved everyone a lot of trouble."

"Someone survives against those odds, there must be reason for it."

"Guard said you don't touch the nobles."

"He's got that right. Whenever someone tries to stop those young punks, if they don't just stab you there and then, their fathers come in and make you wish they had."

"So, the nobles do whatever they want?"

"It is the way the world works."

"It isn't right."

"You may want to be careful how loudly you say that," Gordie said, "there are some who would make trouble for you for that."

"More than this?"

"A lot more." Gordie got up. "I have to get on shift. They will give you another day here then you are out on your own. You might want to give some thought to leaving town."

Zeb didn't tell him he was on the way out of town when they attacked. It was no co-incidence they attacked him then. The mage watched him. He was going to be angry. Zeb pushed himself to his feet and drank down the water again. He wrapped a blanket around himself and forced himself to walk to the door.

"Hey," he called, "I need to leave. Can I get some clothes?" One of the men in white came and looked at him.

"It's your funeral," he said, and pointed to a box filled with clothes. "See what you can find."

Zeb found some clothes that fit well enough and dragged himself out of the surgery.

Somehow he made it down the hill to the wagon yard. A broken wagon was overturned and the door to the house smashed in. Zeb picked up a piece of wood and walked into the house. He dropped the wood when he stepped through the door. There was no one alive in this house. Hal's body leaned against a wall in a pool of blood. Master Candler had been hacked and chopped until he was almost unrecognizable. Zeb didn't want to see any more. All he could think about was Lamb's body torn apart by the wolves, only this time it was Joan. He fell to his knees and keened his grief.

"If this is how you protect your people," he shouted, "you deserve to die." He heard a noise at the door and tried to force himself to his feet.

"Good God, Arthur," Daniel said, "what have they done to you?"

"They killed them," Zeb said, "Joan and my father, just because they were weak."

"I am sorry about your father, but Joan is safe," Daniel said. "Your father wouldn't come. He said he had too much work to do."

"Take me to Joan," Zeb said pushing himself to his feet.

Daniel put an arm around Zeb and walked him through back alleys to the school.

"We are all staying here now, those who haven't left the city." He looked at Zeb. "Marriette is there too."

The walk took longer than Zeb remembered, but they finally arrived at the school. Two of the young, self-appointed guards stood by the front door. They held no weapons, but Zeb was sure the rest of the gang was within easy calling distance. They nodded at Daniel and one whistled. A moment later, Bill appeared and helped Daniel mostly carry Zeb to a room in the back. The school was crowded with people of all ages; most were too busy to do more than glance at Zeb as he went by.

Joan appeared by the time Zeb was laid on a cot. She took one look at him and burst into tears. She knelt beside the bed and cried onto Zeb's chest. He put his arm around her and held her tight.

"Thank you," he said to Daniel, for more than just bringing him to the school.

Daniel nodded and left them alone.

"Father's dead," Joan said into Zeb's shirt.

"I know," Zeb said, "I saw. Hal is dead too. I have brought too much grief and pain to you and my friends. I should have stayed and died in the mountains."

"No!" Joan pounded his chest. "I am glad you came back. None of this is your fault."

"I'm under a curse," Zeb ignored the pain shooting into his head.

"It still isn't your fault."

"It is, Joan. I have done terrible things, and now I am paying the price."

"I don't care what you have done, you're my brother, and you have done nothing but good since you came back."

Zeb sighed and closed his eyes.

"I wish it was that simple, but there is more to it." He must have fallen asleep then, because the next thing he remembered was Joan forcing him to eat soup. He thought Marriette came by and watched him for a while, but he wasn't sure. What he was sure of were the nightmares that tormented his sleep. The mage showed him images of his father being hacked to death, of Joan being raped and murdered, Marriette lying dead in a back alley.

"You are mine," the mage whispered through the dream, "I will destroy everyone around you. Everything you own will be dust."

Zeb tried not to sleep, but his body betrayed him and sent him to be tortured by the mage. In spite of this, Zeb grew gradually stronger. Joan was there whenever he woke with soup or water. Soon he was able to sit up and eat bread, but the stronger he got the worse the torment got. He began hearing the whisper while he was awake. Joan would lean over to pour him water and he would see blood pouring from wounds on her neck. It was too much.

"I will do your bidding," he said to the mage the next time he slept.

"I will call you when it is time." Zeb felt the mage's triumph and then he was alone.

Zeb woke feeling stronger than he ever had. No underlying pain sapped his strength. He hadn't realized how much his defiance had been costing him. Joan poured him a mug of water, and as he reached for it light shone from her. He took the water from her and felt the light's warmth on his hand. Where Brother Stephen's light had blinded him, Joan's gave him hope, that at least for her, there was more than this dark future.

He was soon up and out of the room. Zeb wandered through the school amusing himself by comparing the degrees of light in the people around him. Most had a faint glow about them, a few had no light at all, while a small number, like Marriette, shone as bright as Brother Stephen ever had. Zeb found the company of the brightest lights hard to bear. The light wasn't physically painful, but it was a constant reminder of his choice to serve evil. He was sure the people around him could see a black shadow surrounding him.

No one treated him any differently, though, as if they couldn't really see him. Zeb went back to doing the sword drills he had neglected since the winter with the bandits. At first, he was clumsy, but soon the bar of iron that he had the smith put a hilt on whistled through the air. The young people stood and watched wistfully, but Zeb refused to teach them. In the forest, his refusal was about maintaining power over the men that he saw as 'his'. Now he didn't want to pull anyone else into the darkness of his life.

Neither Joan nor Marriette came to watch his practice, so Zeb worked harder and harder on his drill until he spent almost every waking moment pushing his body to the limit.

"You're scaring me," Joan said one night, as she sat on the end of his bed. "It is like you're avoiding me."

"I don't want to hurt you anymore."

"But you are hurting me," she cried. "You are the only family I have left, and you don't want to be near me. Am I so terrible?" Hearing Joan ask the same question he had been asking himself was a sword thrust to the heart.

"You are the most precious thing in my life," Zeb said, "but everything I own turns to dust, everything I claim is destroyed. I don't dare love you."

"Love isn't claimed or owned, brother. It is given, and whatever you are, whatever you do, you have my love, always." Joan put her hand on his cheek for an instant. "Even if you don't trust yourself, I trust you." She left him alone in the dark with the warmth of her light still on his face.

THE LOVERS

Marriette threw herself into the life of the school. She met all the students and agreed to the stronger security arrangements. Daniel had brought Joan to the school protesting all the while. Only Marriette's obvious need for her friend convinced Joan that she should stay. When Daniel had returned the next night with the horrible news Master Candler and one of Arthur's friends had been slaughtered by an enraged gang of young nobles, Joan had fallen to the floor wailing in grief. To Marriette's self-disgust, her friend's agony was the remedy for Marriette's own uncertainty.

She had sat up with Joan through the night and into the next day. She learned much of Joan's grief was anger at her father for not coming with them, and even at Arthur for not being there. Yet when Daniel brought Arthur in the next day, Joan gave herself entirely to his care. She spent every hour she could in Arthur's room giving him water or soup. Marriette had looked in once or twice, but looking at Arthur made her feel guilty for being the cause of all his grief and pain.

If she had just given in to her father, no matter the consequence, none of this would have happened. Joan would still have both her brother and father. Torrance would not have had his life torn to pieces. Everyone that Marriette loved would be better off if she had just given up. She tried to distance herself from her friends around her, but it was too late. The people at the school constantly needed her approval for some idea or other. They wanted to show her what they had learned already. In spite of her failures, the school had become a community. The people were filled with hope and certainty that life was going to get better. Marriette couldn't bring herself to tell them it was all a lie.

She avoided Arthur especially, because she found herself with feelings for him that she couldn't deny. She secretly watched his drill, and compared him with Torrance's awkwardness. All her resolution to continue as if she was still married to Torrance was crumbling. What was worse was the knowledge that she had angered the king. Each day she waited for the royal guards to march up the street to arrest her and drag her to prison, or worse: to arrest her friends and leave her alone.

She continued with her morning meditation and prayers, but for all the comfort they gave she might as well have been doing accounts. Marriette cried out into the void looking for some answer, some hope that she would be able to save her friends, but there was no answer, no light to warm the space in her soul.

Arthur had been up and about for a week, and Marriette was still torn. Her sleep was interrupted with dreams of slaughter. Joan had gone to talk to Arthur. She felt her brother was avoiding her. So Marriette was alone when Bill came to get her.

"Ye better come, Lady," he said. "There's someone to see you." He led her down to the small room that he and his girls lived in.

"The girls are with Licia, so you have some privacy." He pushed her into the room and closed the door behind her.

She almost didn't recognize Torrance. He looked years older than when she saw him last only weeks before. His shoulders still had the defeated slump and he was walking with a cane again.

"I had to see you, and damn the king," he said.

"I've missed you," she said.

"I'm sorry, I never expected this. I had no idea she hated me so much." Torrance's eyes were haunted. "Though we were never husband and wife, I treated Sylvie horribly. What made me think that I could just use another person, then cast them off like old clothes?" His shoulders shook with sudden sobs. "I have failed her and you and everyone who depended on me. You would be much better to just forget about me and find someone else."

Marriette went to hug him, but he moved away.

"No, I can't, I mustn't. It will just make more trouble for you with the king."

"I don't care about the king," she said. "He tried to make me his ward, and I refused. I don't think I am one of his favourite people anymore." She began to weep in her turn. "I've made a mess of everything."

"You!" Torrance said. "You have been the only light in my life." He began to laugh as tears streamed down his face. "Look at us, each trying to prove we are worse than the other." He touched Marriette's face. "I have loved you since I saw you at the altar. Your courage and beauty took my breath away. They still do. If I was to die this moment, I would think myself fortunate to have known you."

"You are my husband, for better or worse," Marriette said, "I will have no other, not now, not while my heart beats."

"I better go," Torrance said reluctantly, "if the king finds out he will be furious, especially if he is making you his ward."

"Where will you go?"

"I need to find Sylvie and make things right."

"Find her?"

"Tamas sent us off together, with a guard to make sure that we shared a room. Sylvie wasn't interested in sharing my bed. She just wanted money. She was furious when she learned that I had been stripped of my wealth and was poorer than she was. I think the guards outside the door were the only thing that kept her from killing me." He lifted his cane, "I have needed this ever since. When I woke in the morning on the floor, she was already gone. The guard just joked about me liking it rough then left too. I just figured good riddance. If I couldn't be with you, I didn't want to be forced to be with anyone else, especially not Sylvie. I think I need to find her and do what I can to help her rebuild her life."

"Only you would be thinking of helping someone who destroyed you." Marriette hugged him gently. "Go, then. Go with my love."

Torrance opened the door and walked out into the night while Marriette wept. Then she dried her eyes and went back to work. If Torrance could do it, so could she.

Marriette sat in on a few classes that were designed to give the students a working literacy. She was impressed with the patience of the young monk who was the instructor. When that class was done, she went to get a meal at the area that had become the unofficial mess hall. It was where the students who were learning to cook for more than one family practiced their art. Marriette sat with her tea and listened. People talked about what they were learning, but they also talked about what had brought them to the school in the first place. Marriette was humbled by the depth of suffering these ordinary people took for granted. They had lost friends, parents and children in the course of their lives, yet here they were still trying to make their way.

Marriette began to take all her meals in the mess hall. The braver students started including her in their conversations. They had far ranging opinions and weren't afraid to argue once they got over their shyness around 'the Lady'. She told the people to call her Marriette. She sought out Joan and tried to encourage her friend to become a deeper part of the community. She still missed Torrance, but the pain became manageable.

A week after Torrance's visit, a white faced young man told Marriette that she had a visitor. He led her to the small room that she used as an office. Duke vonFromme was looking through the books on her shelf.

"I haven't seen a better collection outside of the church or my own library." He picked out a book and flipped through it.

"Most of them are on loan from the church," Marriette said. "May I ask to what I owe the honour of this visit?"

"The king asked me to look in on you and the school. He is concerned about the well-being of his ward."

"The last time I spoke to the king, he didn't seem anything but angry with his ward."

"Even kings may get angry, but the burdens of rule demand more." vonFromme shrugged and put the book back on the shelf. "The deLanguiers estates must be managed properly if the realm is to prosper."

"I see," said Marriette, "so if I just give them to the crown, then the king will leave me alone?"

Duke vonFromme looked startled. "Just give them..." He shook his head. "I am afraid that it is a bit more complicated than that. The king needs you. You're something of a symbol. Your present position is very unusual and making the Council nervous. Do think about the consequences of your actions. As the king's ward, you will have great powers to help the people you care about. Without those powers...." he shrugged again.

"Why is it always threats?" Marriette asked. "The person I care most about would be beyond the help of even the king's ward, and you don't talk about what I must give up."

"Without the king's approval, you cannot run this school."

"There are hundreds of people now who have some part in this school, thousands who see it as a symbol of hope for their future. Not all of those people are destitute. Ask the king to consider the cost of shattering the dreams of thousands of his subjects."

"You play a dangerous game."

"The king may play games with people's lives," she said, "I am not playing a game."

The duke left soon after.

Marriette sat deep in thought for hours. Then she sent for Arthur, Joan and others who were leaders in the school.

"The king is angry with me," she said without preamble. "He wants me as his ward, and he sent Duke vonFromme to apply pressure. There will be repercussions from my refusal. I don't know what they will be, but our people should be warned so they can choose to stay home if they wish. For myself, I am staying here and continuing to do what I can to keep our home running."

"I'm with you," said Joan.

"And I," Arthur said. The others also agreed.

Marriette expected the number of people at classes would shrink, but instead she was inundated with requests to let new students in. The days passed, and even the street outside the school became crowded as the city folk rallied around the school. Marriette worried about such a blatant defiance of the king, but she couldn't stop it if she tried. The hope that people had that this learning would create better lives for them became a mighty river sweeping Marriette along.

Three days after vonFromme's visit, a castle guard knocked on the door of the school and left a message for Marriette. It was a royal summons to appear at the Hall of Justice as a witness in the trial of Torrance leBraun for the murder of Sylvie Figsdotter.

Marriette asked one of the young men to find a carriage for her and changed into the best gown she had left. Joan found her waiting impatiently.

"This is the cost of my defiance," Marriette said. "He will destroy what I love a piece at a time."

"Let me go with you," Joan said.

Marriette nodded. The carriage came at that moment and they rode up to the Hall of Justice.

The hall was filled with an angry buzz. Marriette couldn't tell if it was anger at Torrance or at the king. The guards saw her and let her in.

"Ye can't bring the girl," said one bluntly.

"Are you going to explain to the king why you wouldn't let his ward's maid accompany her?" Marriette said, silently asking Joan's forgiveness. She felt a squeeze on her hand and knew her friend understood.

The guards conferred for a moment then let Joan in.

"Just you keep an eye on her," was their only comment.

Marriette worked her way up to the rail. Torrance stood in chains in the prisoner's box. He looked even worse than he had the night he had come to see her.

She prayed that he would know that she was there, but she could see no difference in him.

The king sat in the Justice Seat and Tamas was talking. The marshal stood unmoving behind the throne.

"So, in defiance of the king's justice," Tamas said, "which allowed him his freedom after his crime, leBraun sent the woman he married away, and when she refused to stay away from her lawful husband he killed her and tried to hide her body...." Marriette tuned him out and listened to the people around her.

"He should have just killed her the first time," one said.

"Don't know what the fuss is about, she was just a servant," another said.

"He ain't noble no more. He has to live with the law, same as the rest of us," a third said.

When did such a divide between noble and common person arise? How can they think that murder is wrong for some people and not for others? She knew what the anger was about now: Torrance had failed to live up to their ideas of 'nobility'. He had tried to do the right thing and failed, and in doing so had broken their hope that the nobility were somehow better people. Why else would God have made some nobles and some common?

Tamas spoke through the rest of the morning. Most of what he said put the worst interpretation of everything Torrance had done. His careful treatment of his people, his marriage to Marriette became twisted by the Justicar into treason and sedition. Even the school came under fire. Marriette worried about her friends, but there was nothing she could do for them now.

Through the afternoon, a young man tried to undo all the damage the Justicar had done. The young advocate was unbearably nervous. He got names mixed up and facts in the wrong order. She felt sorry for him. At the end of the day, she turned to go home, and discovered the guards from the door standing at her back.

"We are to show the king's ward to her room," one of the guards said, "preferably, in a quiet, dignified manner."

Marriette took a deep breath, then let it out and nodded. She followed after the guard.

"You too," the other guard said to Joan.

They were taken to rooms that were as luxurious as anything Marriette had ever stayed in.

"The door will be locked for your own safety," the guard announced and left the women alone.

"Let me help you with that dress, my Lady," Joan said. Marriette was about to protest but Joan put a hand up to her ear.

Joan helped her out of the dress and into a warm robe. She stirred up the fire then they sat and watched each other wait.

A servant in royal livery came in with a tray for Marriette, which she shared with Joan when the door was closed. They went to bed soon after, sure the next day was going to be at least as challenging.

Morning came early, with a palace servant bringing one of Marriette's own gowns from her house. She didn't question the servant, just had Joan help her into the gown.

This day they were guided to a section of the Hall with padded chairs. Wine and food was available for the nobles who came to watch Torrance's final fall into disgrace. Marriette refused the wine, but made herself eat to keep her strength up. Tamas was going through the old evidence. The marriage certificate was brought out again, and the register. The priest was noticeably absent.

"Dead is what I heard," said one of the people around her. Marriette wondered if they were going to blame Torrance for that too, but no mention was made of the priest. The original judgment was recalled, but no mention made of the untimely death of her father. The people surrounding her went over it in ghoulish detail.

Again, when the day was complete, guards walked Marriette and Joan to the room. A meal was provided. They were just debating going to bed when there was a knock on the door. The king entered with Tamas at his shoulder. Joan knelt while Marriette glared at the king.

"We are glad to see our ward is comfortable," the king said.

"Your ward would be much more comfortable if you ended this travesty of justice," Marriette said.

"You see, Tamas, I try to help the poor girl, and this is the thanks I get."

Tamas smiled at Marriette, "I understand her anger, Your Majesty," he said. "She has been betrayed by so many people that she can no longer recognize when someone honestly means her well. Tomorrow you will testify," he said to her. "You will detail how your would-be husband visited you and ravished you."

Marriette opened her mouth to protest, but the king held up his hand.

"Think first, girl," he said. "We don't need to send royal guards to close your school. Fire is a terrible thing, and no one would dare lay it at my feet. Testify as Lord Tamas has said, and you can keep your school and play at improving the poor as much as you wish. Deviate by so much as one word, and your precious school will go up in flames. Tragically, no one will survive. You have no hope of opposing me on this. Help us, and we will even allow you some say in who your husband will be." The king looked hard at Joan. "Convince your mistress. Your life depends on it."

Without another word, the king and his Justicar left the room.

"I would die for you," Joan said. "So would all the others."

"For what?" Marriette said. "They will have Torrance one way or another. They've won. I will be theirs to play with from now on." Marriette went and lay down on the bed to wait for tomorrow when she would commit the final betrayal of her love.

In the morning, she woke to find another of her dresses laid out for the day. Marriette almost cried when she saw it was the gold gown. Joan helped her dress then walked with her to the gallery. The archbishop waited in the gallery.

"No one is to talk to her," ordered the guard.

"You would deny this young woman spiritual comfort?" the archbishop asked. Though his voice was quiet, he might as well have shouted his question. People all around listened for the guard's answer.

"The king ordered—"

"The king's word may be law in this realm, but I answer to a higher king, as do we all. Even the king's word is not enough to keep me from my duty. Unless you wish to ask the king if he wishes to have his kingdom put under the ban." The guard went pale as murmurs surrounded him.

"Keep it short."

The archbishop drew Marriette away from the listening ears.

"Lord Torrance asked me to convey to you that you must save yourself. Say whatever they tell you to say. He knows the truth, as do you. In days such as these, that is enough."

"I will do what my lord commands," Marriette said, "though my heart may break in the doing."

"What is this?" The king came into the gallery. "I said no one and I meant no one!"

The archbishop put his hand up to stop Marriette's words.

"Do you deny the church's right to offer spiritual comfort to all her children?" The archbishop's cold voice rang through the hall.

"You don't know what you are interfering with, old man," the king said. "Archbishops can be replaced."

"Do you remember King Thomas?" the archbishop asked. "How long did his reign last after the church withdrew its blessing?"

"You wouldn't dare!"

"The letter waits to go out. You may finish this farce, though you will have much to answer for on the day of your judgment, but if you try to stand between the church and her duty, we will find out if you will last as long as Thomas."

The king spun and walked to the Seat.

"Court is in session," he called. "Call your witness, Justicar."

"Lady Marriette," Tamas said.

JUDGMENT

Zeb watched Marriette and Joan leave then went to talk to Daniel.

"I need to look different enough to enter the Hall of Justice," he said. "After last time, I don't think they will be too eager to allow me in." He explained that Marriette and Joan had been summoned. "This is their last chance to break her."

"What about Torrance?"

"He is already dead. They just haven't killed him yet. It is Marriette they are after."

"Why?"

"Because she is the one who gives people hope. As long as people have hope they won't just knuckle under to the nobility. Breaking Marriette will show even the nobility the king is to be feared and obeyed."

"So, what are you going to do about it?"

"Friend, you don't want to know." Zeb looked at Daniel. "Get everyone out of here. I don't want a single person in this building by nightfall. Whatever happens, it's going to be messy. Tell anyone who asks that you don't know me, or tell them I was always crazy. It's not far from the truth."

"Good God in heaven, what are you planning?"

"I can't tell you, but come to the trial and you will see."

Daniel gave Zeb some ragged old clothes and used ink to dye his hair black.

"Go with God," Daniel said.

"Where I am going, there is no God."

Zeb went through the back streets to the Hall of Justice and joined the line of people who wanted to see this noble who had fallen so far. The people were angry at Torrance. He had tried to change the way the nobles treated people and failed. Zeb couldn't tell if they were angry about the attempt or the failure. Now that he saw the light in people once more, he avoided the ones who shone the brightest, since they illuminated his own darkness. The guards gave him no trouble and soon he was standing at the rail listening to the Justicar delight in destroying Torrance.

Zeb felt the eyes of the mage on him and heard the whisper.

"Not yet, not yet."

Marriette and Joan sat closer to the Justice Seat. He kept an eye on them through the day. Zeb wasn't surprised when the guards showed up to escort the women away. He went away and spent the night in an alley picturing the king in his mind. Why did this man have any more right to live than the others Zeb had killed? He thought of Marriette pale and trembling and stored his rage up.

The next day, Marriette sat across the room in the section separated off for the nobility. She didn't look any better for the beautiful dress or the comfortable seats. At the end of the day, Zeb again went to the alley. This time storing his rage wasn't enough.

"Isn't it enough for you that one of Your children is being destroyed? Don't You care that she has already suffered more than any mortal should? I am what I am and will live with what I deserve, but she! She shines so bright with Your light I am amazed the whole kingdom isn't blind from it. You do nothing. You say you are love, but how is *this* love? They will break her, and everything good in this place will break with her. They deserve what I will give them."

Zeb paced up and down the alley ranting at the walls while tears poured down his face. "What do I need to do to convince You?" A faint star shone through the clouds. "That is always Your answer. It isn't enough." He finally slept, still weeping unacknowledged tears.

In the morning, Zeb was almost the first in line for entry to the Hall and found a spot behind Torrance where he could watch the broken man and still see Marriette across the way. She was with the archbishop as he argued with the guards. Zeb's rage almost broke loose when he saw how pale the light in Marriette had become. He was too late. They had broken her already. The only thing left was vengeance. The king came in, while the archbishop talked with Marriette. Zeb saw how she glowed for a moment before the light sunk even deeper. He didn't pay much attention to the argument between the old man and the king. It was about power. Zeb was tired of power. Power bound him to this course of destruction. Power needed Marriette to be broken. This whole sham was about power. He bared his teeth in a growl making the people beside him move away.

The king gave in ungraciously and sat himself in the Justice Seat. The marshal glared at the crowd. Zeb wondered if the man hoped for trouble or feared it.

"Call your witness, Justicar." The king was also trapped in the coils of power. The mage was in control, and no one would escape. It doesn't matter, he's a king. He is supposed to be stronger.

"Lady Marriette," called the Justicar.

"Soon, soon," whispered the voice in Zeb's head.

"Lady Marriette," the Justicar said, "I regret the necessity of putting you through this embarrassment, but there are some questions that I must ask in the interests of justice. Do you swear to tell the truth and only the truth to this court?"

"I do."

"You were a victim of this man's fraud. He married you under false pretenses and made you love him, though he could not truly be your husband."

"That is what you say."

Zeb rejoiced. She wasn't going to make it easy for them.

"You were married to him?"

"Yes."

"He was already married, so your marriage was a fraud."

"That is what you have said."

"You don't agree?"

"The evidence did not convince me."

"You set yourself above the law of this land?" the Justicar sounded indignant.

"Even this court may be wrong," Marriette lifted her chin. "I still hold myself to be his wife."

"In spite of witnesses, in spite of documents?"

"Witnesses may lie, documents may be forged."

"I myself examined them and deemed them to be true."

The king's fingers drummed impatiently. He cleared his throat.

"Ah, yes," the Justicar said, "let us turn to the events after the trial. What did you do at the trial's conclusion?"

"I went to the convent and sought solace in my faith."

"Then where did you go?"

"I returned to the school my husband and I had made our life's work."

Careful, don't bait him too much. There is no room for mercy here.

"Did you have any further contact with Torrance leBraun after the trial?"

Marriette went pale and stayed silent.

"I repeat the question. Did you have any further contact with Torrance leBraun after the trial?"

Marriette looked down.

"Answer the question, girl," the king said.

"Yes," Marriette said.

"Describe what happened."

Now, now you pay the price for your defiance. He is going to exact every ounce of humiliation from you. Zeb's hands made the wood railing creak.

"He came by the school. I met him in a room near the back."

"Continue."

"We talked, he was worried about me. I was concerned for him."

"Even though he had a wife?"

"She was not his wife!" Marriette's scream rocked through the hall.

"The king's justice had ordered no contact between you. He was putting you in danger just by being there."

"I didn't care."

"What else happened?" There was an eagerness to the Justicar's question. Zeb knew this was the one he had been leading up to. This was the one that would break her.

She gazed a long time at Torrance. Zeb thought he could almost read her mind. She was asking forgiveness. He almost missed the tiny nod that Torrance gave her. She looked at Joan then; some signal Zeb missed passed between them. Then Marriette stared straight at the king.

"Nothing happened." The king looked like she had struck him. He expected a different answer.

"Nothing happened?"

"Nothing."

"You have sworn to tell the truth."

"I have."

"I can bring a witness who will swear to hearing your screams and cries for mercy from your husband."

"I am sure you can. Yet still, nothing happened. I wished it had. I wish the lies that you would put in my mouth were true, that I had just one more chance to love my husband. Though you may burn the world down around me, I will not lie."

"Enough," the king roared. "Remove the witness."

Marriette stood and turned her back on the king and the Justicar. They turned white at the insult.

"Marshal, bring the Sword of Justice," the king said. "It is time to be done with this." The marshal walked to a table where a long, plain sword lay and picked it up to carry it to the king who would hold it across his knees while he pronounced sentence. Marriette turned between the guards who flanked her.

"Torrance, I love you," she shouted.

"Time," the voice in Zeb's head screamed.

He jumped over the rail and kicked the marshal in the back of his knee. Zeb snatched the sword and hammered the marshal with the hilt while the guards were distracted by Marriette's shout. Zeb swung the sword until it wailed. Guards ran from all corners, while the Justicar backed away. People in the galleries screamed. Zeb started toward the king.

"No." Torrance stood between Zeb and the king with his chains held up to block him. Zeb smashed through the chains with the sword, cutting deep into Torrance's chest.

"Sorry, friend, but I must do this," Zeb said as Marriette wailed. The guards were thick around him now with both spears and swords. Zeb didn't care. He smashed their weapons from their hands and left them bleeding on the stone floor. The king looked frozen in shock on the Justice Seat. Zeb guessed he was used to the marshal taking command in an emergency. Zeb stalked up to him whipping the sword around him. More guards tried to form up between Zeb and the king, but they were helpless before his onslaught. Bolts from crossbows skipped across the flagstones. Zeb ignored them.

In a panic, the people tried to escape the hall.

"Stand!" Zeb shouted in a voice that shook the building. "Watch justice at work. Here is a king who coerces lies in his own court, who plots the destruction of his own people. Do you know what this trial is about? Her!" Zeb pointed at Marriette who had broken free from the guard and sat weeping and oblivious over Torrance's body. "The king is afraid of her dreams." Zeb jumped up on the dais and stood over the king, who finally moved. He scrambled around the other side of the Justice Seat as Zeb aimed a cut at him. The bolts from the crossbows struck him now, but he paid them no more attention than bee stings.

"How does it feel, King?" Zeb asked as he chased the king around the platform. "How does it feel to know that you have been betrayed by the people closest to you? That the only true man in your kingdom lies dying by your sword? You condemned him, humiliated him, stole from him, and he still tried to save your life. How does it feel, King, to be the destruction of your people?"

Zeb grabbed the king by the throat and forced him to kneel on the floor.

"Answer me."

The hall went silent as the people waited for their king's answer.

"If what you say is true, I have failed my people. I deserve death for my crimes. Strike true." He pulled his robes apart and looked up at Zeb with tears running down his cheeks. Zeb lifted the sword to strike. The mage panted with anticipation. Joan sat with heartbroken tears on her face. Zeb looked up at the sword and saw for the first time that it was a simple cross hilt.

"Choose," said a quiet voice in his heart.

"Kill him, kill him, kill him," the voice of the mage ranted in his head.

"No! I will not do this!" Zeb tore down the last barriers in his spirit and let the light flood in.

It swept over him showing him the faces of the people he had slain. Zeb wept for each and every one. He saw them as the Light saw them, as vessels that could choose to be filled. He claimed his love for Lamb, for Joan, for his father, his friends. He knew their love for him, the Light's love for him, even now, after all the millennia. How could he have turned his back on such love to live in darkness and fear? He'd refused to serve a God who would deign to love humans, but this wasn't service. It was joy.

Then he looked at the king kneeling before him. The possibility for true greatness lay in him. This king was no darker than Zeb. As God's light illumined all the places that Zeb feared being exposed, so it could fill this man. The light knew fear and pain and even death, yet death couldn't bind it. The Light's love filled him until he could not hold it anymore and it burst out of him.

THE WORLD

Marriette stumbled to the witness box. She wished the stones would open up and swallow her. The Justicar asked his questions and she fought to stay true to Torrance. She refused to admit that Torrance wasn't her husband, but it was a hollow victory. She and the Justicar danced around the questions. He was getting angrier with her, but she couldn't bring herself to care. When he got to the question that he and king had told her to answer, Marriette realized they didn't want to kill Torrance; they wanted to destroy him. They wanted every memory of him fouled with their lies. She looked at Torrance, begging him to forgive her for disobeying him, but she wasn't going to lie. If she saved herself at the expense of everything she loved, would she be any better than the king?

"Though you may burn the world down around me, I will not lie." Marriette defied the Justicar as she begged forgiveness for condemning her friends to death.

The king shouted at her but she got up from the box and deliberately turned her back on him. Guards flanked her, but they weren't holding her. Marriette's resolve failed and she turned to tell Torrance one last time that she love him.

The world went mad. Someone jumped over the rail and snatched the sword from Marshal, who was bringing it to the king. The man whipped the great blade around like it was grass. Marriette recognized Arthur, though he had dyed his hair and changed his clothes.

While the guards ran to protect the king, Torrance moved even faster from his prisoner's box. He jumped up and tried to cast his chains around Arthur to stop his madness. Arthur slashed the chains to pieces leaving Torrance lying on the floor with a gaping wound in his chest. Marriette screamed and ran to Torrance. She picked him up and rocked him, but his eyes were already glazing over. She had lost him, finally and irrevocably. Nothing mattered anymore. If there had been a weapon at hand she would have plunged it into her heart to stop the pain, but there was nothing in reach and she wouldn't leave Torrance's side.

She heard the shouting and panic, but even Arthur's shout that shook the stones she sat on didn't lift her face from the cold face of her husband. The silence, though, made her look around. Arthur stood breathing hard and stuck with more bolts than she could count. He held the sword with its point at the king's throat, and waited along with everyone in that Hall for the king to answer for his crimes.

"I have failed my people," said the king, and Marriette's heart went out to him. Here was a man faced with his ultimate failure. He pulled his robes apart for Arthur to strike. Marriette couldn't bear to see one more person die, so she looked away. The Justicar watched, looking like her father at his worst, eager to inflict pain. Then she heard something she didn't expect.

"No." Arthur screamed "I will not do this." He lifted his head and looked at the sword. Light filled him. It leaked out his wounds and turned the bolts that punctured him to ash. His face, which had been empty while he fought, filled with joy. Arthur faced the king then dropped to his knees. The sword he held sliced into the stone until it formed a cross upon which he leaned.

"You fool," the Justicar said and waved his hand at Arthur. "Obey me!" Arthur didn't stir, but the Justicar's outstretched hand began to wither. Before he could scream, the mage fell into dust. Kris vonFromme stood behind him with a dagger in his hand.

"I have no desire to be king," he said. He pulled the ring off his hand that made him the king's heir and dropped it to the floor. He walked over to the archbishop and knelt at his feet. The old man touched the noble's head then looked at the king.

The king reached out from where he knelt and touched Arthur's shoulder. Arthur became light and stood. He towered over the king, his wings almost touching the ceiling of the hall.

"What are you?" asked the king.

"I am what my God made me," the angel's voice sounded like the great choir at the cathedral.

"Why didn't you kill me?" asked the king. "I deserve to die."

"All mortals die, but you have work to do before you can rest."

"What would you have me do?"

"Sit in that seat, and dispense justice," the angel said, "God's justice."

The king sat in the seat and looked at the sword that stood before him. One edge faced him, the other the people.

"I see," the king said, "two edges, justice needs to go both ways."

The angel nodded.

"What about them?" asked the king, pointing at Marriette, who still held Torrance. "Of all the people here, I have wronged them the most."

"I will do what I may." The bright figure came and knelt beside Marriette. "Brave one," he said to her, "may I?"

The light bathed her soul, and she breathed in something like roses from the angel. She didn't trust herself to speak, just let Torrance down on the floor and stepped back. The angel knelt with his head tilted to one side as if he was listening to a distant voice. Then he put his hand on Torrance's heart.

"Be whole," sang the angel, and the wound was gone. Torrance sat up and Marriette threw herself into his arms.

Yet, in the midst of the cheering that broke out there was still the sound of weeping. Joan knelt on the floor holding her head and crying for her brother who was gone. The angel floated over to her.

"Little sister, let me offer what comfort I may." It enveloped Joan in a hug until she was hardly visible in the light. Then the angel gradually faded, leaving the young woman with both tears of grief and overflowing joy on her face.

"Archbishop," the king said, "before you hear my confession, I have some things that won't wait to be set right." He looked at the sword at his feet again. "How could I have been so wrong?" He stood and walked over to Marriette and Torrance and knelt at their feet.

"Please, forgive me."

Torrance lifted the king to his feet.

"My King," he said.

"What God has joined let no man put asunder," the king said. "Let it be known that the marriage of Lady Marriette and Lord Torrance is a true union, blessed by God." He looked at the archbishop who nodded. "All your estates and titles are returned to you, and Marriette, you may do with your estates as you will."

"I think the school can put them to good use."

"We will talk more about the school," the king said, "for now, I am in need of an heir. Until my queen bears me a child, you will be my heir." He smiled crookedly. "You are still stuck with being my ward." He put out his hand and a guard handed him the ring vonFromme had dropped. The king put the ring on her hand. It sat heavy and cold on her finger.

"I will pray for an heir for you, Your Majesty."

The king laughed. He walked over to where his cousin still knelt beside the archbishop.

"You are released from your vows to pursue whatever direction God gives you," he put his hand on vonFromme's shoulder. "You have my blessing, cousin."

Next, the king went to Joan.

"Your brother saved me," he said, "at great cost to himself. What may I do for you to honour his memory?"

"He told me that you could become a great king in time," Joan said, "that will be enough."

"Yet, I am compelled to do more." He touched her on the shoulder. "Lady Joan, there are some estates in the north that will need a firm and loving hand. They are yours, if you will so honour me." Joan looked at him and smiled, she hugged the king. He was surprised, at first then hugged her back. "You honour me beyond measure."

The queen rushed in, and, seeing her husband, rushed to him and embraced him.

"I feared for you," she said.

"You were right to fear," he replied, "I have much to amend."

"I will be by your side," she said, "I am your wife as I am your queen."

THE HIEROPHANT

"Forgive me, Father, for I have sinned." Harald had sat in this confessional more times than he could count. It was a ritual, part of his life as king and man. Today was the first time he truly felt the weight of his sin. He could barely find the words to describe his failure.

"I twisted justice to fit my certainty of his guilt. I was so sure that Torrance was a traitor I was blind to the traitor at my side. It was like his words were poison, and the more he spoke, the more I wanted to hear."

"They very likely were poison," the archbishop said from the other side of the screen. "He was a powerful mage."

"I should have known!" Harald felt it tear at him. "I should have known he was false."

"How?"

"The more he talked, the more I felt like my father. The more I felt like a king. I should have realized...."

"Perhaps, or perhaps you are human and prone to failure as we all are."

"I was about to have him killed, the truest man in my kingdom."

"One of the truest, certainly."

"And Marriette, I tried to make her lie about her husband. I didn't want a public scandal over his treason. If he died for murder it was as good as dying for treason. She told me repeatedly what was true and I wouldn't hear her. I was so sure she hated our country because she hated her father."

Harald fell into silence. The archbishop said nothing.

"I was an arrogant, uncaring man, Father," Harald said finally. "I wasn't interested in the truth. I only wanted to protect my kingdom, my power. My pride is what led me to fail. I was so sure, and if I was sure, it must be the truth, right?" He laughed and it tore at his throat. "That is the heart of it, Father. Maybe if I'd talked it out with you, maybe if I'd listened more...."

Tears ran down his face. Harald hadn't cried since his mother died. For all that the council and others distrusted his youth, Harald had never doubted his ability to be king. Now he knew without a doubt how he'd failed. The tears finished and left him with a yawning gap in him. How could he rule again after this?

"The angel said you would be a great king," the archbishop said, "but you've been found wanting in the test. Humility is good; self-loathing is another kind of pride. You must be reforged. By God's grace you are forgiven, and by God's grace you have been given absolution, but also a great penance...." his voice trailed off.

"Yes, Father," Harald said. "Whatever God demands, I will do."

"You must give up your throne until you have completed a pilgrimage to Banstophe and confessed to the Holy Father there. He will bless a token for you to bring here so you might be restored to your throne."

"Banstophe?" Harald said. "That's on the other side of the Vandelusian Empire. It will take months to travel there. It isn't the right season to sail...."

"You will not travel as a king," the archbishop said, "you will be a pilgrim and walk your penitence across the world. You will be forged again in the fires of God."

Harald shivered as he heard echoes of the angel's voice in the archbishop.

"When must I leave?"

"Three days," the archbishop said. "In three days, you must set your foot on the pilgrim's path." His voice returned to normal as he added, "and when Sarandia insists that she will travel with you, do not say no. You will need comfort as well as testing."

"Who do I leave as Regent?" Harald asked.

"You've already made that decision," the archbishop said, "though she won't thank you for it."

"Oh, no," Harald said.

***

"Oh, no," Marriette said, "you have to be kidding."

"Sorry," Harald said, "I made you my ward, and I released vonFromme from being my heir. I cannot take that away from him. There is no one else. You will have Torrance to guide you and the council, though they may provide more confusion than guidance." He tried to smile at her. "Please, Marriette, not for me, but for the sake of the people you love. Belandria needs someone like you on the throne."

She looked at the heavy ring on her hand. The same one vonFromme had dropped on the floor. For a second, Harald was sure she was going to refuse him, but Torrance put his hand on her shoulder.

"Whatever you decide, love," he said.

"With you at my side, I think I can do even this," Marriette said.

Harald felt a tiny part of his burden lift. His kingdom, no, the people of Belandria's kingdom, was in good hands.

"Follow me," he said, and led them to the council chamber. Every seat but leBraun's and deLanguiers had a person standing beside it. Torrance walked around the table and stood by his seat.

"Why is she here?" seGraine said.

Harald didn't respond but led her around to his chair—a smaller copy of his throne—and sat her in it. There was a second of stunned silence then the room erupted.

Harald let the talk go on as the old men who'd doubted him were faced with a young woman in the ruling seat.

Finally, Harald nodded at Marshal, who thumped his staff on the floor. The booming noise settled the talk and the men sat down, except for the archbishop.

"It's customary to wait for our monarch for permission to sit." He looked at Marriette. Harald saw her start to turn red, then focus and look around at the occupants of the table. One by one, they stood again.

"Thank you, gentlemen," Marriette said, "please be seated." She waited as they made themselves comfortable before continuing. "I am surprised by this situation, as you are; nonetheless, I am here and, God willing, I plan to acquit myself with honour and humility. I will count on your advice in the coming time. Be forewarned: I will not count deprecation of my abilities as advice. I can't force you from this table, but I can, and I will, ignore any voice that sees fit to waste my time by doubting a mere woman's fitness to rule as Regent. If you feel I am in error, you will speak up and explain the error and the reason you think it is one."

"Surely, we won't have to put up with this situation for long?" reTaggin said.

"I am headed on a pilgrimage to Banstrophe," Harald said, "and will be gone for months, if the journey goes well, longer if it does not."

"What!" the old man turned red. "Will everything stop because you must go on some foolish expedition."

"I suggest," Marriette said, "that you add your prayers for a safe and quick return to mine."

There was a general laugh around the table.

"You will swear fealty to Marriette as your Regent before I leave this room," Harald said. "If you feel that you cannot do so, you are welcome to leave this table. However." He lifted his hand as reTaggin started to stand, "if you do so, there will be no return when I take the throne again."

The old man slowly lowered himself back into the seat. One by one the men around the table swore their allegiance to Marriette as the Regent of the Throne of Belandria.

"What if you don't return?" seGraine asked.

"Then Marriette will be Belandria's first Queen. I must leave you to prepare for my journey." Harald bowed and walked out of the room as a murmur of conversation began. He felt guilty for throwing Marriette to the lions, but he had no choice.

Marshal fell into step behind him, and Harald stopped.

"Sorry, old friend," he said, "you must stay and protect Marriette. She is going to need you."

"I am bound to you," Marshal said.

"You are, but I must ask you to stay with her. The throne is more important than I am. In two days time, I will not be king. I will not be king again until I return. I need you here to guard the throne and the one who sits in it."

Marshal knelt on the floor.

"By all that I am and the binding that is upon me, I will guard her." He stood again and looked uncertain.

"What is the problem, old friend?"

"I'm not sure I'm the best one to guard her," Marshal said, "I failed you in the Hall of Justice."

"Who else is there?" Harald said. "I know you have no apprentice yet, perhaps it is time to train one, not because I don't trust you, but because you don't trust yourself. As this journey is my penance, that will be yours."

Marshal shook himself.

"Take care of yourself, Son. Try to remember something of what I've taught you." He walked back to the door of the council chamber and stood immovable and on guard.

For the first time since he was crowned, Harald walked alone through the halls to the rooms he shared with Sarandia.

THE FOOL

Three days after the visitation from the angel, Marriette stood with the king as he shrugged his pack into position again.

"I am not the king," he said, "I am just one more penitent making a pilgrimage."

"I wish you would be the king," Marriette said, "I don't know I am ready for this."

"Think of all that you can do in my absence."

"I do," she said, "and that's what terrifies me."

"Listen to your advisors, but follow your heart," the king said. "You must rule until I have done my penance and have made myself right with God."

"It still seems like a very hard thing, to send you halfway across the world."

"I made a very bad mistake, I, and my country need time to heal. Take good care of our people."

"It will be a long journey."

"It will." The king reached out for his queen's hand. "With my queen at my side, I will be fine."

"Goodbye, then, Majesties, and God speed."

"Thank you, my child."

The king and queen, dressed in the simplest of clothes, set out hand in hand on their journey.

"Well, Your Highness," Torrance said. "What is on our schedule for today?"

"Now that I am Regent to the throne," she said, "there are all kinds of important things to do." She kissed Torrance long and hard. "I think the first on the schedule is the question of an heir." She let her hand wander across Torrance's chest. "I really want one."

"Then let us go and begin our day," said Torrance taking her hand. They turned and walked back to the city as the king and queen vanished in the distance.

THE READING

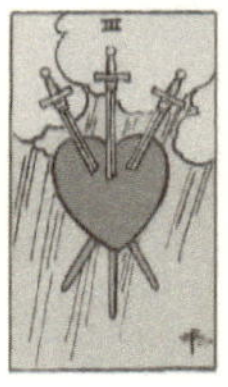
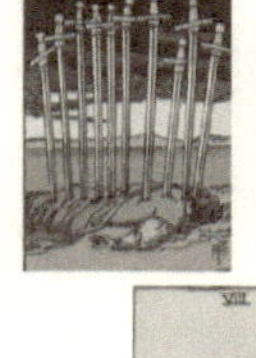

18. The Crux 15 Strengths and Weakness 16 Things Overlooked 9. The Outcome

The Chariot	Hanged Man	Queen of Wands	Ace of Pentacles
Victory Will Force	Letting Go	Attractive	Material
Hard Control	Sacrifice	Wholehearted	Trust
Self-Assertion	Reversal	Energetic	Prosperity

13. Future Challenges 11. Perception 17 Distant Future 8. Hopes and Fears

Two of Swords	The Devil	The Star	Six of Swords
Blocked Emotion	Bondage	Hope	Depression
Stalemate	Ignorance	Inspiration	Recovery
Avoidance	Hopelessness	Generosity	Travel

1. The Present

Ten of Swords

Bottoming out

Victim Mentality

Martyrdom

3. The Block

Seven of Cups

Wishful Thinking

Options Dissipation

4. Near Past 2. What is Seen 5. Near Future 6. The Environment

Three of Swords	Eight of Swords	Ace of Cups	The Tower
Heartbreak	Restriction	Emotional Force	Sudden Change
Loneliness	Confusion	Intimacy	Downfall
Betrayal	Powerlessness	Love	Revelation

12. Past Challenges 10. Foundation 14. Secret Friends/Enemies 7. Reality

Nine of Swords	Death	Five of Cups	The Fool
Worry	Ending	Bereavement	Beginning
Guilt	Transition	Regret	Faith
Anguish	Inexorable Forces	Loss	Apparent Folly

The deck is a 1910 Tarot Deck which began the trend of modernizing the Tarot Artwork, adding complexity and depth to the cards. There are innumerable decks available to suit one's needs and tastes.

The spread is a modified Celtic Cross. Any errors are my own. Tarot is very much about intuition. The cards simply help.

ACKNOWLEDGEMENTS

No book is written without help, and that is especially true of this one. It started long ago as a short story, grew into a short novel and good friends at the time Caitlin Smith and Megan McLaurin encouraged me to add the tarot as a backbone to a longer work. I wrote the outline and they helped me put the reading together which is the underpinning of the story.

Years later I wrote the first draft of the novel you have in hand. It's been read by Jan Hinds and Dean Croke, Dean especially is always a great help. From there it went through another incarnation and passed through a reader's group at Critique Circle.

I submitted to a couple of small presses and got valuable feedback. After yet another revision I sent it to Serena Antal, who is my proofreader extraordinaire.

ABOUT THE AUTHOR

Alex is an author, editor and reviewer living in Winnipeg, Manitoba overlooking the Assiniboine River. He has two dogs who drag him out for walks, a wife who makes him read out loud and a scotch collection to celebrate the successful completion of his next goal.

ABOUT THE ILLUSTRATOR

Jian Guo (breathing) is an architect, painter and designer from the People's Republic of China.

OTHER BOOKS BY ALEX

Wendigo Whispers

Generation Gap

The Gods Above

The Heronmaster

Blood and Sparkles and other stories

Princess of Boring

By the Book

Sarcasm is My Superpower

Tales of Light and Dark

Like Mushrooms (poetry and photography)

Playing on Yggdrasil

The Unenchanted Princess

Alex also has stories in:

Words on the Rocks

Beyond the Wail

Collidor Stream Collection 2016

COMING SOON

This summer I'll be releasing the first of my thriller novels set in a fictional town in Northern Manitoba. I'm tremendously excited about the cover. Keep an eye out for *Wendigo Whispers*

In the fall, I will be releasing *Becoming Marilyn* which is what I've called a side-quel of *Sarcasm is my Superpower*.

Of course, I will continue to post short stories on my blog page http://alexmcgilvery.com

You can sign up for my newsletter and get early peeks at new books, stories and have a change to beta read for me and be part of the next book. http://alexmcgilvery.com/newsletter

A TASTE OF THE NEXT BOOK

REGENT'S REIGN

1

The dress that had looked so beautiful that morning when her maid dressed her, now weighed on Marriette like a heavy chain. The delicate hand on her husband's arm was all that maintained her balance as she navigated the rough cobbles that was the street in this district of Bellopolis. The Church was opening a school based on what she had done in the warehouse district. The Bishop had asked Marriette to open the school. As the King's Ward and Regent, Marriette couldn't just attend, she needed to bring her entire circus with her.

Marshal prowled up ahead of her. He examined everything from the crowds to the windows overlooking the street. There were men out there in the crowd watching too. Three more followed behind her. Torrance held her arm, but at her left the secretary of the day walked with a disproving look etched on his face. From the slippers he wore, he rarely left the palace walls. A maid walked back behind the soldiers and a carriage rumbled along in case the Regent became tired.

The Regent was way beyond tired, but she wasn't going to give in and ride. Her people had turned out in hundreds and thousands to see her. Marshal wouldn't let her greet individuals, but she smiled and nodded to those who waved. Only another block to the new school and at least she would be able to just stand instead of walk. There might even be water.

Marshal stiffened and strode to the side of the road. A man quailed under the warrior's glare. With good reason, Marshal was the tallest and biggest man Marriette had ever seen. It appeared from where she stood as if another poor soul forgotten the edict and carried a belt knife.

As the man wilted three more men burst out of the crowd carrying knives that might as well have been swords. Marriette drew breath to warn Marshal, but the men behind her were faster.

"Attack!" one of them shouted. Marshal pushed the man he was talking to away and dashed toward the three. One turned to face him while the other two charged toward Marriette. The soldiers behind ran to place themselves between her and the threat. Torrance pulled her back toward the carriage holding his drawn sword in his other hand. Another three men with knives jumped out of the crowd at her. The first impaled himself on Arthur's sword. The second tangled in the body and he, the dead attacker and Torrance went down in a heap.

The third man grinned and stalked toward Marriette. She backed up and tripped on a cobble. The dress made it impossible for her to find her footing again. Marriette landed hard on the pavement. A crack sounded from the hand she managed to get behind her and pain shot up into her shoulder. The attacker twirled his sword and let his grin widen.

Marriette's skirts were up past her waist with her right hand broken and trapped, her left hand scrabbled uselessly at the mounds of fabric. The maid screamed and ran at the man with the knife. He swatted at her, but missed. She stabbed at him with a comb, but it bounced off leather armor under his clothes. He swore at her and swung again, but once more just missed. She scratched his face with the comb and blood ran into his eye.

The attacker who had fallen with Torrance and the first man pushed himself to his feet and ran past the one who was trying to kill the maid and miraculously not succeeding. The secretary placed himself between Marriette and the man, but the attacker punched him with the hilt of the knife and didn't miss a step. He threw himself at Marriette and plunge the knife toward her heart. She tried to roll out of the way, but the dress held her like chains.

White hot pain skewered her as the knife cut through the jewelled bodice. One jewel turned the blade just a hair so it didn't find her heart. He raised his hand to try again but Torrance's sword skewered his knife hand and twisted the knife away. Her husband's boot connected soundly with the assassin's head and the man rolled away his eyes already glazing over.

Torrance knelt beside her and tried to stop the bleeding. The secretary tore his shirt sleeve away and handed it to Torrance. It wasn't going to be enough. The pain moved from being white hot to ice cold. Marriette shivered on the street. She tried to lift her hand to touch Torrance's face, but even that was beyond her strength.

An old woman pushed her way out of the crowd and knelt opposite from Torrance.

"Let me help her," the woman said.

"Please!"

She put her hands on Marriette's wound and sang notes that set Marriette's teeth on edge. She wanted to scream or cry, but no sound would come out. She had no air in her lungs and she couldn't draw any in. The old woman leaned down and blew into Marriette's mouth. Rank breath filled her and lifted her ribs.

She could breathe again.

Marshal loomed over the old woman.

"Stop," she said and put her hand out in command. The pain vanished with the word. The Marshal frowned but stepped back.

"Rest," the old woman said, "and you'll be fine." She pushed herself to her feet and curtseyed to Marriette, then walked off to disappear into the crowd.

"We should have held her for questioning," Marshal said.

"She saved my life," Marriette said. The maid came over and arranged Marriette's skirts carefully.

"We must get you back to the palace and out of this dress," the maid said.

Two men from the carriage lifted Marriette and carried her to the carriage. They handed her up to two other men who laid her on one seat.

"Thank you," Torrance said, "we'll be fine now." The men nodded and closed the door after the maid climbed in.

"You are still holding your sword," Marriette said.

"I will carry it until you are safe within the palace walls. He sat at Marriette's head and planted the tip of his sword between his feet.

"It's a shame about the dress," the maid said, "that colour is especially nice on you." She used a damp cloth to clean Marriette's face.

"You are brave," Marriette said to the girl. Though if she looked harder the girl was close to her age.

"You are my Queen," the girl said, "I couldn't let that horrible man hurt you."

"But you could have been killed." Marriette touched the maid's cheek. "I would be terribly upset if you died because of me."

"You're a Queen," the maid said, "people are supposed to die for you."

They arrived at the palace and servants came with a chair to take Marriette into her rooms.

More maids fussed over her while the maid who had ridden with her back from the attack broke down into tears and begged to be excused.

"Come back when you're ready," Marriette said. "I'm sure you saved my life." The maid curtseyed and ran off weeping. Strange that she would show and upset until they were safe, but everyone was different.

The dress vanished and Marriette placed in a bath with hot water. A young girl sponged the blood from Marriette's skin and looked with wide eyes at the scar that marked the top of Marriette's breast.

"When?" the girl asked.

"Just a short time ago," Marriette said, "I was dying. I knew it, then an old woman came and healed me before disappearing again. Marriette ran her finger along the scar and a faint echo of pain twinged her chest.

"Maybe she was a saint!" the girl said.

"Perhaps."

"The Doctor is here to see the Regent."

"Bring me my robe," Marriette said. "Let's get this over with."

The doctor was a man of indeterminant age who leaned on a cane. An assistant carried a large bag.

"Let's see now," the doctor said and made opening motions with his hands. Marriette pulled her robe open far enough to show the scar. "Does it still hurt?"

"If I put pressure on it."

"Hmmm," the doctor peered at the scar with his hands behind his back. "Not a complete healing then, but enough to stop the blood loss. Did you have trouble breathing?"

"Before she helped me," Marriette said.

"As I though, the knife punctured your lung. You are fortunate, your Majesty, even I would have a hard time preserving your life in such circumstance." He stepped back from her and tilted his head. "You must drink water to replace the blood you lost. I will speak to the kitchen about sending you plenty of red meat as well. Walk around if you must, but do not lift anything with your left arm for at least a week."

"I barely lift anything with either arm," Marriette said.

"Then you should have no problem," the Doctor nodded in satisfaction. "If the pain returns or you bleed, have me summoned at once. You will want to avoid more such adventures if you wish that child to be born healthy and whole." The doctor reached back his assistant put a package in his hand. "For mild pain, make a tea of this and drink it with honey. Don't overdo it." He put the package on a table beside the chair, then bowed and left, followed by his assistant.

"Your Majesty!" the young girl who had helped her in the bath looked at her with a glowing smile. "An heir, your husband must be very pleased."

"I'm sure he will be once he knows," Marriette said as she tugged her robe closed. The Doctor never touched her, or anyone else that she'd ever seen. Yet he knew things about her that should be impossible. She'd only started to wonder this very week. She smiled and wrapped her arms around her. "Please go ask him to attend me here." The girl curtseyed and ran out of the room. The other maids helped her don a dress so she was properly attired for her husband.

Torrance strode into the room and knelt at Marriette's feet.

"I should have been faster," he said. "I let them slow me down."

"You slowed them down as well," Marriette said, "and you were there when I needed you."

"After you were wounded," Torrance clenched his fist in the fabric of her skirt. "I was sure I had lost you."

"We owe a debt to that woman."

"Marshal is out of sorts because none of his men can find her."

"I will deal with Marshal in time." Marriette put her hand on her husband's shoulder and played with the hair that curled there. A few grey hairs among the dark.

"I have more momentous things to discuss," she said.

"More important than you almost dying on an assassin's blade?"

"Much more important," Marriette said, "It appears that you are to have an heir."

If Torrance's head had snapped up much harder, he would have broken his neck. Tears that he hadn't shed over her on the road sprang to his eyes. Marriette couldn't think of any more words that she wanted to say. She pulled him to her as the maids discretely left the room.

It didn't take Torrance nearly as long to get the dress off her as it had taken the maids to put it on.